FOOL'S GOLD

ALSO BY ALBERT DIBARTOLOMEO
The Vespers Tapes
(released as *Blood Confessions* in paperback)

FOOL'S GOLD

Albert DiBartolomeo

St. Martin's Press
New York

Editor: George Witte
Production Editor: Eric C. Meyer
Copyedited by Janet Field
Design by Judy Christensen

ISBN   0-312-09058-7

First Edition: March 1993

10 9 8 7 6 5 4 3 2

Books are available in quantity for promotional or premium use. Write to Director of Special Sales, St. Martin's Press, 175 Fifth Avenue, New York, NY 10010, for information on discounts and terms, or call toll-tree (800) 221-7945. In New York, call (212) 674-5151 (ext. 645).

FOR SUSAN

I would like to acknowledge the following people: Jerry and Kate Hinkle for their title suggestions, George Witte for his sensitive editing, Joe Bartolomeo for his stories, Gene Mirabelli, Carol Bonomo Albright, John Paul Russo for writing back, my friends at Drexel University and Molly for listening, and Jimmy, Joel, Carmen, Rachel, Elizabeth, Tony, and my parents for so much beyond words.

1

IT had to rain, Benny Bean thought. And that chick had to live in Longport, New Jersey, so he had to drive the sixty boring miles from Philly. Over the Walt Whitman Bridge, then the fifteen minutes on Route 42, then the Atlantic City Expressway, where there wasn't anything to look at but fields and trees and maybe, if you were lucky, some dead deer by the side of the road that got smashed by a big truck or something. The scenery didn't do anything for Benny, even if the trees were red and orange from winter coming, and neither did the loud music coming from the tape deck he paid absolutely zero for, a little gift he had made to himself after ripping it out of a Saab on Spruce Street in Center City. But he kept the music on anyway because the quiet bothered him more.

It didn't help either that Benny wasn't feeling a hundred percent. The car, like small rooms, made him feel cooped up, like he was back in that closet his old man used to lock him in when he was a kid. Benny could see himself on the closet floor, hugging his knees, with his father drunk again on the other side of the door. He could almost smell the moth balls and the leather of the shoes and hear his father's drunken mumble.

Benny rolled down the window and spit, as if the memory were a bad taste in his mouth.

The only good thing about the ride to Longport was that it was to a rich house with a Jacuzzi and a swimming pool and a whole lot of nice items in it that Benny could steal. Plus, it was only fifteen minutes from Atlantic City, where Benny liked to do some dice or cards. He had taken the chick there twice, but both times he had dropped something like a thousand bucks shooting craps and playing blackjack.

Talk about bad nights. He had to steal some poor chooch's Monte Carlo to get some of the money back the first time and then a nice new—what was it?—a BMW, yeah, with leather seats the second. Both didn't have shit for alarms, your standard Pep Boys do-it-yourself crap, which Benny got by in seconds, not even thinking how good he was. After delivering the cars, Benny hung around Selligrini's shop in that junkyard near Fishtown not far from the river and watched the Monte Carlo get chopped in less than two hours. Selligrini and his men were real pros, those guys handling the power ratchets and blowtorches like surgeons on speed. The BMW they painted red, changed the license plate, and Selli asked Benny if he wanted to make another hundred for driving the car to somebody in New York. Sure, Benny said, he wasn't doing anything. He drove the BMW up the New Jersey Turnpike, smelling the fresh paint the whole way, and handed it over to a guy in Queens. He took the train back.

At Thirtieth Street Station, Benny copped a briefcase from the floor while the owner was talking to the lady in the information booth, Benny so close to the guy as he took the case that he could've kissed him. It was one of those briefcases with the combination locks, which Benny breezed past in twenty seconds with the help of a screwdriver. He didn't find much in the case, just a pocket calculator and a bunch of papers.

Selligrini was on vacation in Vegas for two weeks, and because Benny was such a good customer, Selli gave him the keys to the gate and the shed just in case Benny grabbed something and wanted to bring it in to hide. Last summer, when Selli returned from a trip, Benny surprised him with a Lincoln *and* a Trans Am, both tucked nice and neat behind the shed where you couldn't see them even if you were in the junkyard, let alone from the small back street, which nobody hardly drove up anyway. And the summer before that, while Selli was in Cancun, Benny helped his friend Skinny Fuji kick a heroin habit by locking him in the cinder-block shed for a week. Benny could still hear Fuji's maniac yelling.

Benny reached the turnoff for Longport in the late afternoon. The rain was still coming down in that steady way that made Benny think it was going to rain forever. The gray sky made the bay look like the water from his mother's emptying washing machine when she did Benny's laundry.

He reached the town a few minutes later. Benny never saw so many nice homes, all of them looking like they just got painted yesterday. And look how clean everything was, with no trash in the streets and no graffiti. Next to Philly, Longport was as clean as an operating room.

When Benny stopped at a traffic light, he watched the windshield wipers scrape back and forth across the glass, doing it without blinking, even though his eyes burned. It was a long light, and as his eyes watered, Benny whiffed the moth balls and the shoe leather from the closet when he was a kid.

What he could use, Benny thought, were a couple lines of coke and then some strapper's head to bash in with a plumber's wrench.

It was almost dark now, as Bean parked a few blocks from the house. He took the pry bar from the floor, slipped it up his sleeve, and got out of the car whistling, glad to be on his feet again and out in the air. He put up an umbrella he bought from a gook on a corner back in South Philly. Benny normally didn't use an umbrella because he thought they were sissy. But in the rain without an umbrella in a place like that, he might look suspicious. Just like he was careful how he dressed, leaving his leather jacket home with the black jeans he liked. But he kept the boots because he liked the inch and a half taller they made him, putting him over five foot by just that much.

Benny walked toward the ocean. No one was around. The people who lived in the houses were only there on weekends, maybe, or inside because of the rain, or at the casinos in Atlantic City losing some of their big money. Maybe they were even out on the boats some of them had, like the chick's father, who took Benny out on it with the rest of the family that one Saturday. The father stayed in the cabin the whole time and hardly said a word. That was last summer, right before Benny went to prison a second time for trying to steal a Mercedes. Lucky for the overcrowded situation in the jail and the court ruling that said you could only have so many guys in the prison, because Benny was out in less than a year.

On the boat, Benny kept his pants and his boots on the whole time, while everybody else wore swim suits, getting red like lobsters. But he took off his shirt, wanting to scare those geeks with the muscles he developed in the can a year ago and with his tattoos, the one with the knife through the heart his favorite. But then he got seasick and the only thing that mattered to him was getting back to land before he puked his guts out. He didn't make it. For the last hour, he hung his head over the side of the boat and threw up, his brain loose in his skull and rolling around in there like a bowling ball. Some of them joked about it. He's throwing up his liver and they're laughing and smirking behind him, even the chick. Benny didn't forget that.

He walked to the wooden steps that climbed the sand bank, went up them, paused on the short deck to look up the shoreline to the house, then walked down the steps on the other side to the deserted beach. His boots dug into the sand, and when he walked to the water's edge his heels sunk into the wet sand there, making neat tracks. He tried to look like he was just out for a stroll, in case there was somebody with nothing better to do than to watch him.

Benny turned around after a few minutes and walked on a slant across the sand toward the house. He climbed another set of wooden steps with thin grass coming up through the boards, then down the other side, the bank mostly blocking out the sounds of the waves when he stepped back on level ground. There was the house, the back of it facing the beach, with no cars in the driveway at the side, just like when he checked out the place those three times. Keeping his eyes peeled, Benny walked the rest of the way to the back door. Night had come on the whole way now, and if anybody saw Benny from the other houses seventy-five feet away they were animals who could see in the dark.

Benny looked through the panes of the door but saw only blackness; then he did a circuit around the house. Crouched low, his feet sinking into the flower beds and making sucking sounds in the mud, Benny looked through the windows. Most of the rooms were dark, except for a table lamp left on in the living room. It didn't look like anybody was home, but when Benny returned to the back door he knocked just in case. He could hear the rain gurgling in the drain spout nearby and the drops hitting the water of the swimming pool to his right. No one answered the door, and Benny smiled. He headed for the patio.

Benny jimmied the frame of the sliding patio doors with his pry bar and lifted a door off its track so easily that he thought he was blessed. He stepped in the house and went straight to the alarm control in the kitchen nearby. Benny punched the illuminated numbers he had memorized and then written down in the bathroom right after watching the chick do it one night. He just hoped the code was still the same and then knew it was when the flashing light went off.

"Hello?" Benny called, just to be safe. "Anybody home?"

All he heard was the humming refrigerator and the ticking of the clock on the wall. Benny walked toward the living room, his wet and muddy shoes squeaking on the ceramic tile and leaving tracks. The living room was the same as before, and the way he used to think about it in his cell when he imagined himself walking through it, taking the goodies. Benny thought the room was out of one of those house magazines. Like the kitchen, it was spotless and looked unused. There were pieces of crystal in two rich-looking wall cabinets and these figurines that Benny knew were porcelain because he copped a couple once from another house. There were a couple of urns, too, that looked like they came from some museum.

Benny picked up the nearest urn and tossed it into the closest cabinet of figurines; then he picked up the other urn and threw it at the other cabinet. The cabinet glass shattered and the urns smashed apart when they hit the floor. Benny smiled and then went upstairs.

In the master bedroom, Benny stuffed the jewelry into his pockets and then opened the dresser drawers and pulled out cashmere sweaters, knit shirts, silk scarves, tennis whites, panties in all colors, and tossed them over his shoulders. But he didn't find anything there. He treaded on the clothes as he crossed the room to the other dresser, this one belonging to the man. Benny emptied the drawers in seconds and found three hundred dollars in twenties in the sock drawer.

"Nice." He kissed the money.

Benny next went to the other rooms. One looked like it belonged to a kid, and there was nothing in it to take; and the other was the chick's room, but it didn't look used. He figured maybe she had her own place now, or maybe was just living at college. Maybe she got married or something. They had seen each other for only about two weeks while she was on summer vacation and working as a waitress in a restaurant on Ventnor Avenue, where Benny met her and, the next day, convinced her to go out with him. They had some laughs, Benny got to see the layout of the house, learned the alarm code, and he even banged her a few times before she said she didn't want to see him anymore. Benny acted a little disappointed, but he thought, No big deal. It wasn't like he was crazy in love with her; he couldn't be after that boat ride, which, when he remembered her laughing with the others as he puked, he wanted to smack her for, but he controlled himself because he was already thinking about robbing her house. He wanted to stay friendly with her as long as possible, a nice guy, somebody who she wouldn't immediately think of when she or her parents came home and discovered the burglary.

There was nothing to steal in the room, and Benny went downstairs.

In the den, where Benny had laid the chick on the sofa one night as she dug her red fingernails in his ribs, he went straight to the desk, turning on the little brass lamp he thought he might take. He rifled the drawers, but one was locked, and no matter how much he pulled on the handle it wouldn't move. He tried the pry bar but couldn't get it into the crack between the drawer and the frame. Benny went into the basement, looked among the tools laid out nice and neat on a rack of metal shelves, and grabbed a large screwdriver to take back to the den. An electric drill with a three-quarter inch spade bit in the chuck caught his eye, and he brought that up, too.

He was glad he did, because the desk was made of some tough wood. Benny worked the screwdriver into the seam but he couldn't splinter the wood where the tongue of the lock caught. He dropped the screwdriver, picked up the drill, unwrapped the cord, and plugged it into the wall socket. Benny quickly drilled three holes around the lock and then easily broke it completely out with the screwdriver.

"Bingo."

Benny pulled the drawer all the way out and dumped the contents on the desk top. There were important-looking papers he threw in the air and a velvet-covered box at the bottom nearly as big as the drawer. Opening the box, Benny saw a couple sheets of paper and, under them, a bunch of silver and gold coins, most of them in their own little plastic case. There was also a plastic tube with a cork in the end holding small gold coins.

Benny whistled. One look at all those coins told Benny they had to be worth a lot of money. But he didn't realize how much until he unfolded the two sheets of paper and saw that the coins were listed on them in a column, with dates, and with "condition," and "value as of 1/89," at the tops of the next two columns. Benny whistled again when he read, "1795 gold half eagle," and to the right of that, "Fine," and, in the last column, "$5,000." There were some gold dollars and two "double eagles" with values of between $750 and $1,000. Some "quarter eagles" worth $800 were listed. Then there were a lot of "silver dollars" ranging between $25 and $250. One of the silver dollars, with the word "Gobrecht" in front of it and "1836" to the side, had the figure "$3,700" in the last column. After all the columns, at the bottom of the second page, were the words, "Krugerrands—20." These must have been the twenty gold coins in the plastic tube that Benny quickly counted. Yeah, twenty. Then there was something handwritten in ink, which said, "Spanish doubloon" with four dollar signs beside it, but no number. Benny didn't know what a doubloon was but the dollar signs made him think it had to be worth a nice hunk of change.

Doing some quick arithmetic, Benny realized he had something like thirty thousand dollars worth of coins in his hands, not counting that doubloon thing.

"Beautiful, beautiful."

Man, this was the break Benny needed. Feeling pretty good, he put the box of coins on the chair and picked up the drill again, an idea coming into his head. Benny quickly cleared the surface of the desk with a few swipes of his hand and squeezed the trigger on the drill, bringing it up to speed. The bit was a little dull and the wood smoked as Benny drilled a splintery hole through the desktop. Benny pulled out of the hole and began another. That one smoked too as Benny drilled, wood chips scattering outward from the bit. Once through, he did one more hole, and then left the drill embedded in the desk.

"Laugh now."

With the smell of burnt wood in his nose, his pockets jiggling with jewelry, Benny took his coins from the chair and started on his way out. He felt terrific, like he had just had some great sex or had just coldcocked some prick who had given him a hard time.

But just as he stepped into the kitchen, he saw a blur to his left, and almost immediately something crashed against the side of his head as somebody clobbered him.

2

THE boy was sweeping the sidewalk again in front of Paul Fante's wood shop in Northern Liberties when he arrived in the morning. While on the telephone the day before, Paul had glanced out the window facing Second Street and seen the boy solemnly pushing the shards of a broken beer bottle to the gutter with a worn broom. Paul had been curious, but by the time he finished the business on the telephone, the boy was gone.

Now here he was again, dressed in the same filthy and tattered jacket and pants, sweeping in the drizzle.

When Fante parked at the curb, the boy glanced up, his eyes fearful and guarded, and then he looked down again to his sweeping. He slowly worked his way south, making careful swipes with the broom, as though he meant to sweep all the way to Market Street, seven blocks distant.

Paul stepped out of his pickup truck as a car pulled up beside him. It was Andre, his helper.

After saying good morning, Paul motioned toward the boy with his chin. "He showed up again. Shouldn't he be in school?"

"I don't think he has a home to go to, let alone a school."

"Don't tell me that."

"You already know it."

"But I don't want to believe it."

"This is modern America. People living on the street, even children."

"He has to have a home."

"I don't think so. I asked him about it but he just gave me that look."

"What look?"

"Kind of scared, kind of sheepish. I don't think he talks. Did he talk to you?"

"He barely looks at me."

"Maybe he's mute. I know he can hear because yesterday, after asking him about five times, he showed me his name, but only when it looked like I was getting mad."

"*Showed* you his name?"

"It was on a ratty piece of paper he took from his pocket."

"What was it, his name?"

"Tut."

"Tut?"

"Like the king."

"That's his name? Tut? You sure you read it right?"

"T-u-t. That was it."

"Tut." Paul looked down the street at the boy, patiently sweeping with his back to them, his clothing the same grimy color as the gutter he pushed the bits of trash toward.

"I asked him his last name but he just looked at the ground like he didn't know what I was saying."

They watched the boy sweep for a time; then Andre crossed the sidewalk to open the shop. Instead of going into the shop with him, Paul went up to the boy, sweeping now in front of the meat wholesaler. "Uh, Tut?"

11

The boy wheeled and looked at Paul, panic on his dirty face.

"That's your name, right? Tut?"

The boy didn't answer or nod, only clutched the broom handle to his chest, looking downward somewhere to Paul's side.

"Well, if it's not, let me know."

The boy did not move. His shoes were mismatched and his hair looked as though he had cut it himself with a pocket knife. Paul noticed a patch of ringworm at the boy's temple.

"Look, did you eat?"

Tut's head seemed to tremble no.

"Here." Paul took five dollars from his pocket and put it into the boy's dirty hand. "Get two cups of coffee and something for yourself to eat."

Tut stood still.

"See the diner up the street with the sign?" Paul pointed. "Go ahead."

The boy hesitated, then moved from his spot, and shuffled up Second Street, dragging his broom behind him.

There was always a moment of mild surprise when Paul entered his wood shop, as though things should have somehow changed overnight. But all the machines, the stacks of material, the projects being made, and the piles of sawdust were exactly where they had been when he left the night before. The mingled odors of wood, glue, and varnish were still thick. It could not have been otherwise, Paul knew, no elves to rearrange things during the night, but he somehow expected a difference. Or wanted one, he thought today—a change, a little less of the everydayness, the "same old same old," as his neighbor Mr. Mitchell put it. Standing briefly at the door, as if he had not quite decided to stay, Paul felt suddenly bored and fatigued by the idea of spending the rest of his life in just this same way, having to continue for money, responsibility, or just out of habit, but continuing day in and day out without wavering.

At the back of the shop, Andre ripped a sheet of plywood on the table saw, filling the air with dust. Paul went into his tiny office, closing the door against the noise and the dust to listen to any messages on the answering machine and attend to the paperwork. Paul made more money now than ever, but he had more headaches. He often missed the days when he could come into the shop and work at his own pace, doing one of the small showcase cabinets he used to make with such care. He would sometimes bring his wife and girl along on a Saturday and would carve or do inlay or just reglue chairs, "quiet work," as his wife straightened out the office and his girl played in the wood shavings or built houses with the cutoffs. But those days were gone because they were gone.

Paul did much less actual woodworking himself now because business matters always needed attention, and that took up much of his time. Andre and a retired man, who came in several days a week, did most of the woodworking, and Paul rarely went to the shop alone on Saturdays now because of what he remembered, his girl building her houses out of wood scraps.

There were no messages on the answering machine.

Paul took out the specs for an office job, made some quick sketches, and then estimated the materials needed, the labor to build, and the cost to have the unit spray-lacquered outside. He added all the numbers together and circled the total.

The table saw quit and Paul heard a rapping at the shop door. It was Tut returning with the coffee. Tut entered the shop, ducking through the doorway as if it were too low. He held out his fist, a few dollars showing outside his balled fingers.

"Keep the change," Paul said, taking one of the cups. "You didn't eat anything, did you?"

Tut didn't answer, only looked to Paul's side toward the floor, his hand still held out with the money in it.

"Look, if you want to sweep the shop, go ahead. After that, you have to go. Okay?"

Tut seemed to nod.

13

"All right, give Andre his coffee, and put that money in your pocket." Paul walked into his office.

He remained at his desk for two straight hours, doing drawings and cut lists, estimating bids, answering and making phone calls. The paperwork gave Paul a headache. While he rubbed his temples with his eyes closed, Andre showed up at the door, a mallet in one hand, a chisel in the other.

"You finished the lion heads?" Paul asked.

"Not yet. I just wanted to tell you that the kid's done sweeping."

Paul stood up and handed Andre five dollars. "Give it to him and tell him to go."

Andre took the money but did not move, studying the edge of his chisel.

"What is it?"

"Nothing."

"Is it the kid?"

"It's the kid."

"Look, we don't know that he doesn't have a roof over his head."

"But it doesn't look like he does."

"He's got to have some relatives."

"Maybe, but he's not living with any of them from what I can see."

"Then take him home with you."

"I don't think Charlotte and the kids would appreciate that."

"So what do you expect me to do?"

"Maybe he could sleep in the shop?"

"Sleep in the shop? No, I don't think so. Anyway, we'd have to lock him in here, and I don't think he'd like that."

"You want me to ask him?"

"How's he going to answer you if he can't talk?"

"Winter's coming; it's going to be cold."

"Andre, we can't have him sleeping here. What if he turns on a machine and hurts himself?"

"I guess you're right," Andre muttered. "Damn shame," and he left the office.

Yes, Paul said to himself, damn shame, and yes again as, shortly later, Tut walked by the office and out the door, dragging his broom.

Paul had returned to his paperwork, but he could not concentrate. He was relieved when his uncle Rick telephoned.

"Busy?" his uncle asked.

"Not for you," and Paul meant it, his affection for Rick long-standing and deep.

"We decided on the honeymoon." Rick had divorced a few years ago and was about to marry again in a few weeks; he had asked Paul to be his best man.

"Good. Acapulco?"

"Italy. She wants to see the original David and the Pope on his balcony."

"You might get blessed."

"I could use it; maybe it'll help me win the lottery, or maybe just the street number."

Paul laughed and felt a rush of warmth for his uncle, affection that went all the way back to Paul's childhood when Rick came to live with Paul's family after Rick's mother threw him out of the house for practicing his saxophone late in the night and for what Rick called "general delinquency." The brother of Paul's father, Rick lived with the family for several months, sleeping in the other twin bed in Paul's bedroom. He spent his workless days playing the saxophone in a sleeveless undershirt and khaki pants, smoking cigarettes, reading worn paperback books in bed, writing in a notebook, or talking to Paul in long, nearly incomprehensible riffs which were hypnotic, as compelling as any fairy tale or children's story, even though Paul understood little. Rick would come in late at night and Paul would hear him on the stairs, climbing slowly, and then entering the room. He was often humming tunes. Rick would not turn on the light, pulling off his clothes in the dark, and he would lie back on the twin bed too small for him,

15

a blade of silver light from the street lamp coming in at the window and cutting across his chest. Often, he would light a cigarette, the match like a sudden balloon of light expanding quickly against the darkness, then nearly as quickly shrinking back to darkness but for the orange ember, which flared brighter and caused Rick's face to glow momentarily as he inhaled. The invisible smoke seemed to lightly cover Paul's face. "You awake?" his uncle would often say. And Paul, not quite ten years old yet, would say yes, and for a long while that seemed enough for Rick, just that answer, as though all he needed at the time was the knowledge that he wasn't awake in the deep night alone. "Still awake?" his uncle would say later, but after Paul's yes this time, his uncle would launch into one of his riffs of fantastic, mysterious, spellbinding talk, none of which Paul could ever recall in any detail but which always struck him as marvelous and somehow essential to Rick. Paul would fall asleep to that voice in the dark, feeling safe. In the morning, Rick would already be awake when Paul woke, reading in bed with a cigarette in his mouth, scribbling in the notebook or cleaning his saxophone. Later in the day, they might go together to the playground and toss a ball back and forth or go to the local library. Once they went to the Art Museum on the Parkway, where they strolled among the paintings and sculpture. Rick also took Paul to a fight at the Blue Horizon in North Philadelphia and to a circus, both after the week Paul had to stay in the house for stealing the chalices from the Church of the Epiphany with Frankie Vespers.

Paul could not explain what influence Vespers, a "bad kid" in the neighborhood, had over him, except that Paul wanted Frank to like him. When Vespers suggested they steal the gold chalices and sell them to a fence he knew, Paul found himself agreeing to do it. The church was unlocked then, and Frank stole the chalices in less than a few minutes while Paul stood lookout. Frank gave the chalices to Paul to hold without explaining why, and Paul didn't know why until word went through the neighborhood that there had been a desecration

16

of the church—someone had violated the sacred altar and the tabernacle and stolen the chalices. Some of the neighbors thought that the thieves should be stoned or burned alive when caught. Paul heard his mother and the woman who lived next door discussing these gruesome retributions while they hung laundry in their backyards. "They should burn in hell," his mother said. At that moment, the chalices were sitting in a pillowcase in Paul's closet. He knew then why Vespers had given the chalices to Paul to hold: Paul had the evidence. He ran from the house looking for Frank; when he found Vespers, Paul told him that he wanted to give him the chalices and that he no longer wanted a cut of the money Frank would get after selling them. Fine, Vespers had said, and told Paul to bring the chalices to him at seven o'clock that night. Paul felt relieved by that, but when he went home he found that his mother had decided to do spring cleaning and had begun with his room. She had found the chalices. "It's you?" she said, angry, hurt, shocked. "My own son, my good boy? You did it?" Paul could only gape at her, shame and fear hot in his belly. Before he could think to tell her about Frank, Paul's mother told him to return the chalices to the monsignor at the rectory, confess his sin of theft, and beg forgiveness. "I'm going to call the Father in an hour to make sure you have," his mother said. The church was only ten minutes away, but it took Paul nearly the full hour to work up the courage to walk there and up the rectory steps. But when the janitor answered the door, instead of asking for the priest, Paul thrust the pillowcase into his hands and ran. He told his mother that he had given the chalices to the monsignor, but she called the rectory anyway and learned otherwise. Paul's mother punished him by making him stay in his room all day and then in the house all week, allowing Paul out on Sunday only for Mass. Before the priest began his sermon, he alluded to the stolen chalices, saying that they had been returned by the person who stole them. But the priest feared that the thief was not "wholly contrite, not sorry enough in his heart." If the thief was present, "and I believe he is, couldn't he show God that he is truly sorry by standing up right now and acknowledging his sin?" Paul froze and did not take his eyes from the back of the woman in front of him; she swept her eyes about the church along with most everyone else, looking for the thief to show himself. Then Paul's mother elbowed him. He ignored her. She elbowed him again. He remained rigid, looking neither right nor left, his rapidly beating heart making his entire body pulse. Then his mother took Paul by the elbow and, standing, yanked him to his feet; then she sat down. Paul felt on fire, as though already burning at the stake with thousands of eyes watching. People murmured; a few children laughed briefly. Paul looked at no one. "You may sit now, son," the priest called from the pulpit. Paul could not move and his mother pulled him down to the seat by his arm.

The trips to the fight and the circus, Paul realized later, had been attempts by his uncle Rick to ease the sting of that church experience. "Big deal, chalices," Rick had said when he heard about it. "It's just metal they put wine in. Look at it this way, Paul, you're a star now, famous; you've got reputation. You did something that sets you apart."

Despite what his uncle said, Paul could not see past the humiliation in the church to anything positive.

After three months with Paul's family, Rick announced one morning that he was going to drive to California with a bunch of his friends. The next day, Rick left the house when a large car with four men wearing sunglasses and smoking cigarettes pulled up out front. Rick slid into the car and waved briefly to Paul on the sidewalk, and the car drove away. Paul did not see his uncle for years.

Rick spent a year as a house painter in Santa Barbara and then returned to Philadelphia; "after a period of craziness," as Rick put it, he moved to New York, where he tried to "get serious" about a music career but failed. "I only had to see what it took to be serious to realize that I wasn't serious enough. I was only a dabbler," he told Paul. After New York, Rick returned to Philadelphia for good, and worked at a number of odd jobs for five or six years before going into the clothing business. Not until Paul had become an adult and spent a good many evenings in Rick's house would he know that Rick had spent some of those years in "activities" that, but for luck, Rick said, could have put him in jail. He did not elaborate.

"Anyway," Rick said over the telephone, "I was wondering if you might want to meet me for lunch tomorrow or the next day."

"Sure, sounds like a good idea. Let me get my schedule straight and I'll call you."

"Good. So call me."

They hung up.

Paul tried to do the paperwork again but could not focus enough to accomplish anything. Giving up, he went out into the shop, hoping to clear his head. Andre stood at his bench, cutting a mortise in a trestle table support. The mortise was sharp and clean, without ragged edges. Andre's personal chisels lay on his workbench in their leather pouch. German steel, German made, he had told Paul; they were old, too, when steel was harder because of a higher carbon content, and so the chisels needed sharpening less frequently.

"Paperwork blues again?" Andre asked, without looking up from his work at Paul, standing near.

Paul nodded.

"Make something. Doesn't that usually help you?"

"Usually."

"Why don't you make one of your showcase cabinets with some of that wood you've been squirreling away for years."

"You convinced me."

Paul went to his special wood pile and selected for the cabinet door a two-foot two-inch-thick piece of walnut that he would resaw and glue back together in a bookmatch. He then picked the wood for the cabinet sides, making sure the arch patterns of the grain were similar, and found a board for the top and bottom. For the cabinet back, Paul searched for clear, straight-grain ash that would create "light" inside the cabinet because of its blond color.

Paul made a quick sketch, figured the measurements, and went to work. First, he surfaced the wood on the joiner, as loud as a subway train, and then went to the planer, even louder, and reduced the wood parts to their final thicknesses: one inch thick for the top and bottom of the cabinet, three-quarters of an inch thick for the sides and door frame, one-half inch for the back panel. Paul cut all the carcass parts to length and width on the table saw, the sawdust flying back at him, and then ripped and crosscut the rails and stiles for the door and back panel frames. He would mortise and tenon the rails and stiles using his own chisels, which were not as sharp as Andre's but nearly so.

As Paul ran the glue edges of the boards carefully over the joiner, Andre tapped him on the shoulder.

"What?" Paul shouted above the noise of the machine.

Andre cocked his head toward the office, his eyebrows slightly raised.

Looking toward the front of the shop, Paul saw Claire Lawrence standing outside the office, smiling at him. She wore a skirt and blouse, and, with her hair free and nearly touching her shoulders, Paul nearly failed to recognize her. Bright sunlight from the large windows facing Second Street framed her, and she looked radiant and beautiful against the dark walls and clutter.

"I let myself in," she said as Paul came up. "I hope you don't mind."

"Not at all," Paul said, aware of the sawdust on his bare forearms, on his clothes, and probably in his hair, feeling embarrassed because of it.

Paul first saw Claire on the South Street Bridge three weeks ago during his morning run. He glimpsed her sunlit profile as she stood stretching at the iron balustrade. They made brief eye contact as she turned from the dull river to watch him pass. Paul looked away and did not think of her until some days later when she ran past him outside of Franklin

Field. After several strides, he recognized her back and the straw color of her hair. She ran with an easy athletic rhythm, almost grace, and the space between them steadily widened until she turned a corner on the University of Pennsylvania's campus and vanished. Approaching the burned-out supermarket at Twenty-third and South the following morning, Paul saw her limbering up on the sidewalk. He nodded to her, and moments later she fell in stride with him, asking if he'd mind if she joined him. Paul said no, and they ran together through West Philadelphia, turning at Thirty-eighth Street, and returned to Center City on Market. They ran together most mornings since then, though without talking much. He knew she lived somewhere on Pine Street, and she told him she had run track and thrown the javelin in high school, as though to explain her excellent stamina. Paul told her he lived near Bainbridge Street and went to the gym four or five times a week. He did not tell her that he exercised so often because of the fatigue that resulted, that he jumped rope, rowed, and punched the heavy bag with a savagery as if to burst its seams so that when he returned to his empty house he'd be tired enough to face it, his emotions dulled by weariness. Mostly he and Claire exchanged pleasantries. But a few days ago, Paul mentioned that he owned a wood shop, and almost immediately Claire said that she had been wanting to have a wall unit custom-built for a long time now and asked Paul if he wanted the job. He'd be happy to do it, he said, and went to her house last evening to take measurements. After he finished making a rough sketch and penciling in lengths and heights, Claire offered Paul tea or coffee. He agreed to tea, and they spoke during the short time it took for the tea to brew and for Paul to drink it. When Paul walked home through the October night twenty minutes later, Claire's image lingered with him the entire way.

"I was in the neighborhood to drop my car off at the mechanic's," Claire said, "and thought I'd stop by to give you your deposit."

"Come into the office." Paul walked past her into the bright room and sat at the desk, offering the chair at the drawing table to her.

"So, this is the shop," Claire said, looking in her purse for her checkbook. "It's bigger than I thought."

"And we still don't have enough space."

Claire found the checkbook and asked Paul how much he wanted as a down payment. He gave Claire the price of the unit he had figured that morning and asked for a third of the cost. "That's standard," he said, uncomfortable with the money talk.

"Fine," and Claire began to write out a check.

"It'll take four to six weeks. That's standard, too."

"No hurry."

Claire handed the check to Paul, who folded it and put it in his pocket without looking at it, as though it were something slightly obscene best gotten out of sight quickly.

"Well, thanks," Claire said. She began to move toward the door.

"Heading back to work?"

"The salt mine, yes."

"Uh, need a ride?"

"Thanks, but I think I'll walk because I'm missing my aerobics class tonight. I'm having dinner with my father." Claire's face went momentarily somber, her eyebrows coming together in a frown. "He's been acting strange lately; actually he hasn't been himself since the divorce. But this entire last month, he's been odd."

Paul gazed at the floor, not knowing what to say.

But Claire brightened as quickly as the cast had come over her features. "Well, thanks again," she said, holding out her hand to shake.

Paul took it and found Claire's grip firm and warm. He opened the door for her and she stepped out, smiling once at him before turning toward Spring Garden Street and the El. Paul watched Claire walk down the street. She turned briefly at the corner, as though she could feel Paul's gaze. She smiled and waved.

Claire Lawrence, Paul thought; then the ringing phone called him inside.

3

COPS? Benny thought, when he felt the blow. Then, as he slumped toward the floor, he thought cops didn't usually hit you like that without a warning. Maybe somebody *was* in the house after all, all this time, listening to Benny break up the place, maybe watching him and just now working up the nerve to crack his head. Or somebody followed him into the house. Whatever. The main thing was Benny got clunked, making him drop the box of coins out of surprise and some pain. He heard the box hit the tile, and then watched half-shocked as this strange guy maybe in his fifties and wearing a suit—a suit!—reached down and grabbed it. The guy didn't say a word and started for the door. But not wanting to give up the coins so easily, Benny dove after the guy and grabbed his leg before he moved out of reach. The man fell and the box of coins flew across the kitchen. Benny started to scramble up the guy's back to slam his head into the floor, but the man twisted onto his side and swung back with—what was it?—a fire poker. He struck Benny on the head and shoulders four or five times before Benny let go of the leg to cover himself. The man whacked Benny twice on the arms and then crawled across the floor toward the coins. He had nearly reached them when Benny lunged and grabbed his leg again.

"Goddamn!" the man shouted, and swung back again like a jockey beating a horse to make it run faster.

Benny covered his head again and the poker struck him across the knuckles, which hurt more than the hits to the head. He felt the pain shoot up his arm and into his head, where he saw stars. The man crawled toward the coins again, and Benny, his hand killing him, followed on his knees. The old guy grabbed the coins and stood up. He took one step, but Benny lunged again and caught him by the ankle.

"Let go!"

"Fuck you!"

Benny heard the poker break the air before it hit him again. The man went a little berserk now and hit Benny again and again on the head, the shoulders, the arms, the back, just flailing away, until Benny said Fuck this to himself and let go. The guy dropped the poker and hurried through the family room and out the patio doors, Benny listening to his footsteps fade.

Benny slowly rolled over onto his back and stared at the ceiling, his head feeling hot, his hand killing him.

"Shit."

The house was very quiet now; Benny could hear his breathing and the rain in the drain spout outside. He felt almost comfortable, the floor tiles warm on his back, until he ran his fingers over his scalp and felt the lumps and the blood. Lucky it was only a fire poker the old guy hit him with and not something heavier, like a baseball bat, which is what anybody serious would've used, like Benny.

Benny pulled himself up and sat with his back against the refrigerator, waiting for his head to stop spinning before getting to his feet. He walked weak-legged to the sink, turned on the water, and stuck his head under the tap. The cuts stung, but he let the water run over his head for awhile before turning off the faucet. Later, Benny wondered what the owners would have thought if they came home just then and found him at the sink—that he busted in their house to wash his hair? He almost laughed about it.

Benny found a couple of dish towels in a drawer and used them to dry his head. It didn't even feel like a head, it was so lumpy and dented; it felt like a cantaloupe going bad. It hurt to press the towel against the lumps, but Benny could take pain; as a matter of fact, he was good at it.

Least he still had the cash, Benny thought. But his thirty thousand in coins was gone and whatever that other doubloon thing was worth. Who the fuck was that guy?

Turning from the sink and about to leave the house before somebody came in, Benny spotted what looked like a small wallet on the floor. He picked it up, his head throbbing when he bent down. It was one of those business card holders and inside there were a bunch of little white cards, all the same. Benny read the information from the top card.

"Henry Lawrence?" he mumbled, and then thought, I got my ass kicked and my coins boosted by a guy named Henry Lawrence, an insurance salesman? It didn't make any sense. But that didn't matter. Benny had the guy's name from the card, his company, the company's telephone number, and—some luck was still on Benny's side—a Philadelphia number with the word *Home* beside it. That, and getting the coins back, was all that mattered.

In the car after he left the house, the dish towels streaked with his blood beside him, Benny looked at himself in the rearview mirror and decided that he didn't look that bad. He was feeling a little better, too, and thought he'd go to Atlantic City, start tracking down this Henry Lawrence and maybe see if Audrey was around.

Twenty minutes later, Benny pulled into the Bally's parking lot, let a valet deal with his car, and headed for the casino. He detoured to a pay telephone in the hotel lobby and, after

26

dropping over a dollar in change in the slot, called his widowed mother in Philadelphia.

"Ma, it's Benny."

"Benny, you coming to dinner?" She sounded as though she had been drinking again.

"No, I'm in Jersey seeing some friends."

"Are you coming tomorrow? I have your laundry all cleaned."

"Thanks, Ma. I'll try to get there. Listen, I want you to do me a favor. You got the phone book there, the white pages? Look something up for me, would ya?"

"Sure, Benny, what is it?"

Benny had to spell Lawrence's name four times and his mother had to write it down, and then she had to find her glasses so she could see the tiny print in the phone book, and then she had to remember where *L* came in the alphabet, so that by the time she finally found *Lawrence,* Benny wanted to strangle her.

"Here it is. Howard Lawrence," his mother said.

"Henry, Ma. *Henry* Lawrence."

"Oh." She muttered the name as she looked again. "I found it. There's two. You want the numbers?"

"Yes, Ma, I want the numbers and the addresses."

"All right." The first number did not match the one on the business card, but the second one did. Benny listened carefully to the address, making his mother repeat it twice as he wrote it down on the card. "How many times you want me to say it?"

"That's good, Ma, thanks." Benny said good-bye and hung up. He looked at the address, knowing the apartment building: the Dorchester on Rittenhouse Square in Center City Philly. You had to have money to live there. So why was this Lawrence doing burglary and hitting Benny on the head? Maybe that's how he got rich, a professional thief? The guy sure didn't look like a pro, and he swung that poker like a fairy. But so what? The main thing Benny had to do was to figure out what his next move should be, whether Lawrence was a professional or not. The guy could be racing back to Philly right now to see a fence or a coin dealer, who would cash the coins. But cashing the coins would be doing Benny a favor; it would save him the trouble of doing it. All he had to do then was to get to Lawrence before the money disappeared. Even if the money went into the bank, which Benny didn't think would happen, he knew he could strong-arm the guy to get it, no sweat, and probably have fun doing it.

But that was going to have to wait just a little while. Benny had begun to feel dizzy, and the only thing he wanted to do at the moment was put his head in Audrey's lap and rest. Or get a massage from her, but nothing sexy. Didn't she say she was working Bally's this week? Benny went to look for her in the casino.

He did a couple of circles around the blackjack and craps tables, which were pretty quiet, but did not see Audrey. Benny checked the lounge, but she was not there either. He ordered a rum and Coke and decided to wait for her to show up, knowing that if she was working now she would come down to the bar afterwards, because that's what she always did. He had met Audrey at the bar a few years ago with Freddie Whale, the loan shark, and Benny's good friend Gus. It was right before Benny's first stint in Holmesburg, where he used to lie on his bunk thinking about the things he had done to her and the things he would do to her when he saw her again. Benny marked Audrey for a hooker as soon as he saw her because he had previous experience with them. Benny had girlfriends, he was even serious about some, but he liked hookers, too. Why not? You could do things with a hooker you couldn't do with your wife or somebody you were serious about, and which if you did it wouldn't be the same. Audrey was somewhere in between, half-hooker, half-girlfriend. The hooker half still jazzed Whale once in a while, though it was only Whale who ever mentioned it to him, not Audrey. The girlfriend half let Benny give Audrey things for her birthday and take her out to dinner and sometimes to a movie now and then. At first, she was just a whore, and Benny paid her for the works, did everything. But the more he saw her on later trips to the casinos, the more he liked her; and the more he liked her the less he treated her like a whore and the less she treated him like a trick. He would see Audrey now sometimes and not even touch her, or if he touched her it was just to hug her, be friendly. Sometimes they kissed and Benny tasted Listerine on her breath. He made Audrey swear that she didn't have AIDS, made her get blood tests every month, and made her promise that any john she took on had to wear a rubber no matter what they wanted to do. Audrey had promised. But whenever Benny banged her now, he used a rubber because he knew that if a hooker was looking at a couple C notes, even less, most of them would let a john have what he wanted, not wearing a lube being the least of it.

"Hiya, Benny," Audrey said, coming up from behind him.

Benny jumped a little in his seat and turned.

"What happened to you?" Audrey's smile with the gold tooth vanished. "Those bruises."

"There's a lot more on my head."

"Are you all right?"

"I probably got internal bleeding."

"Oh, Benny, let's go to the hospital."

"No, I'm all right. But if I could lay down in a big bed, I'd feel better."

"Okay, come on." Audrey took Benny by the arm, and they walked out of the casino and down the corridor to the elevators.

Stepping off the elevator at the fourth floor, Benny followed Audrey down the hall. She stopped at a room, pulled a key from her purse and opened the door. The room had a beige carpet and a lamp on each side of the bed, a couple of cheap dressers, and a small round table; it smelled the same as the casino. The room faced the ocean and the Boardwalk directly below. Benny parted the curtains a little and looked out the window. He couldn't tell where the ocean ended and the sky began; it was just black out there beyond the white breaking waves and the beach, which he could see because of the bright lights from the Boardwalk. Looking down at it, Benny saw a few people here and there, most of them walking with umbrellas.

Benny turned from the window and lay down on the bed. Audrey began to remove his boots. "Leave 'em on," Benny said.

"I'll rub your feet."

"Leave 'em on."

"Suit yourself." Audrey crawled up the length of the bed and lay down beside Benny, but propped up on her elbow. "So what happened?"

Instead of telling her, Benny took the jewelry from his pockets and told her to take whatever she wanted.

"Really?" Audrey giggled.

"G'head, take anything."

Audrey sorted through the jewelry, trying on the rings and the bracelets, holding up earrings and necklaces and asking Benny how they looked. He said everything looked beautiful even if it didn't. What did he know about jewelry? Audrey settled on a round five items, leaving the rest for Benny to fence or pawn.

"Now, let's relax." Benny ran his fingers over his scalp, lightly touching the bumps.

"Anything I can do to make you relax better?" Audrey smiled and placed Benny's hand on her thigh.

"Baby," Benny said.

That evening, not long after he returned to Philly, Benny sat with Freddie Whale at one of the tables in the club on Dickenson Street. It was dark outside, and the light in the club wasn't that much better. The club was a pretty dingy place to begin with; the walls above the dark wood paneling were covered with yellowed paper and the wood floor had no finish on it, so the few lights dangling in the ceiling didn't help much. In the daytime, a lot of light came through the big plate glass windows, but at night you felt like you were going blind.

Guys sat at some of the other tables, one of them that nut

Cosmo, so Maglio had to be in the back room. Old one-legged Lenny was making sandwiches behind the small counter now, and Benny saw him go in the back a couple times with things to eat and drink. Nobody talked too loud, like they were at a wake, but that was because Maglio was there. They didn't want to annoy him. After Tucci got whacked at the airport, which everybody knew was Maglio's doing, dead guys started turning up all over South Philly and Jersey. Maglio was cleaning house. There were jokes that if Maglio didn't like your shoes, he'd have Cosmo put a bullet in the back of your head. Benny believed it, and he knew Whale did, because Benny could always see the fear in Whale's eyes when Maglio came up.

Whale was drinking Sambuca and smoking his cigar, one fat arm on the table, the other in his lap. He had a fat neck with a couple of warts on it, a big head with little ears, and the kind of hair with the baldness racing up two sides of his forehead, leaving a section of hair in the middle. When you saw Whale, Benny thought, you knew why they called him Whale. He was big, mostly in the belly, and had to sit back from the table because of it.

Benny had dropped by the club on his way uptown to the Dorchester because earlier in the day Gus had told Benny that Whale had a job for him.

"What were you doing today?" Whale asked, blowing out cigar smoke like a bus.

"Little a this, little a that," Benny said, lying. "Nothing special." No way Benny was going to tell the fat guy about the coin job, knowing Whale would want a piece of it, thinking he deserved it because he had this idea that Benny worked for him. Which was true in that Benny pretty much did whatever Whale asked him to do and then was paid for it, but Benny worked for himself mostly. Well, maybe not mostly, but he did a lot of jobs on the side that he wasn't told by Whale to do. He was his own man. And after he got the coins, he might just go into his own business and kiss off Whale for good.

"The nothing special fuck up your face?"

"I got in an argument on Broad Street with a couple of weight lifters."

"Weight lifters, huh?" Whale looked at him. "Dope."

Benny didn't care what Whale called him, just so Benny got past him with the lie without being cross-examined.

"Gus said you had a job for me," Benny said, wanting to get the bullshit over with so he could leave and take care of the coins.

"Yeah." Whale flicked ashes off his cigar, hanging over the side of the table even though there was an ashtray right in front of him. "It's a boat."

"A boat?"

"Don't you know what a boat is?"

"Sure, I know."

"It's at the Penn's Landing marina, belongs to some prick who owes me money."

"I don't know how to drive a boat," Benny said, thinking about the time he went out on the ocean and got sick, and how he'd wanted no part of boats ever since.

"Nobody *drives* a boat, you moron. You sail it."

"I don't know how to sail one."

"Who asked you to? I don't want you to steal it. Just damage it a little."

"Oh." Benny was relieved. "How little?"

"Firebomb it."

"That's not little."

"I want to see it on the TV news, burning in the river."

"There's lots of boats there. How do I know which one?"

"They got names. This one's Typhoon; it's written on the sides and back in big letters."

"Typhoon?" Benny wondered how it was spelled but didn't ask, not wanting Whale to say he was stupid.

"Yeah. Torch it. But make sure nobody's on board. I don't want to have to worry about a murder getting connected to me like that other job you did."

"Aw, you're bringing that up again?"

32

"A day don't go by when I don't think that's going to come back to haunt me."

"Nothing ever happened. It all worked out."

"Lucky for you."

What Whale reminded Benny of just about every time he saw him was the time a few years ago when Benny was supposed to mess up this guy's car for being late in his payment to Whale. Benny could've just smashed the windows with a tire iron and slashed the tires like a punk, but instead he cut the brake lines of the car and the pickup truck the guy owned. When the guy drove, the brakes would give out a few blocks later and he'd smack into the back of a bus or something, maybe get banged up a little, then he would just have to be reminded that next time would be worse. Benny thought it was a smooth idea. The guy did drive away in the truck the morning after the fixing but he must have realized something was wrong and stopped, using the emergency brake, Benny figured. But that wasn't the big problem. The big problem was that the guy's wife and kid got in the car and wound up skidding into the Delaware River, where the kid drowned. Whale saw it on the news and freaked, not just because he thought the cops might find out about the cut brake lines, investigate, and pin a murder on him, but because he thought the guy wouldn't pay him now. As Benny said, though, nothing ever happened, and it all worked out. That's why Benny couldn't figure why Whale brought it up all the time, except to break Benny's balls.

"So, how much for the boat?" Whale asked.

"How 'bout if I tell you later?"

"What, you need to think about it?"

"I have to check out the situation, see what's what."

"Just do it and we'll work out the money later."

Benny didn't like that but didn't say anything; he would have if he wasn't thinking about the coins.

Lenny thumped over on his fake leg and put the sandwiches they ordered in front of them. "He wants you," Lenny said to Whale, tipping his head toward Maglio's back room.

Whale nodded, and Benny noticed the fear come into his eyes. "Call me after you do it," he said to Bean, before heaving himself up from the table and whaling across the room.

Benny imagined throwing a harpoon into the fat bastard's back.

Relieved that Whale was gone, Benny took a few big bites of his sandwich, wanting to finish it quickly so he could get down to the real business, the coins. But halfway into the ham and cheese, Gus came in, nodded to the guys by the door, couldn't miss Benny, and came over. Benny was glad to see him; Gus was one of the few friendly guys in that joint. They had been in prison together when Benny went for the first time, the same cell even, and Benny liked Gus a lot. Sometimes Benny thought the only thing that would make him cry was seeing Gus in a casket.

They shook hands. "Your face?" Gus asked.

"It's a long story."

"I got time."

Benny put down his sandwich and leaned toward Gus. "Feel my head."

"Feel your head?"

"G'head, feel it."

Gus rubbed his fingers over Benny's scalp. "It's all lumps."

"I got those today." And then, talking low but not whispering, not wanting to worry the goons, who sat too far away to hear anyway, Benny began to tell Gus how he broke into a house and copped the small cash and the jewelry, and how he found this batch of coins but didn't get away with them because, get this, some old guy beat him over the head with a fire poker and took them.

"Aw, shit, you're kidding me," Gus said.

"No. Can you beat that?"

"Who was it?"

"First, I thought it coulda been a professional thief who got to the house right after I did and let me do all the work. Only thing was, he wasn't interested in anything but the coins. I could tell by the way he fought for 'em, the way he knew they

34

were in the box I had when he hit me. Which didn't explain much or even matter. He had my coins, that's all that mattered. I did the work to get them and I want them back."

"Well sure, but how you gonna do that? You don't know the guy from Adam."

Benny took the little folder of business cards from his pocket and showed Gus. "It musta fell from his pocket when we were fighting. I did some investigating and already got his home address, the Dorchester uptown."

Gus read the top card. "Henry Lawrence." He handed the cards back. "When you gonna see him?"

"Real soon."

"Need any help?"

"Thanks, but no. I can handle it."

"Let me know what happens."

"Naturally."

"Good." Gus paused, glancing at the door to the back room. "Whale get called in?"

Benny nodded. "He told me about the boat job, but I'm not crazy about it."

"How much did you ask for?"

"I didn't, but it'll have to be something nice. Like, I figure, eight hunnert."

"Eight hunnert? He won't go for that, Benny."

"Gus, I'm gonna have thirty thou soon, and I'm going to need some big incentive to do any kind of job. I might not do anything, just take a vacation."

"Whale'll laugh at eight hunnert, Benny."

"Tough."

"Whatever you say, big man." Gus motioned to Lenny, then called a roast beef sandwich to him. Lenny barely nodded.

"By the way," Benny said, "I didn't mention the coins to Whale."

"Okay. It's safe with me."

It was Holmesburg prison they were in together. Benny could still remember it like it was yesterday—the cockroaches, the yard, the cafeteria, the showers, the men. Instead of Gus's cologne and coffee, he now smelled the lousy food, smoke, disinfectant, insecticide, shit. He thought about how crazy with the heebie-jeebies he got those first few days, locked in a cell with Gus, who was doing six years for involuntary manslaughter after having dropped a guy over the side of the railing along Thirtieth Street near Chestnut, where the railroad tracks ran forty feet below—a job he did for Freddie Whale, but which he never mentioned in court, of course. Gus only got charged with the involuntary manslaughter and not murder because his lawyer convinced the jury that Gus had only wanted to scare the guy by dangling him over the railing but he slipped out of Gus's hands, fell, and broke his neck, which was true.

Benny saw himself now in the prison those first days, yelling, climbing the bars, pounding the walls, the other inmates yelling to shut up or laughing crazily at his craziness. Gus had to grab Benny from behind and put a choke hold on him which, after Benny went spastic, knocked him out. Benny woke calmer, with Gus looking down in his face, telling him it was going to be a long sentence if he didn't settle down. Benny told him that he was all right, but during those first few weeks he got the heebie-jeebies often and so intensely that he *asked* Gus to do the sleeper number on him, which Gus did, wrapping his big arm around Benny's neck and squeezing the jugulars and the windpipe together between his forearm and his biceps until a curtain came over Benny's eyes. He never knew how long he was knocked out unless he checked a watch; sometimes a minute, sometimes longer, depending on how long Gus squeezed. But whatever the length, Benny always felt calmer when he woke up, the willies gone. Even after Benny started taking the Valiums he bought from the guys who dealt them, he asked Gus to give him the sleeper now and then because it was instant and total.

Benny fought often during his early weeks in prison until word got around that he was connected to Gus. No one bothered Gus, partly because he was large and muscular, but mostly because he was one of Maglio's men and Maglio was the big mahof in Philly after Carmine Tucci. The association protected Gus and, through Gus, Benny.

Gus finished his sentence a half year after Benny. Benny visited him every two weeks and, upon Gus's release, met him outside the prison with an almost brand-new Buick Electra that Benny had gone all the way to Delaware to steal. Benny had filed off the serial numbers and had Selligrini paint it. "It's yours," he said to Gus, handing him the keys. Gus seemed happy to get the car, hugging Benny for it. After Gus got settled, he introduced Benny to Freddie Whale. It was a good relationship for a while, with Benny even having some good times with Whale, but that didn't last, and now it was pretty obvious that Whale didn't like Benny too much.

Benny waited for Gus to get his sandwich from Lenny, and they ate together, talking about things you forgot about a half minute after saying them. When they finished eating, Benny said he had to go; he wanted to deal with Lawrence and did not want to still be around when Whale came out of the Maglio room. Maglio might come out with him, and that guy gave Benny the chills.

"So I'll be seeing you," Benny said, standing up from the table. He waved a ten at Lenny and dropped it beside his plate, thinking it was way too much for a ham and cheese sandwich and a beer, but what the hell, the guy had one leg.

"Good luck," Gus said.

"Piece a cake." And Benny walked out of the club.

4

AFTER parking his car on Eighteenth Street near Delancy, Benny Bean walked the block to Rittenhouse Square. Surrounded on all four sides by some of the priciest real estate in the city, the square had walkways criss-crossing it, big trees, large areas of grass, and a bronze statue of a lion snarling at a snake. Benny entered the square, well-lighted by lamps, and walked through it toward the Dorchester on the other side. A few people were sitting on benches or strolling on the walkways. But they wouldn't be for long, Benny thought, because it had begun to drizzle again.

His plan was to sit somewhere not too conspicuous where he could watch the entrance to the Dorchester, so that if Henry Lawrence came out or went in Benny would see him. Benny had telephoned Lawrence just before leaving South Philly to see if he was home—not to talk—but no one answered; Lawrence was either out or not answering his phone. Benny figured he was out. If Benny didn't see Lawrence tonight, he'd come early the next morning and wait again; then he would play it by ear. Lawrence would have to show up sometime, unless he had never returned to the city with the coins. Benny didn't want to think about that.

He considered going up to Lawrence's apartment, but that meant he would have to get past the doorman Benny now saw and the people at the desk in the lobby, which would be more trouble than it was worth at this time. Waiting for Lawrence might take longer but it was safer, though the hedges that ran almost entirely around the park kept Benny from seeing the entrance to the Dorchester while sitting on a bench. He didn't want to stand around in front of the building because he would draw attention and allow somebody to identify him if they saw Lawrence get banged up.

Luckily, a thin street cut between the Dorchester and a row of townhouses, connecting Rittenhouse Square with Twentieth Street; a street lamp had blown out there, and the darkness made it a perfect spot for Benny to watch the entrance to the building and, through the floor-to-ceiling windows, the lobby.

Not wanting to be seen by the doorman, Benny walked through the park to Walnut Street, turned at the church, and hurried up Walnut to Twentieth. He turned down Twentieth, walked behind the Dorchester to the little street between the apartment building and the townhouses, and turned toward the square. He picked the darkest spot on the street and sat down on the sidewalk beside a set of front steps, with his back to the wall. He messed up his hair and tugged his clothes out of order so that anybody passing would think he was a homeless person or a drunk. Benny hoped he would not have to wait long and get slowly drenched by the rain.

But it was Benny's lucky night. After sitting only fifteen or twenty minutes, Benny saw two people come from the park and cross the street to the Dorchester. One was Lawrence, Benny had no doubt, the other a woman. Benny wanted to jump up right then and slam this guy who took his coins, but even if Lawrence wasn't alone, Benny wouldn't have been able to rough him up there because the doorman stood nearby under the entrance canopy.

Benny heard Lawrence's voice as he and the woman stood talking under the canopy. Lawrence talked loudly, as though he might be a little drunk. But he did not talk long before he kissed the woman on the cheek and went toward the entrance doors, nodding to the doorman as he passed.

"Goodnight, Dad," the woman called.

That figures, Benny thought.

Lawrence turned and waved briefly and then went through the doors, Benny following him with his eyes as he walked past the reception desk to the elevators.

After the elevator doors closed behind Lawrence, Benny looked back to the daughter and saw that she had walked away from the front of the Dorchester and around its side as she, too, watched Lawrence. Benny pressed himself against the steps as she walked past him on the other side of the street, preoccupied, her head now pointed at the ground. She did not seem to notice Benny.

As soon as the daughter turned the corner at Twentieth Street, Benny stood up. He figured he wasn't going to see Lawrence again tonight because Lawrence would probably stay in. He wouldn't be able to cash the coins at that hour anyway, or the coins were already cashed, in which case Benny would only have to twist the old guy's arm for the money. Benny would return tomorrow morning early. In the meantime, he started after the woman, thinking he might need to know where she lived in case things had to get complicated.

After following Lawrence's daughter home the night before, and doing a little peeping Tom to see if he had to concern himself with a husband or some other guy—it looked like she lived alone—Benny had gone home himself and gotten a good night's sleep. He woke up at seven, way earlier than his usual, but he felt good, excited even, thinking about what he was about to do.

Benny put on sweat pants and a sweat shirt and drove

uptown, parking on Nineteenth Street near the diner at Spruce at about eight o'clock. People were already jogging around Rittenhouse Square, so Benny fit right in. To keep from missing Lawrence, Benny ran only two sides instead of jogging all the way around the square and then cut through on a slant, corner to corner, making his route a triangle. He jogged at a slow pace, and even walked some, keeping his eyes on the front of the Dorchester the entire time. After five triangles, as Benny came out of the corner at Walnut Street, he spotted Lawrence just as he entered the square at the corner across from his building. He carried a briefcase. Benny continued in the direction he had been running and soon reached the entrance to the square where Lawrence had entered. He stopped running and walked after Lawrence, now at the center of the square. Lawrence walked to Eighteenth Street, left the square, and turned north. When Lawrence turned down Sansom Street, Benny hurried, wanting to catch him there because few people would be on Sansom at that hour of the morning.

Benny jogged after Lawrence, went past him a few steps, stopped abruptly and spun. He punched Lawrence in the stomach, brought his knee into the guy's face as he folded over, and then busted him in the mouth as he came up, throwing him back against a trash dumpster and knocking the briefcase from his hand. Lawrence wobbled a little with his back against the dumpster for a second or two, then slid straight down onto his butt. Blood ran from his nose and mouth onto his tie and light blue shirt.

"How's it feel?" Benny said, squatting down and taking hold of Lawrence's tie.

Dazed, his mouth open, Lawrence's head rolled as Benny jerked on the tie. Lawrence did not answer.

"I think I broke your nose," Benny said, "and guess what?" He stuck his fingers into Lawrence's mouth and yanked out two loosened front teeth. "You can kiss these good-bye." Benny flipped the teeth over his shoulder.

41

Lawrence's hand came up toward his mouth but fell as the teeth hit the sidewalk.

"All right, geek, look at me." Benny jerked the tie.

Lawrence's eyes were almost like Benny's when he did the downers and the vodka together, just these two openings in his head that let in different colors of light. Benny had to get Lawrence's attention and did it by knocking the back of his head against the metal dumpster, then jerking the tie again, choking off Lawrence's air.

"Do I look familiar? I'm the guy you bopped at the Jersey house. I don't care what you were doing there, but you took my coins and I want them back. Very simple. Now, tell me they're in the briefcase so we can call things even."

Lawrence managed to shake his head no.

"No? That's a shame." Benny slammed Lawrence's head— *bong!*—into the dumpster. "Now what do we do?"

Lawrence blinked, trying to breathe as Benny strangled him a little more.

"You go into your fancy building all fucked up in the face like this, then come out carrying a bag a minute later to give to me, it won't look right. So I think you better meet me somewhere, say, in the playground at Ninth and Fitzwater at, what, one-thirty. Near the monkey bars. That'll give you time to get cleaned up and get the coins or the cash, I don't care which. Got that? Say yes."

Lawrence nodded, panicky, his face nearly purple now.

"Good." Benny let go of the tie and immediately Lawrence grabbed at the knot and pulled it open so he could breathe. "And I don't have to tell you about going to the cops. You rat on me and I'll rat on you, and you're the one with the evidence, prick." Benny grabbed the briefcase and opened it. No coins, just papers. He dropped the case and stood up. "One-thirty, Ninth and Fitzwater. Don't be late. If I don't see you, you'll be very sorry." Benny hurried away and down the street, not looking back, but knowing Lawrence wouldn't be getting up any time soon.

Instead of going back to his apartment right away, Benny

drove down Broad Street, turned at Snyder Avenue, and stopped at the Melrose Diner at Fifteenth and Passyunk for some breakfast. He sat at the counter; he wasn't too hungry, but he ordered some scrambled eggs and toast anyway. After eating, he walked back to his car and killed some more time by going to the supermarket at Eleventh and Reed to get a few things he needed. He stuck a couple of bottles of aspirin in his jacket pocket before going to the checkout line.

He was taking the groceries out of the car in front of his apartment when he heard his name. Turning, he saw Gus coming his way on the sidewalk.

"How did it go, Benny?"

"Well, there's a guy lives in the Dorchester who got his face busted on the way to the office."

"So you got him."

"I got him good."

"You get the coins back?"

"This afternoon. I'm meeting him at the park at Fitzwater."

"What if he's got cops with him?"

"That's why this is so beautiful. If he goes to the cops, it's like telling them he stole the coins. He'd ruin himself, his reputation, all that. No, he won't have any cops with him."

"Thirty thou's a lot."

"Don't I know it. I could lay back a while on that."

"I still can't believe first your bad luck, then your good luck."

"Nuts, ain't it?"

"Least it looks like it's working out."

"Won't be long now."

"Well, I'm in a hurry to see Whale, Big Bean. So, see you later."

Benny liked when Gus called him Big Bean. They shook hands and Gus continued down the street.

Benny killed the rest of the time by first lifting some weights and then taking a nap. He woke up at twelve-thirty, took a shower, snorted just a little coke, and then drove to the playground, parking on Ninth Street. Benny reached the playground right at one-thirty but Lawrence was not in sight, so he waited around on one of the benches watching kids play, their mothers standing around talking or sitting on the benches. The kids made a lot of noise, screaming and laughing, and the mothers kept their eyes on them so they wouldn't do anything stupid and get hurt. It was about twelve years ago, Benny thought, that he used to play touch football in this playground with friends he knew. He was a quick kid, being small, and caught pretty much everything thrown to him. He played some baseball there, too, shortstop, but he wasn't much of a hitter. He wasn't too hot on sports in general, not like some of the guys he knew, but he liked to bet on sports. He had been betting since high school, where he did not often go to his classes, believing them a waste of time. You needed money to do everything, and you didn't make any money sitting in a classroom learning about history or algebra. So Benny started to push some pot and pills and to teach himself how to steal cars. He hooked up with Selligrini and, at first, used to bring him cars where the driver had left the keys in the ignition. But then Selli gave him a set of slim-jims and let Benny hang around the junkyard, where he practiced popping the locks on rack after rack of car doors. Selligrini taught Benny how to hot-wire and how to bust out the entire key ignition to get to the wires when you couldn't get to them under the dash in the later-model cars. Benny learned how to get past alarms by crawling under the cars and snipping the wires to the battery or to the horn or siren. Benny became so good that he could break into a car and drive it away in less than forty-five seconds—maybe twice as long, if that, if he had to deal with an alarm. The great thing was Benny always had a buyer in Selligrini and so the cars he stole were never on the street longer than it took Benny to drive them to the junkyard down there near Fishtown.

The police caught Benny only twice, once while he was joyriding in a stolen car when he was young, the other while he was on his way to Selligrini's junkyard. The last time Benny had trouble was when that guy with the silent beeper alarm came out of his house and pointed that big nickel-plated gun at Benny like Clint Eastwood when Benny was crawling out from under the guy's Mercedes. The guy happened to work in the district attorney's office and saw to it that Benny went to jail. During this recent stay in prison, most of the prisoners were hardcore and violent criminals, so Benny was locked up with mostly multiple rapists, killers, and armed robbers. With no Gus there to protect him or to knock him out with the sleeper hold when he got crazy, the time for Benny had been constantly tense and frightening. Benny's nerves still had not recovered. But district attorney connections or not, Benny was released from the overcrowded prison in six months because of a court order limiting the number of prisoners in it.

Benny looked at his watch. Two o'clock. If he's fucking me, Benny thought, I'll kill him.

Earlier, Benny had had no doubt that Lawrence would meet him with either the coins or the money, so now that the guy didn't show, even when Benny gave him until two-thirty, Benny couldn't believe it. He thought Lawrence understood him perfectly about everything and was too scared not to give up the coins or the money. Who did this guy think he was dealing with?

Fifteen more minutes, Benny said to himself.

Lawrence didn't show after the fifteen minutes and Benny went to the nearest pay phone and called him. Then Benny got his second surprise when Lawrence answered the phone.

"Hey, what the fuck are you doing there?"

Lawrence knew who he was. "I—"

"Where are my coins?"

"Don't you have them?"

"How the fuck would I have them? I'm waiting for you."

"Wasn't that your man who grabbed the coins from me?"

"The fuck are you talking about?"

"About an hour ago."

"Make sense, fucker."

"If he wasn't your man, then I think I was mugged."

"Don't give me that shit."

"I'm telling you the truth," Lawrence said.

"I don't give a fuck if it's the truth or not. You took my coins and I want them back or the money they were worth."

"I swear, I started over, and in broad daylight—"

"You fuck me, I'll fuck you worse. I want thirty thousand from you one way or the other."

"I don't have that kind of money."

"No? Well, you better find it," and Benny hung up on the bastard. This guy needed more incentive, Benny thought. Then he remembered the daughter, seeing her and Lawrence the other night kissing good-bye outside the Dorchester, how Benny had followed her home because he thought there was a chance it might be useful to know where she lived. He never thought he would have to go to her house. But early that evening, as night fell, he went.

Benny parked his car practically in front of the chick's door, saw that the lights were out in the house, cased the area, then sat in the small park across the street, waiting for her to come home from work. When the daughter came up the sidewalk around six o'clock, Benny didn't think of touching her at all then, not there where people could see him, especially if she screamed. If he only wanted to bop her, rough her up a little, and say a few words so Lawrence got the message, he maybe would've taken the chance, because it was dark enough, and nobody, least of all the cops, would put much time in looking for him or anybody for a simple assault and battery. But this Lawrence had to get a big message, had to know who he was fooling with, had to have something more than Benny's fist hanging over his head. So he let the daughter go into the house, and would give her, say, ten minutes before he went up to her door. He had noticed the Halloween decorations in some of the windows the first night and hatched a few plans.

But just as Benny was about to start for the house, the daughter came out and hurried up the street. Benny thought for a moment to rush after her, but then he realized this was better. He waited another minute before leaving the park.

Shortly later, Benny ducked into the alley behind the daughter's house with his sack of tools and other items.

So he wouldn't break into the wrong house, Benny counted the same number of doors from the back end of the row as there were from the end in the front facing the street. Seven. A lucky number, especially when Benny saw that the yard was unlighted.

Benny had to climb over a pile of rubble in the alley before reaching the house. A couple of cats scooted up the alley past a milk crate. Benny took the crate and used it to stand on as he felt on top of the cinder-block wall before pulling himself up. Some people put spikes or broken glass up there to discourage burglars, and some of them strung razor wire, the worst stuff you could run into. The top of this wall was clean, and Benny placed his sack on it, then pulled himself up. He hesitated before dropping down because he knew a guy who jumped from a wall once into a mess of razor wire strung on the ground like a giant Slinky, cutting him all up in the legs and just missing his jewels. Then there was another guy Benny knew who dropped down without looking and had ten penny nails go through both feet, like Jesus Christ, the house owner having put some boards in his yard with the nails hammered through.

Benny eased himself down into the yard. No wire or nails or anything but hard dirt waited for him. No dog either. Benny took his sack from the top of the wall and crossed the yard to the house. The back door was steel, and Benny left it and moved to the barred window close by. He saw no alarm wire or tape. It seemed the only thing keeping him out of the house was the grate covering the window.

With these old row houses, the bricks were soft and often crumbled around the aluminum anchors as you pulled the bars away from the wall. This house was no different. Benny didn't even have to use much pressure with his small crow bar; the anchors let go so easy it was a shame, especially if Lawrence's daughter had paid a lot of money to have the grate put in. The hardest part was keeping the iron grate from dropping straight down and making a lot of noise or smashing Benny's toes. But Benny had some muscle and was able to let the bars down slowly and quietly.

Benny turned the grate on its side and leaned it against the wall, using it as a ladder to stand on as he jimmied the window with his putty knife. It was a double-hung window with one of those cheap latches that locked in the center where the top of the lower window met the bottom of the upper. All Benny had to do was slip the putty knife between the window rails and move the thumb press of the lock to the side. It took him maybe twenty seconds. Now he only had to worry about a motion detector, which he bet this chick didn't have, and a dog, which he also bet she didn't have, since there was no smell of dog shit in the yard. Benny lifted the window but hesitated before climbing in, letting anything he hadn't considered to show itself. Nothing happened, and Benny dropped his sack into the house, pulling himself in after it. Once in the house, he closed the window.

He had climbed into a kitchen, its darkened layout made visible by light coming through the entryway. After taking his Beretta from the shoulder holster—a gift from Gus—Benny started toward the front of the house. A room divider with books and a stereo system and some knickknacks in it marked the living room off from the dining room. On top of the wood table sat a bowl of fresh fruit and some mail. Benny read the names on the letters: Claire Lawrence. He was in the right house, all right.

Benny went into the living room. Drapes covered the windows, so nobody could see him from the street. A lamp burned on an end table by the sofa. On the table sat magazines and—what was this?—a picture of what looked like a much younger Lawrence and a little girl standing with a kite between them at the shore. How nice. A thick Persian rug that might've been worth stealing if Benny was there to steal, which he wasn't, covered most of the open floor. By the window stood a small drop-leaf desk with a chair in front of it. A key stuck out of the lock. What was the use of a lock if you were going to leave the key in it? Benny turned the key and pulled down the drop leaf. Inside were a bunch of pigeonhole compartments with envelopes and paper in them, and a couple of drawers. In one drawer were pens and other stuff, and two checkbooks were in the other. Benny tore off the top two checks and then looked at the balances: nearly two thousand total. This chick had to have a MAC card, Benny thought, and he hoped he'd find it; he could always squeeze her for the access numbers.

After checking that the place looked the same as when he came in, Benny went upstairs. First, he looked in the three bedrooms for anybody and then he went into the bathroom. Keeping the door open, he took a leak. When he finished, he flushed and went into the bedroom he knew the chick used because of the clothes over the chair in the corner and the shoes on the floor, plus the wicker laundry hamper with the lid off and the used clothes filled to the top.

Benny dropped his sack on the floor and turned on the bedside lamp. He went through the drawers of the dresser, looking for cash and credit cards. He didn't find anything there, and the jewelry the daughter had in a box on the dresser wasn't worth taking, all of it cheap. But Benny spotted another box in the small bookcase along the wall. Inside the box, sitting under three new twenties and a book of postage stamps, were a group of plastic cards, two credit cards and one a MAC.

"Bingo."

Benny scooped out the stamps, the cash, and the cards and jammed everything in his pocket. Then, taking one last look around, he took a pair of black panties from the top of the clothes pile in the hamper and lay down on the unmade bed. Benny turned off the bedside lamp, covered his face with the panties, and waited for Lawrence's daughter to come home.

5

AT the end of the day, as Paul emptied his pockets at his bedroom dresser, he noticed that Claire had neglected to sign the check she had given him as a down payment for the wall unit she wanted him to build. He thought about telephoning her then, but decided instead to bring the check and a pen along on his run the following morning, thinking Claire could sign the check when he met her on the street. But Paul did not see her. After he returned to his house, Paul telephoned Claire, and caught her just before she left the house for work. She had overslept and missed her run, she told Paul. He mentioned the unsigned check, and Claire apologized, suggesting they meet that evening in Rittenhouse Square where she could sign the check. Paul said, "All right," and they agreed on a time.

Paul returned from the shop earlier than usual and needed to kill an hour before meeting Claire. He lay on the sofa in the darkened living room and watched the television news, the cold gray light from the box spilling onto Paul's out-stretched body like a lethal dust. The professors at a local university had gone on strike, the city was set to go bankrupt in two months, and a ten-year-old boy in New Jersey had been sexually assaulted and beaten to death. Only the boy touched Paul. Whenever he heard stories of that nature—crimes against children, the elderly, the weak and defenseless in general—Paul wished the worst sort of punishment for the criminals, the most brutal, prolonged physical torment. He imagined administering the punishment himself.

Paul had been on the television news once. A news team had filmed him after the car his wife had been driving, with their daughter beside her, plunged into the Delaware River. Paul did not allow himself to think about that.

He got up from the sofa, did several sets of push-ups, showered, dressed in clean clothes, and started off for Rittenhouse Square.

"Why woodworking?" Claire asked after signing the check.

They were sitting on a bench in Rittenhouse Square beneath a huge sycamore, their arms folded against the chill. A few other people sat on lamp-lit benches lining the crosswalks, and several men in tattered clothing slept on benches in the shadows. Strollers passed without hurry, one woman mumbling to herself. A pair of mothers walked by with their children dressed in Halloween costumes, and Paul felt a momentary stab of hurt remembering his own girl on past Halloweens and his wife dispensing candy through the early evening to costumed children who had come trick-or-treating to their door.

Paul forced himself back to the present. "Why?"

"Of all the things, I mean."

Paul thought for a moment. "I like it."

"That's the best reason. I write user documentation for software programs, and what you do seems much more interesting."

"I suppose it depends what side of the fence you're on."

"Sometimes I feel compelled to become a ditchdigger."

"A ditchdigger?"

"Well, maybe not a ditchdigger, but a job where, when you do it, you have something tangible to show for your efforts."

"Aren't your software manuals tangible?"

"I put together words with a team of writers, and you can't touch words. It's the ink and the paper that are tangible, not the words, not the idea. You can't hold an idea. Not so with a chair, for instance. From what I see of your craft, you take raw wood, cut it up, put parts together, and some hours later you have a functional object or a piece of art, or both, that can and does last for generations."

"But you must like your work some."

"Oh, I do. I didn't want to sound as though I was whining."

"You didn't."

"I don't like whiners." Claire paused. "No, I'm stimulated and challenged by my work, only a little unhappy that, unlike a bricklayer, I can't say, 'See this building. I helped build it. Those are my rows of brick.' Do you see what I mean?"

"Exactly." And Paul did, smiling to himself that Claire had articulated far better than he ever had the reason he had chosen to work with his hands.

"How long have you been a woodworker?"

"Ten years." Paul mentioned that he had earned a liberal arts degree from a local college, that he "knocked around" doing odd clerical jobs for about five years, and that, laid off from the public schools as a library assistant, he began professional woodworking, which had been a hobby until then.

Claire followed with some of her own history. She told Paul that she had gone to school at Columbia in New York, where she studied biology; after graduating, she took a job as a research assistant with a company in West Philadelphia, studying various diseases in rats and rhesus monkeys. But she found this depressing. "All that sickness and death in those animals, which I was directly responsible for." She quit the research job and worked in bookstores for a number of years before returning to school for a master's degree in technical writing, "which makes boredom a virtue. The flatter the language, the better." On the personal side, Claire went on, she read a lot and liked to travel. She told of trips to Canada, California, Mexico, and one she made by herself to Peru at the end of a marriage that had been "a mistake. I went to clear my head, to view my marriage from another environment. I climbed Machu Picchu and rode in a large motorized canoe on the Amazon at night. In the jungle, the sky seems closer and the stars are dense. The sounds are thick and constant—bird calls, monkeys, insects. A tarantula was in my bungalow the first night. One confession: despite the views that made me leave my research job, I ate the monkey the tour guides served us for one meal in the Amazon. I was starving after a long trek through the jungle. So much for principle."

"A monkey?" Paul asked.

"Can you believe it? If you're thinking that because humans are related to the primates, eating the monkey makes me partly cannibal, I've thought about that, too. By the way, your arms look succulent."

They laughed.

Somewhere in the middle of their conversation, Paul began to notice Claire's intelligent eyes, her even teeth and long fingers, her smell; he grew nervous, suddenly aware of his own looks and the way he sounded. For three years, he had not been in the company of any woman other than his mother for longer than ten minutes; he could not seem to manage it. Not that he didn't try. Prompted by both Andre and his uncle Rick, he had gone to Center City night spots in the past year but wound up leaving those dark places, with their blaring dance music and odors of cologne and beer, minutes after arriving. His uncle Rick had arranged blind dates for him, attractive and charming women in their own way, but Paul could not resist collapsing into himself; he became somber, could barely talk, and felt the whole sad futility of the thing like a great weight on his back. Mumbling apologies, Paul had fled the women.

But as he sat with Claire, his hands growing cold and his underarms moist, his stomach somewhat queasy, he felt the mild anxiety he knew to be connected only with a situation where something mattered, where emotions were at stake.

"When I returned from Peru," Claire said, "I still felt the same about my marriage. It was over. And I was glad that I had kept my name."

Not wanting to go in the same direction and talk about how he had become single, Paul said that it was getting a little too chilly to stay outside and asked Claire if she wanted to go to the diner on Nineteenth Street. "For tea or something."

"Sounds like a good idea."

They stood up from the bench and started down the walkway toward the street but had not left the park when Paul noticed Tut walking furtively toward them, peering into the trash cans and at the ground around him.

"I know this boy," Paul said as they drew closer to Tut. Paul quickly told Claire how Tut had appeared recently in front of the wood shop, sweeping the sidewalk.

"Is he homeless?"

"It seems that way."

Tut drew closer, reaching into the trash cans to examine their contents. He did not see Paul and Claire until Paul called his name. The boy's head jerked sharply and his entire body spasmed; then he froze, looking at the ground to the side of Paul's feet, cautious and fearful.

"What are you doing up this way, Tut?" Paul asked.

The boy did not answer.

"He never talks," Paul said. "At least no one around the shop has heard him."

"Can we bring him with us to get something to eat?"

Paul hesitated, imagining Tut, looking as though he had just come from rolling around in a dirt pit, in the bright fluorescent light of the diner. "Sure, if you want."

Claire approached the boy. "Tut?"

He shrank back slightly.

"Tut, this is Claire, a friend of mine," Paul said.

54

Tut did not seem to care.

"Would you like to eat with us?" Claire asked.

Only Tut's eyes moved.

Claire touched the boy lightly on the arm. "Come on, Tut," she said softly. "You'll like it."

Tut allowed himself to be urged away from the trash can, and then the three of them left the park, walking quietly, as though silenced by a common anguish.

At the diner on Nineteenth and Spruce, they took a booth by the window. Claire and Paul sat on one side, Tut on the other; he sat completely mute, his eyes down or gazing at the red neon outline of a flying horse hanging on the wall at the rear. A waitress brought the menus, giving Tut a startled look when she placed one before him; then she receded. The diner's specials were represented in the menu by photographs, and Claire asked the boy what he wanted to eat. His eyes went wide at the pictures of the food, but he remained silent.

"I'm sorry," Claire said. "Just point, then. Anything you want."

After a long pause, Tut moved his dirty finger over the menu, stopping at a photograph of a platter of roast beef with gravy, mashed potatoes, and green beans.

Claire smiled. When the waitress returned, Claire ordered a hamburger and fries for herself and the roast beef platter for Tut; Paul ordered a salad, for which he had no appetite. After the waitress had gone away, Paul stood up to show Tut the men's room so that the boy could wash his face and hands, both smudged with grime. "Tut," Paul said, and motioned for him to follow. The boy slid from the booth and shuffled alongside Paul to the rear of the diner. Tut's awed eyes widened and his lips parted as they drew closer to the neon flying horse.

Paul held the door open, but the boy hesitated, looking in at the toilet and sink with nervous caution as though, once in, Paul would slam the door shut and he'd be trapped.

"Wash up," Paul said, nudging Tut into the bathroom.

Paul left Tut standing before the sink and mirror, the boy's eyes watching the edge of the door as Paul slowly swung it shut. Paul waited outside the door a moment before walking back to the booth. When Tut did not emerge after a few minutes, Paul returned to the bathroom, rapped softly on the door, and then went in. He found Tut still motionless in front of the sink.

"Well," Paul said, entering. He let the door swing closed after him. "First, do you have to use the toilet? Do you have to pee?" Paul thought he detected a slight shaking no of Tut's head. "Okay, then let's wash those hands."

Paul stood beside Tut and turned on the faucet; he adjusted the temperature, then took Tut's filthy hands and put them under the water. Tut pulled back a moment but then allowed Paul to keep his hands under the water, rinsing them. Paul put soap from the dispenser into his own palms and washed his hands with the idea that Tut, who looked as though he might stand unmoving forever, would mimic him. Paul knew that Tut must have had experience washing his hands, that he had once lived in an actual house with running water, that somebody had cared for him at least minimally. He imagined that Tut had once been a child like other children, had played games, gone to school, had a bed to sleep in. But with the boy stuck in fear and amazement before the sink, Paul could not be sure now. Darkened with city grime, his clothes ratty, shoes barely in one piece, Tut seemed aboriginal, feral, born in an alley or subway and raised, perhaps, by stray dogs.

"Come on, Tut, wash. I know you're not stupid." He couldn't be, Paul thought, to live by his wits as he did, seeking shelter and food every day, avoiding the reach of harm. Paul spread the soap over his fingers and rubbed briskly, trying to make it appear fun as he had years ago with his own child. He thought of her now, sitting in the bathtub, adrift in her own world as completely as her toys were in the water, speaking gibberish or singing songs of her own invention. Paul remembered her as she helped him wash the car she would die in, and his knees went weak. He leaned against the sink for a time, collecting himself, and then finished rinsing his hands. As he began to dry them with the coarse paper towels, Tut began to wash.

"Your face, too," Paul said, and left the bathroom.

"Is he all right?" Claire asked when Paul returned.

"Yes."

"Are you? You look kind of odd."

"I'm fine."

The waitress brought the food, and just as Paul moved to retrieve Tut from the bathroom, the door opened and the boy shuffled over to them. His hands were clean to the wrists, but the dark film began there. He had cleaned his face, but at the hairline and ears Paul noticed the shadow of dirt. Tut sat behind his steaming platter of roast beef, potatoes, and string beans, staring at the food, transfixed.

"Go ahead, Tut, eat," Claire said.

Tut grabbed the fork beside the plate and began to shovel the food into his mouth.

"That he understands," Paul said.

"I can see."

Claire slowly ate her hamburger and fries and Paul picked at his salad, barely tasting the unripe tomatoes or the iceberg lettuce and avoiding the brown withered mushrooms. Both he and Claire watched Tut devour his food; at least for now, the boy seemed unaware of his surroundings or even these two people sitting across from him. Tut did not use the knife and stuffed the thin slices of roast beef into his mouth intact, no matter what their size. Thick brown gravy dripped down his chin, which he sometimes wiped with the back of his wrist and sometimes did not. He scooped up wads of mashed potatoes, made them vanish, and stabbed at the string beans with the fork, eating them with the same doglike eagerness. Watching Tut, Paul feared that the boy might choke. But he continued to eat relentlessly without any harm and finished before Claire and Paul. Claire slid half her fries over to Tut, and Paul gave the boy the nearly untouched salad. Tut glanced up at both of the adults once, as if to make sure of their meaning, and then started in on the fries and the salad, eating all of both, except the withered mushrooms.

"So there's one thing he won't eat," Claire said.

Tut finished the salad and the fries and then turned his attention to the milkshake Claire had ordered for him. He gulped it, halted, waited several moments with knitted brows, gulped the shake again, waited, and gulped again until he had finished the shake. Paul realized that the brief headache from drinking something too cold had stopped Tut from drinking the shake in one long gulp. Claire did not ask Tut if he wanted dessert, but when the waitress returned, Claire ordered the boy pie á la mode. Unoccupied while he waited for the dessert, Tut became sheepish and wary again; he jumped at sudden noises from the kitchen or at people walking by outside the window and hunkered lower in the seat as if to hide himself. By the time the dessert arrived, his chin nearly rested on the table. But when the waitress placed the apple pie topped with scoops of vanilla ice cream in front of him, Tut's eyes brightened and he sat up. He seemed to forget everything but the food as he gobbled it with what still seemed like fierce hunger. Paul and Claire watched again in silent amazement.

Shortly later, the three of them stood on the sidewalk outside the diner in the glare of its fluorescent light. It had gotten colder since they entered the diner. Claire looked earnestly at Tut, who stared at the ground, while Paul looked away from both of them. He wanted to be elsewhere now, because he knew it would come to this. They would have to send Tut back to the streets, to rummage through trash cans for pizza crusts and half-eaten sandwiches, constantly looking over his shoulder for dangers. The thought made Paul both angry and sad.

"Tut, where do you stay?" Claire asked.

Tut silently watched one foot kick the other, then grind something imaginary beneath his sole, then kick again. Paul wondered if Claire had forgotten Tut did not talk or whether she hoped her voice would somehow unlock the boy's.

"Where does he stay, Paul?"

"I don't know. Somewhere near the shop, I think."

She looked at Tut again. "Do you want us to take you to your home, Tut?"

Tut glanced up briefly, did not meet Claire's eyes, then looked at his feet again.

"What should we do?" Claire asked.

"Maybe we can take him to my shop. He can make a bed out of the shipping blankets." That would make Andre happy, Paul thought.

"I'll make some phone calls in the morning and see about getting him off the street."

"Okay." Paul started away toward his neighborhood, but stopped after several steps when he realized Claire and Tut had not started with him. Turning, he saw Claire with her hand on Tut's shoulders; he was still rooted to the sidewalk in the restaurant's glare, his head down, still kicking one foot into the other.

"Come on, Tut, we're going to take you to the shop," Claire said. She took him by the arm and urged him from the sidewalk and into the street.

Fifteen minutes later, they reached Paul's row house with his pickup truck parked in front of it. Paul felt relieved that the night was too cool for his neighbors to be sitting outside as they frequently did when the weather allowed; he did not want to have to explain this boy and Claire to them. Paul slid into the truck and unlocked the passenger door from inside. Claire pulled the door open and stepped aside to allow Tut to enter first. But he did not move.

"It's all right," Claire said.

Even as Tut allowed Claire to press against his back, he resisted getting into the truck. He held onto the frame of the door, and his frightful eyes darted about. When Tut finally got into the truck, he sat on the very edge of the seat but would move no further inside.

"Ok, I'll get in first," Claire said, taking Tut by the arm and allowing him to step out onto the sidewalk. Then she slid in beside Paul. "Come on, Tut, join us."

Tut remained fixed. Claire called to him. But instead of getting into the truck, Tut stepped away from it. As Claire said his name again, he took another step back, then another, the steps unsure, as though he hadn't quite made up his mind about them. Claire leaned away from Paul and toward the door to call Tut again. As she did, Tut took one more tentative step backward, turned, and ran.

"Tut!"

Tut ran down the sidewalk, scooted between parked cars, crossed the small street, and ran down the sidewalk on the other side. Paul had already spun the steering wheel right and left, jerked out of the parking space, and sped down the street after the boy. But Tut had turned the corner at Nineteenth Street, heading north, back toward Center City, and by the time Paul and Claire reached the intersection seconds later, the boy had vanished.

The street crossing theirs ran one way south, and a bus headed toward the intersection. They could not see Tut on their side of the street, in the street, or on the other side as they crossed after the bus whooshed by. Paul sped straight down the street between the row houses toward Eighteenth, turned north, sped past Graduate Hospital to Lombard, and turned left. If Tut had run straight north on Nineteenth Street or cut down to Eighteenth at either South or Bainbridge, Paul would have a chance of meeting him, so he pulled up along the curb at the edge of the hospital's parking lot. Paul and Claire stepped from the truck and looked up and down Lombard Street and toward Ninteenth, but they did not see Tut. They stood looking much longer than the time it would take for someone walking from Paul's house, let alone a boy running, to pass where they stood beside the truck.

"What are we doing?" Claire said at length.

Paul looked at her. "I'm not sure."

"We're chasing a kid who hardly knows us. It's no wonder he ran."

Paul took another look up and down the streets, and only now wondered what he meant to do if he saw Tut. Grab him, toss him in the truck, take him to the shop when the boy was so plainly afraid?

"What was I thinking?" Claire leaned against the truck.

"You wanted to help him."

"But I acted like I wanted to save him, adopt him."

"It's kind of you."

"I don't know what it is."

"Do you want to drive around some, farther in town?"

Claire shook her head. "No. He's afraid to go with us, that's obvious. But I suppose it's a good thing that he doesn't want to get in a truck with strangers."

Paul nodded and leaned against the truck beside Claire. They did not speak for a time and only gazed at the hospital and the parking lot. An ambulance arrived a few minutes later, pulling up to the emergency ward, and they watched across the hoods of the parked cars as the joking paramedics, without urgency, opened the wide back door and pulled out a figure strapped to a stretcher.

"Let's go," Claire said.

She walked around to the other side of the truck and got in. Paul slid behind the wheel and started the engine as the flashing red light of the ambulance beat against their faces.

6

TUT ran because he got the jumpy feeling because once a man said he had food for Tut and Tut went with him to his house, where the man gave Tut a cheese sandwich, and then after Tut ate it the man hurt Tut and took him back in his car to where he picked him up on the street and gave Tut a quarter and told him not to tell anybody, and Tut cried as the man drove away down the street.

Tut ran away from the man from the shop, who was nice, and the woman he just met, who was nicer, soft and clean-smelling, because when he got the jumpy feeling, that meant he might be hurt, so he ran down the street and turned the corner and ran through the rat dark up the other street with the big bus coming down it with bright headlights and the heads of the sad-looking people inside, the bus loud and stinking as it went by, and the dark falling in again after it, quieter.

Tut cut across the street and ran down a street smaller than the one the man and the woman were just on, but darker, the street lamps not all working, his eyes wet from the cold as he ran.

He started running back toward the park, but then he thought he wouldn't and kept running straight toward where he knew the big street was, with the cars going both ways and the screaming subway train underground and the light almost as good as day, reaching the street in little time, turning into the brightness, and walking now toward the city hall with the statue of a man on top of it and the clock a dot of yellow.

The cars were going in both directions and there were some loud buses, and Tut walked with his chest calming down past a grate in the sidewalk where he heard the subway train scream and rumble bad enough to hurt his ears, making him think of how he used to sleep in the subway before it got too crowded with a lot of bad people—one who tried to set Tut on fire—so he stopped going down there.

He walked toward the yellow clock.

The buildings he passed were different shapes, some tall and square and new, others not tall and new but old and dark, and he passed some parking lots and another subway entrance with the smell of pee coming up from the steps, and then he saw a lot of people in nice clothes out on the sidewalk, with cars and taxis stopping in front of a building with a lot of glass and gold doors and real flames in lamps on the wall and with soft music coming out and people all laughing and smiling.

Tut couldn't cross the street because of the traffic and there were so many people that he had to slow down and find his way through, the perfume smells coming off some of them very strong, and some of them sparkling with jewelry.

Then a man came down off the steps near the doors and told Tut to go away, and Tut headed right into the street between two stopped taxicabs and as soon as a hole in the traffic came he ran across the street to the other side.

Still looking back at the crowd, wondering why they were

waiting, Tut walked into a trash can and knocked it over and a cop in the middle of the street said, "Hey!"

Tut got scared and ran, ran all the way to the city hall where green statues of men and men on horses stood on big stone blocks and stone men and some women were attached to the building with the yellow clock high up in the black air.

The city hall was lighted up all around, especially around the stone men and women against the building and around the statues that stood apart on the sidewalk, making them look real, the horses looking more real than the people.

Tut liked horses.

Some cops had horses and Tut liked to see them, smell them—they were so strong and shiny, except the ones he sometimes saw in the other part of the city, the ones that pulled the carriages, looking tired and sad, with the people in the carriage looking happy.

Tut turned down the Market street and then up the Thirteen street.

It was dark on this street mostly, with nobody around except a few people here and there walking slow or just standing in the dark, looking at Tut with nothing in their eyes as if he wasn't there, most of them carrying some kind of bag, most of them dressed like Tut and wearing broken shoes like Smash Louie, who waved at Tut and tried to make him come across the street—but Tut wouldn't come because Smash took Tut's dollar and forty cents last time.

Smash was old and broken up, with bad sores on his legs, and he just stayed in the dark, cursing at Tut.

Tut went past the old, dark buildings with the black windows and hurried through the Chinese streets and then across the biggest street he had ever crossed, the cars going both ways, and then through more rat dark and past old buildings with no one at all around, not even a dog.

He passed the electric station humming behind the tall fence and soon he reached the big street he walked down a lot and turned toward the river, wishing he had a bike to ride or somehow could get to his place soon because he was tired and sleepy now and felt too weak to do anything, even run, if anybody wanted to hurt him.

Soon Tut was walking at the side of the wide street that ran along the river and he could see the building where the yellow trash trucks came every day going up and down the ramp, but it was quiet now, the gate closed, the yellow trucks lined up in rows and rows.

Sometimes very big trains ran on this street, but they went very slow and a bell rang the whole time, not like the trains that went fast over the bridge not far from there.

Tut wondered if those trains went to Florida because Florida was where his mother went to get a job, leaving that one summer in the bright hot sticky heat and saying she was going to be back in a few days to get him, leaving with that man Mack, who Tut didn't like because he hit his mother after they drank the beer, twisted her arm, hurt her in the bedroom because Tut heard the noises through the door.

They left in a big red car, Tut watching them through the window because his mother told him to stay in the house.

The next day, Tut cooked meat on the stove for lunch and a dish towel close to the blue flame caught fire and when Tut tried to swipe it off the counter it hit the curtains and they caught on fire and very quickly fire started to go all around the kitchen.

Tut got scared and ran from the house and stayed in the playground six blocks away, afraid of what his mother and Mack would do to him, and when he came back at night very hungry there were no windows in the house and no door and black was all around the openings and a big pile of burnt furniture and stuff filled the sidewalk.

He went into the black and burned house smelling of smoke and stayed there until he got too hungry, and then he went out with the four dollars his mother had given him before she left with Mack and he bought a loaf of bread and a small jar of peanut butter at an all-night store and he took that back to the house and ate a peanut butter sandwich sitting at the top of the cellar stairs looking at the deep black water in the cellar that was shining in the light from the street lamp coming in through the broken-open cellar window, and after eating he slept on the floor of his only half-burned bedroom, glad that it was summer and not cold.

In the morning, Mrs. Smith sweeping her steps saw Tut come from the house and her hands went to her cheeks, and then she called Mr. Smith, who came out and told Tut to get into his car so he could take him to the police station, but instead of going in the car Tut ran away, like he did from the man and the woman who fed him at the bright restaurant with the red flying horse.

He wished he would see a real flying horse, maybe there were some.

Tut passed a car-repair place, then a fenced-in lot, then an office building with a few lights on, then nothing, then the lumberyard, then the park, then nothing again, then the factory, then just little buildings here and there.

Tut passed the diner where he sometimes bought an egg sandwich on a roll and a carton of milk and where they let him sweep the sidewalk so he wouldn't have to pay and where he checked the dumpster at night for food and lots of times found halves of sandwiches and tomato slices and something to drink, but he didn't check tonight.

Tut kept walking and went down a small street, then down another after a turn, then up another street and across a lot, and then through a very dark street until he reached the junkyard, where he crawled through the small hole in the fence and then crawled through the tunnel in the pile of metal to his car sitting without doors and no wheels, with junk all around burying it so that nobody could see it from any direction, not even the guys who worked there in the garage across the lot past the stone shed—Tut was there many times and they didn't even know.

There were rows of car doors in the lot and fenders on racks and bumpers and hoods and windshields breaking up the sun during the day and engine pieces, and when the men were not there on warm Sundays Tut crawled through another tunnel that went to the lot and he would lie on his stomach and look out thinking about Florida, where the oranges grew on trees.

After Tut crawled to his car he turned his flashlight on and lit a candle and put the flashlight away and took a shirt and socks from his pile and put them on because he felt cold, then he went to a spot in the ground where he lifted a piece of cardboard and then a flat piece of metal and then took the metal box he kept there out of the hole and opened it.

There was the penknife he had found, a ring he had found, a chunk of glass with a bug in it that he had picked up from the street, some wire, the piece of paper about Florida he had gotten at the big train station, a candy bar he took one bite out of and put back, and his can of money.

Half of the can was filled with coins, and Tut also had eighteen one-dollar bills, and now he added the money the man from the wood shop had given him today, wondering how long before he had enough for the ticket to Florida.

He looked at the piece of paper about Florida and unfolded it and saw good enough by the candlelight the picture of the ocean and the birds and the blue sky and the orange trees and everybody smiling—they were so happy, especially the girls in the bathing suits.

Tut put the paper back in the box and then the can of coins and then the whole box back in the ground, covering it with the plate of metal and then the cardboard, and then he crawled back into his car, covered himself with a blanket, and went to sleep.

Few words were spoken. Claire had not asked Paul to take her home, but he had. She did not ask him outright to come in with her, but after parking the car around the corner of her house, he walked Claire to her door and followed her inside when she wordlessly left the door open, as though Paul's coming in was understood. Claire removed her windbreaker and dropped it on the sofa, slipped out of her shoes, and went into the kitchen without turning on more lights than the lamp already burning on the end table. She returned with glasses and a bottle.

"Have some cheap wine?" Claire asked, smiling.

"That's all I drink."

Claire poured the wine and handed a glass to Paul. He continued to stand near the entrance with his jacket still on, nervous, looking as though he were about to leave instead of having just arrived. His throat became hot with the wine and he could feel heat in his eyes as Claire put on jazz music.

Claire sat down on the sofa, looking vaguely weary, but it seemed to Paul more of a spiritual lassitude than a physical one. She closed her eyes as Paul stood watching her, undecided about moving, but feeling no great urgency to do anything. He watched Claire breathe. She opened her eyes and looked at him.

"Sit?" she asked.

Paul nodded. He took off his jacket, put it over the wing chair, and crossed the room to the sofa. As Paul sat, Claire put her glass on the end table and moved closer to him. One of her hairs had caught at the corner of her mouth and Paul reached for it, stopped, dropped his hand back to his lap, then reached again, smoothing the hair away. Claire caught his hand, held it briefly against her cheek, and then held it on her knees. She began to massage the fingers and palm. Paul leaned across her to put his glass beside hers and saw a photograph of a little girl beside a man, a kite resting on the ground in front of them, the sea behind, both of them squinting.

Paul thought of his own girl and the kite flying they had done at the Lakes those breezy spring afternoons, the girl's excited chatter, her clapping hands as the breeze took the kite into the sky, her long quiet gaze of wonder as something in her child's brain took the shape of an emotion still beyond language.

"Is this you?" Paul asked.

"My father and me."

"How old were you?"

"Seven or eight. I don't remember."

"You look happy."

"We were. But the string broke and the kite fell in the ocean."

"You remember that?"

"Very clearly. I think I expected my father to go swimming after it and bring it back. When he said he couldn't, that it was too far out, I cried. Not so much because I lost the kite, but because he had failed me."

"Fathers seem invulnerable to children," Paul said, gazing at the rug. "When kids realize they're not, it's a shock."

"My father has the usual human weaknesses," Claire said. "He drinks more than he should, for instance, and he made some terrible investments."

"Mine never had money to invest."

"Are your parents still alive?"

"Just my mother. My father died when I was thirteen."

"That must have been difficult."

"You're told to be a man about it, and you are. Or you try to be."

Claire touched the back of her fingers lightly against Paul's cheek, looking directly into his eyes for something, searching. "I like you."

Paul wanted to say something in return, if only that he felt likewise, but no words came. He looked at Claire's mouth, her throat, then completely away, but back to her mouth again as it floated toward his, touching lightly at first, as though to gauge something there. Paul barely moved, as though testing something himself, like thin ice. He tasted the wine on Claire's mouth and felt several of her hairs against his face. Claire pressed harder. Their lips parted and Paul felt Claire put her hands behind his neck and pull him slowly down as she sank back to the seat cushions, where she lay flat, one knee upraised with Paul's thigh between hers.

They kissed long, Paul's heart pounding. He moved his mouth to Claire's neck, felt with his lips the rapid pulse at her throat, tasted salt. But even as he touched Claire's breasts, opened her blouse, undid the snap of her bra, caressed the hard quarter-sized nipples, took them one after the other into his mouth as Claire's breath caught, Paul felt distant, watching himself, aware of feeling nearly numb to what he knew he should be feeling intensely. They shifted and Paul slid his hand lightly downward over Claire's trembling belly, wanting to feel, wanting to see and touch and taste the rest of her, and hoping mostly that his body would disconnect from his mind and operate on its own, seek its own primal release. He touched Claire on the outside first, then sought the button and the zipper of her slacks, undid them, brushed beneath her warm smooth panties, through the hair and, pausing a moment, into her wet heat. Claire gasped. She lay still for a time as if caught by Paul, his hand motions gentle and unhurried, almost curious. Soon, Claire shifted and moved her hand down Paul's ribs to his hip, then over the front. He felt surprise in Claire's fingers when she touched him, a concentrated groping, and then an urgency as she undid his belt and the rest and slid past the elastic band of his shorts. Her hand felt cool and smooth, and Paul, as his fingers slowed, tried to focus on Claire's touch. But he remained limp, his memory too powerful yet for this. After a time, Paul removed his hand and sat up. Claire let go of him.

"I'm sorry," Paul said.

"It's all right."

"It's not you. I want to, but I can't."

"Really, it's okay." Claire sat up and closed her blouse.

"I haven't been with anyone for a while."

"We'll take it slower some other time."

Paul looked at her for a time. "I like you, too." Saying it now, looking into Claire's eyes, he felt that he could one day love her, or someone like her, that love and the warm comforts that came with it were now possible.

They sat quiet, the music from the stereo the only noise in the house.

"I guess I'll go," Paul said after several tunes played. He stood and fixed his pants.

Claire stood, too. "Running tomorrow?"

"Yes. The usual time."

"Mind if I bump into you?"

"I'll be disappointed if you don't." And then Paul walked to the door, Claire following. He paused to touch her arm before walking out into the Halloween night.

7

WHEN Benny heard the front door open and close below, he jumped out of the bed and stood to the side of the bedroom doorway. He heard another voice down there with this Claire Lawrence, a guy, and put his hand on his gun, thinking he might have to change his plan and deal with him, too.

Because they did little talking and their voices were low, Benny couldn't make out what they were saying. Mostly, he heard the jazz music that one of them had put on, and soon after he couldn't pick up any voices at all. Benny thought maybe the chick had a date and they were warming up on the couch before coming up to the bedroom. Which worried Benny a little. It didn't matter that Lawrence's daughter might see Benny's face, because he could always count on Lawrence to keep everything from the cops, even what his daughter saw, but not somebody else that Benny had no leverage on. So it could get sticky if both of them came up.

But after maybe twenty minutes, Benny heard the voices

again, only they didn't last long. Footsteps went to the front door, and the door opened and closed. Benny knew the daughter was alone now. He listened to her steps cross the floor to turn off the music and then return to the stairs. The upstairs hall light came on, sending light into the bedroom. When Claire started up, Benny got ready, going over in his mind the moves he would make.

At the top of the stairs, instead of coming his way, Claire went into the bathroom. Benny listened to the splashing, the flush, the rustling of clothes, water in the sink. Then footsteps came toward him.

Benny punched Claire in the stomach before her hand touched the light switch. She was bigger than Benny had realized, but she went straight down, her breath gone. Benny knelt beside her and showed her the Beretta first thing.

"See it," Benny said, waving the gun in Claire's face. "Don't make me use it."

She was curled up in panties and a T-shirt, holding herself, her face screwed up with trying to breathe.

Benny took the duct tape from the edge of the bed where he had put it and quickly wrapped some of it around her wrists and fingers, binding them together. Then he ripped a piece from the roll and put it over her mouth. The whole thing didn't take a minute and was done before Claire could do anything about it. Benny stood up and looked down at her, still curled up, but breathing better now and with her eyes wide open, starting to look afraid.

"Don't look so scared," Benny said. "I'm not here to fuck you." As he said it, he looked at the panties and the thighs, thinking about changing his mind. "Come on." He pulled her up from the floor and sat her on the edge of the bed. "I wish you didn't take off your pants, cause now I have to dress you. Where's your stuff?" Benny looked at the dresser behind his back. "You got pants in here? I'll point to the drawer and you shake your head. This one?" Benny touched the fourth drawer with the gun, but Claire indicated nothing. He opened the drawer anyway and saw folded jeans.

"Bingo."

Benny took the pair on top, let them unfold, opened them at the waist, and knelt in front of her. "Okay, lift your feet in."

Claire put one foot in slowly, but paused, and Benny knew the moment before it happened what she meant to do, only it was too late. He had knelt too close to her, distracted maybe by the panties, and instead of putting her second foot in the pants, she brought her knee sharply up and hit Benny squarely under the chin. His teeth cracked together and he pitched backward into the dresser, dropping the gun as he hit his head. Claire stood as Benny fell back; she first kicked at him, aiming for his head and groin, and then stooped for the gun.

The tape Benny had put on Claire's fingers saved him. She tried to pick up the gun while Benny lay dazed on the floor, but there was no easy way to hold it with her fingers bound together and no way at all to get a finger on the trigger; otherwise, Benny might've been a dead man, in the newspapers the next day. When she realized, too, that she could not work the trigger even if she managed to hold the gun, she started to run from the room and down the hall. Benny scrambled up from the floor after her.

He tackled Claire in front of the bathroom before she could turn down the stairs. They hit the floor hard, Benny landing squarely on top. Claire rocked wildly beneath him, trying to free herself, and nearly knocked Benny from her back.

"Stop it!"

But she kept struggling, and Benny sat up on the small of her back, grabbed her hair, and rammed her head into the floor a few times. She made a noise of surprise and pain, then settled.

"You done now?" Benny said, breathing hard, starting to feel the pain in his jaw where she had kneed him. "Because if you're not, I'll crack your head open now like a fuckin' coconut."

Claire made a noise in her throat that Benny took as yes.

74

"Good." Benny stood up. "Don't move." He stepped backward toward the bedroom, keeping his eye on her the whole way down the hall, ready to pounce if she got up. At the bed, he knelt for the gun, grabbed it, and took the jeans back with him. "All right, stand up, and get these on, unless you want to go outside without pants."

Claire's back came up but she stayed on her hands and knees for a few moments before getting to her feet. She faced him. Benny saw that the left side of her forehead where he had slammed it into the floor was bruised and swelling.

"Turn around."

She didn't move, only looked at him.

Benny pointed the gun at her stomach. "Turn."

She looked at the gun and slowly turned her back to him.

Benny moved quickly now. With the pants in one hand and the gun in the other, he stepped toward Claire and put his arms around her waist, his head barely reaching her shoulders. Benny opened the pants at the waist, holding them in the gun hand with just his pinky finger through a belt loop. "All right, in," Benny said, stooping slightly.

Claire did not lift her feet.

"Come on, I don't have all night."

She kept her feet on the floor.

"You either put on the pants or I hurt you some more." She was starting to get on his nerves. Most chicks, you show them a gun, maybe they scream a little, but they do whatever you want, crying a little maybe as they do it, scared to death not to, that you'll hurt them worse. But not this one. This one gave him a hard time the whole way, even in her underwear. "What's it gonna be? Huh?"

That's when Claire swung back her elbow and hit Benny in the nose. She broke through his arms as he staggered and ran down the stairs.

Again, Benny was glad that he had taped Claire's fingers because by the time he caught up to her she was at the front door, trying to turn the locks and knobs with her wrists.

Benny grabbed her by the hair and pulled her away from

the door and into the living room, where he spun her and gave her a shot in the stomach again. As she dropped to the floor, Benny followed her down, turned her onto her back and sat on her waist.

"What the fuck I gotta do to you?" Benny said, putting his hand on her throat. "I don't want to beat you but you're making me." Blood dripped from his nose to his pants. "Jesus, look what you did to me." He wiped blood with his forearm.

Claire's face began to turn deep red from Benny's hand pressed against her throat.

"I can keep pressing until you pass out and then do whatever I want to you, or you can cooperate. Choose."

Claire's face started to go purple.

"Cooperate?"

Benny felt her chin nod against his wrist.

"Good." Benny let go and the chick sucked air. He wiped his nose again and stood, straddling her for only a moment before he moved quickly away to pick up the jeans he had dropped at the foot of the stairs. Benny reached in his back pocket and pulled out his knife, pressing a button on the handle so that the blade shot out. Benny grabbed the girl's bound wrists and quickly slit the tape that bunched her fingers, but not the wrists themselves. "Pull the pants on yourself. And no more fucking with me or, I swear, I'll cut you."

On her back, Claire took the jeans and worked her legs into them, pulling the waist up to her thighs, then arching her back so she could shimmy the pants over her hips. She could not manage to zip and button the pants, so Benny did it for her.

"All right. Now back up the stairs so we can finish this bullshit and get going. Come on." Benny took her by the arm and pulled her to her feet. "Walk." He shoved Claire toward the stairs and as she went up them, a little wobbly, Benny followed, but far enough behind so he wouldn't get kicked another time, if she got that in her head again. Which, if she did, he might just give her a slash with the knife.

76

Claire paused at the top of the stairs.

"In the bedroom."

She turned and walked down the hall.

"Shoes?" Benny spotted a pair of running shoes as he said it and kicked them across the floor to her. "Put these on."

She sat on the edge of the bed and tugged on the shoes with her index finger.

"Finally." Benny took his roll of duct tape from the bed, lifted off a few inches, pressed the sticky side on the chick's forearm, quickly did two turns around her waist, pinning her arms against her body, and then wrapped her fingers again. He put the roll back in his bag and pulled out a white bed sheet and a gorilla mask. Benny dropped the mask on the bed and unfolded the sheet; it had two black ink dots on it close together which, from a few feet away, looked like holes. Benny put the sheet over Claire's head and adjusted it so that the black dots faced forward like eyeholes. To keep the sheet in place, Benny took a large rubber band from the sack and put it around Claire's neck.

"See, it's perfect being Halloween. You're the ghost and I'm the ape, and it looks like we're going to a costume party. Who's gonna see you tied up under there? Nobody." Benny picked up the bag and the mask, gave a look around the room, and then took Claire by the arm and pulled her up. He guided her through the bedroom door and then down the stairs to the living room, where they stopped while Benny put on the gorilla mask.

"Let's go," Benny said, the mask on, his voice sounding funny. He put the gun in the sack and opened the door, and they went outside, Benny holding tightly to Claire's elbow.

It was past nine o'clock, and if kids had trick-or-treated the area none were around now. Benny didn't see anybody, kids or grown-ups, and he felt a little disappointed that no one was around for him to fake with his costumes.

Benny held Claire around the shoulders as they walked to the car, so if anybody did see them they would think the couple knew each other and were going on a Halloween date.

At the car, Benny opened the back door and guided the chick into the seat by putting his hand on her head like cops when they arrested you. Then Benny hurried to the driver's side, opened the door, and tossed his sack of equipment on the seat. As soon as he got behind the wheel, he took off the ape mask, started the car, and drove away from the curb.

During the drive toward the Delaware River, Benny glanced often in the rearview mirror to look at Lawrence's daughter; he rubbed his chin where she had kneed him and felt his nose, which he could hardly breathe through now because of the swelling.

Benny thought that Lawrence would've been proud of the way his daughter fought, even though it almost got her killed.

With the sheet over her head, blinding her, Claire could not run once they got outside, and if she tried, risking a collision with a telephone pole or a wall, anyone seeing her would only think it was a Halloween shenanigan. The tape covering her mouth kept her from yelling out, and she had to submit to this monster, whoever he was, and let herself be taken to his car. Her wrists hurt from the tape around them, her stomach from the punches, and her forehead from being slammed into the floor. She had nearly gotten away, but he was quick, strong for a small man, and smart. How had he gotten in? How long had he been in the house? He had to have been upstairs while Paul was with her in the living room. The idea make her shudder.

As the man drove her away from home, Claire imagined the streets pass, watching in her mind as though outside and above the car. She had driven down Pine Street enough times to know its feel and traffic patterns at that hour, and so she knew with reasonable certainty where she was as they drove. They stopped at traffic lights on Twenty-second, Twenty-first, Nineteenth, and Eighteenth, where Claire heard a siren pass, sure from its sound that they had stopped near Graduate Hospital not far from where Paul and she had stopped earlier in the night to look for Tut. A fraction of a minute later,

Claire knew from the sound of the traffic going in both directions north and south and the rumble of a subway train that they had stopped at Broad Street.

The car soon moved and Claire felt it cross the wide street, rising slightly with the grade, then dip sharply on the other side where a sink hole, filled periodically with asphalt, had existed for years. They soon slowed for a traffic backup starting at Thirteenth Street, and Claire heard the man mutter, cursing, and then pound the steering wheel once, annoyed at the holdup. Where was he taking her? Why? What did he mean to do when they arrived? She should have fought harder, should never have allowed him to take her from the house, no matter what, forced him instead to drag her unconscious from it if necessary. Now he might be joined by someone else and she would have less chance of escaping and remaining unharmed. At the thought, Claire strained against the tape wrapped about her, her brain swirling with the effort, but the tape would not tear and she gave up. While she was bound like this, harm could take any number of forms; Claire imagined the most vicious, but quickly forced the images from her mind before panic could take hold.

They continued moving straight, stopping now and then for traffic lights as, in her mind, Claire saw the street numbers descend. She felt the car thump over the trolley tracks at Twelfth and Eleventh, and after several minutes, at Fifth Street. Shortly later, the stop sign at Second and Headhouse Square halted them, and then, seconds later, the car turned left onto Front Street. Claire felt the gradual decline as they rode toward Spruce Street, where they turned right, as Claire pictured Delaware Avenue directly ahead and the black river just beyond. The car stopped for the light.

Claire heard cars pull up beside them and behind. She screamed under the duct tape across her mouth and rocked violently on the seat, hoping to attract attention.

"Hey, quit that shit."

Claire continued to rock and yell in her throat.

"It won't do you any good, anyway. They're looking at you,

but they think you're goofing off under that sheet. I'm smiling at them now and waving, and, guess what, they're laughing."

The car moved again, and Claire quieted. They turned left and rumbled over railroad tracks, and soon Claire imagined the municipal parking lot at the river's edge where the city tow trucks deposited illegally parked cars. When they slowed for another stop, Claire knew they had reached the traffic light outside the city trash incinerator at Spring Garden Street.

Claire had rarely driven beyond that point on Delaware Avenue, and so when the car moved again the surroundings blurred. She vaguely remembered old buildings, piles of tires, entire acres of shipping containers, warehouses, and, farther north, the old part of the city that used to be called the Industrial Corridor, lifeless and defunct now. With the old manufacturing buildings lining American Street dark and empty, their windows long smashed, a scary desolation pervaded the area.

The car rumbled once more over railroad tracks or ruts in the road, and Claire remembered now that this direction led to the I-95 entrance at Girard Avenue. Fear surged in her, and she rocked and kicked the back of the seat, screaming behind the tape, afraid now that the man was taking her out of the city, north to a secluded rural area beyond sight and sound of anyone.

"Calm down."

Claire continued to thrash.

"I'm not going to hurt you if you stay cool. You think if I wanted to hurt you, I would be taking you somewhere to do it instead of back at your place where it was nice and cozy? Relax."

That made some sense to Claire and she settled. But where was he taking her?

They turned left sharply and soon right, traveling slowly now, as if tentatively, passing over a lumpy road with stones or broken glass scrunching beneath the wheels. The car weaved left and right again, and then again, until Claire had no idea where they might be, though it had to be somewhere near Fishtown, or Richmond maybe. Claire recalled how she had missed the I-95 entrance once and found herself thumping over railroad tracks and potholed streets to wind up between a long warehouse, with the river beyond somewhere, and a gigantic brown brick building six stories high and a football field long. She had seen several vent stacks that ran up the sides of the building to the roof and heard steely noises emanating from the darkness within. Parked outside near the loading dock had been several flatbed trailers with immense spools of rusting sheet metal chained to them. Grim-faced men had stood in the huge loading bay, staring as she rode slowly by. But those men and a stray dog were all the life Claire had seen.

The car stopped and the engine quit. Claire's heart thudded in her ears.

"Now, I don't want any more trouble," the man said. "You get wild and I'll crack you. If everything goes right, you won't be here long." He left the car, locking the door.

Claire listened to his footsteps on the ground, counting them until they stopped. She heard keys jingling and then what sounded like chain against a fence. Claire heard a squeak of metal and guessed that the man had swung open a gate. She fought again against the tape that bound her arms to her sides but could not tear it. Failing that, Claire caught the sheet between her knees and pulled downward as she threw back her head. Caught beneath her and at the neck by the rubber band, the sheet did not move. Claire worked herself onto the floor, trying again to hold the sheet between her knees while tossing back her head to get the sheet off.

"The fuck are you doing?" The man had returned from the gate and opened the car door on her side.

Claire abruptly sat back.

"You want the sheet off? I'll take it off." He grabbed the sheet at Claire's throat and yanked. "There. Happy?"

Claire shook hair out of her eyes and blinked. The light

outside of the car was not much brighter than under the sheet. Claire saw silhouettes of dilapidated buildings, deep solid-looking shadows, the skeletal outline of a tree, a cyclone fence, shapes she could not identify. The only immediate light came from a single pale bulb attached to the side of a squat building beyond the gate.

"Nothing for you to see anyway. Let's go." He grabbed Claire by the elbow and pulled her from the car. Then he walked her across the cracked and uneven sidewalk through the slightly open gate, pausing to close it after them. "So far so good, honey." He started Claire toward the shed.

Claire smelled rust, and in the outer rim of the light from the dim bulb she saw mounds of what she guessed was scrap metal, the piles rising, a short distance from the shed, to the height of her house on Pine Street. She could barely separate the silhouetted mounds from the night sky, but it seemed to her that the piles of metal ran into each other and completely surrounded the shed, except for the space directly in front of it, so that it would be nearly impossible to see into the yard except from the cratered street where the car now sat, and then only obliquely.

The man took Claire to the side of the shed, where a rack of car doors just at their backs rose ten feet high.

"Think about it," he said. "I could shoot you here and nobody would hear or care if they did. So don't run." He worked a key into a padlock run through a large hasp and used another key to turn two cylinder locks in the flat steel door.

Claire considered running despite what he had said, but with her arms bound to her sides she would be easy to catch and subdue or to hit with a bullet. She decided to wait until she had a better chance to escape or to attack him.

He turned the doorknob, pushed against the door, and shoved Claire into the shed, following her. It was solidly dark within and smelled of engine oil and damp earth. He closed the door. It was no warmer inside than out. The man flipped a switch and a light bulb hanging from the ceiling came on.

They stood in a small room, the four walls unpainted cinder block, the floor bare hard dirt. Small windows the height of Claire's chin with sheets of plywood covering them interrupted two walls. A metal desk and wooden office chair sat in the corner; on the opposite wall stood a metal shelf stand with blackened engine parts and cans of paint filling the shelves. Coils of air hose, a pair of snow tires, and a bucket sat along the wall to the left of the shelf stand.

"Here's the deal," the man said. "I'm gonna take the tape off your mouth. You scream, you scream," he shrugged. "It don't matter because there's nobody to hear you. Like I said before, if everything goes right you won't be here too long. But figure on staying the night, which can't be helped. You have to use a toilet, there's a bucket for you. Don't worry, you get used to it. Friend of mine was in here for seven days going cold turkey. Talk about a smell." He moved behind her. "I'm going to cut the tape now, but I don't want any shit. You get another idea about fighting me and not only will you be sorry but so will your father."

Claire went rigid at that, her eyes widening.

"Yeah, you heard me, your father," the man said, slipping a knife between Claire's back and the tape that bound her arms to her sides, then cutting the tape with a jerk. He went around to her front, cut the duct tape binding her fingers and wrists, and then stepped away, letting her do the rest.

Claire peeled enough tape from her fingers to remove it from her arms, then lifted an edge of the tape over her mouth and pulled quickly. She winced at the sting as the tape came off.

"My father?" Claire said, gasping.

"You heard right."

"What do you mean?"

"He fucked with me, that's all."

"I don't understand. How do you know him?"

"You mean a lowlife like me? What's your father doing knowing me? That it?"

"I just want to know what he did."

"He's doing it." The man took a quick step toward Claire and grabbed her by the hair. "Kneel down," he said, putting the tip of the knife at her windpipe.

"What are you doing? Don't."

"Shut up." He tugged her downward by the hair.

"Whatever my father did, I'm—"

"Don't make me cut your face." Pulling on her hair and with the knife at her throat, he forced Claire to her knees, her chin level now with his waist. "Turn around." He yanked Claire's hair so that she turned away from him on her knees, the knife still at her neck. "Lay down."

"Don't."

"Lay down!" The man shoved against the back of Claire's neck, and she had to throw out her hands to keep from falling flat against the ground, ending up on her hands and knees. He put his foot on the small of her back, forcing her to lie prone on the hard, oil-smelling dirt. "Don't move."

Claire lay still, her heart pounding.

"What's your MAC number?"

"What?"

"I got your MAC card, Claire Lawrence. What's the access number, or should I carve my initials in you?"

Claire told him the number.

"Good." He moved away from her.

Claire heard his feet scuff the dirt floor and, before she realized it, he opened the door and stepped out, closing the door quickly. He threw the lock in the hasp, then turned the keys of the two door locks. Claire listened to his steps fade, to the chain rattle in the gate, to the car start and drift away. Then absolute quiet.

Claire rose slowly from the floor, as though the man was still in the room, his knife out. Standing, she brushed at her knees and hands, and rubbed her wrists where the tape had been.

She went to the windows; the plywood covered the entire opening except for two vertical gaps on either side of them, the plywood having been cut too narrow. Putting her eye to an opening, Claire saw nothing but night. She went to the door and pulled on the knob, checking the strength of the frame. The door did not budge. Claire moved around the walls, one to the other, squinting at them for cracks she might widen. But she saw no cracks or loose cement—no source of heat either. She felt chilled and hugged herself. Looking for something to keep her warm, Claire found a filthy shipping blanket under the desk and draped it around her shoulders.

Her father?

Claire did not sleep all night. As she shivered atop the desk beneath the filthy shipping blanket, listening to a periodic skittering from the floor and an occasional car horn from somewhere, the evening played itself over and over in her head—the attack in her bedroom, the near escapes, the ghost costume, the blind drive through the city, and finally the mention of her father. That still baffled her. She could not comprehend what her father, who had never struck Claire as even remotely mysterious, would have to do with a man like that. What didn't she know about her father that would lead to this?

Unable to warm herself, Claire threw off the blanket as dawn light showed at the edges of the windows; she ran in place in the middle of the dirt floor for several minutes and then did a set of jumping jacks, trying at the same time to think of what to do, how to get away.

After the exercise, Claire examined the door and the windows more closely to see if she could escape through either one. The steel door was encased in a steel frame and attached to the cinder block in a manner not visible to Claire; the hinges had fixed pins, so she could not remove them even if she had a screwdriver and hammer. Through the one-inch cracks on either side of the plywood covering the windows, Claire saw bars outside. The plywood was held in place with some kind of square-head bolt; Claire tried to pull off the plywood but could not budge it. She searched the room for any kind of tool but found none. Frustrated and angry, she picked up a greasy alternator from the shelf and pounded the plywood covering the nearest window with it. The noise was deafening, but Claire only dented the wood. She dropped the alternator on the dirt floor and screamed loud and long, hoping her voice would carry beyond the plywood and the glass and someone would hear her. The only sounds that came from outside the shed were distant shifting trucks, horn blasts, and once a helicopter, but nothing human.

Claire pressed her eye to the spaces at the windows a number of times as the gray light of the morning gave way to yellow, but she saw only piles of scrap metal.

She had tried to put it off as long as possible but now, several hours after light came in the cracks at the windows, Claire absolutely had to use the bucket in the corner. She had gone camping once in the Appalachian Mountains with her ex-husband and was not squeamish about such things, but she was bothered that the man might come in while she was in the middle of using the bucket. She did not want to give him the chance to humiliate her. But she had no choice. She went to the bucket.

When she was done, Claire covered the bucket with a piece of cardboard she found against the wall and began to pace again. Minutes later, she saw the rat.

Her breath caught at the sudden movement along the wall as the rat scurried behind the desk. Claire looked around the shed for something to swing but could find nothing—a precaution the man had taken, Claire thought. She squatted to look beneath the desk and saw the rat huddled in the corner, watching her.

Claire quickly pulled the desk away from the wall, and the rat ran to the other corner, squeezing behind a wooden box filled with hubcaps. Claire rushed to the corner and with both hands shoved the wooden box against the wall. The rat squeaked briefly, its head now visible at the side of the box. The head shook for a while; then it went still. Claire continued to press on the box, not wanting to chance that she had only stunned the rat. She let up slowly, poised to crush the rat again should it stir. Claire pulled the box away from the wall and the rat fell onto its side. When its hind legs twitched, Claire picked up the alternator and dropped it squarely on the rat's head, flattening it. Claire became aware of the sewer smell then and, suddenly queasy, went to lean against the desk. Regaining her breath, she heard fumbling at the locks on the other side of the door.

Claire watched the door open several inches.

"Stand where I can see you."

Claire moved several feet toward the wall and stood close to the dead rat.

"Show me your hands." He peered through the small opening.

Claire lifted her hands from her sides and held them out.

He opened the door further and came in with his gun in one hand pointing at Claire and with several white bags in the other.

"You don't need the gun," Claire said, thinking that he did.

"Maybe not, but I like the way it feels. Go sit on top of the desk." He waved with the gun and then closed the door behind him without taking his eyes from Claire.

She crossed to the desk and sat on top of it.

"I brought you something to eat."

"I'm not hungry."

"So don't eat." He tossed Claire the bags.

"I want to know what this is all about." She placed the bags on the desk.

"Do you?"

"Why am I here?"

"Roll of the dice."

"Is it about money?"

"Is what about money?"

"My father. Why I'm here."

"That's none of your business."

"None of my business? I'm the one locked in a shed."

"Life's a bitch."

"If you were me, you would want to know."

"But I ain't you."

"But what did my father do to you?"

"Look. I don't even know your father. But to shut your mouth, he has something of mine which he don't seem to want to give up. So I grabbed you to make him. How all that came about don't matter, and if it did I wouldn't go into it because I don't feel like it. Okay? That's it. No more questions."

"What could he have of yours?"

"Jesus Christ!" The man pointed the gun at the ceiling and fired, the sound loud and sharp, causing Claire to jump. He then rushed across the room and grabbed Claire by the hair, pressing the gun against her cheek. "You want to suck on this, tell me what it tastes like? Huh?"

Afraid, wincing from the pain, Claire shook her head no.

"Then shut up." He let go of Claire's hair, shuffled backward to the milk crate by the door, and sat down.

Trembling, Claire ran her fingers over her aching scalp, still feeling the cold of the gun on her face. She realized then that he *would* kill her. Close up, his face inches from her own, his eyes wild, seething, she had seen his hair-trigger lunacy and rage. He would kill her in a second, Claire knew, kill without feeling, and that frightened her.

Claire saw now that she would have to escape or kill him. Even if this man got from her father what he wanted, Claire doubted that he would let her go. It seemed more likely that he would kill her no matter what the outcome between her father and him. He would want no witnesses.

She had to be careful then. She would have to keep her own outrage in check. She would have to calculate and plan.

The distant wail of a siren came through the walls. The man looked to the bullet hole in the ceiling and then to the door as though the sound of the gunshot had alerted the police. But the siren grew no louder. Turning back, the man's eyes crossed the dead rat and settled on it.

"You do that?" he said, pointing at the rat with the gun.

Claire nodded.

"Nice work."

"It'll stink soon. It stinks now."

"You shoulda thought of that before you killed it."

"I wasn't going to share this palace with a rat."

"I guess it's not Be Kind to Animals Week, is it?" A sneer remained on his face.

Smelling the food, Claire opened one of the bags and took out two white Styrofoam containers. She lifted their lids to reveal a hamburger and french fries. The other bag contained several doughnuts. Claire had no appetite but knew she should eat to keep her strength up. She took a french fry and bit half of it, slowly chewing. The french fries were cold, and the hamburger, too, had lost its heat. Claire ate methodically, without hunger and without tasting much. The man gazed at her, though with little apparent interest.

Claire could eat only half of the hamburger and the fries; she closed the lids on what she had not eaten and put the containers back in the bag.

The man stood up. "Stay where you are."

Claire did not move.

"I'll be back later." Holding the gun on her, he stepped quickly through the door and slammed it closed, locking it.

Claire jumped from the desktop and tried to see him through the crack between the window frame and the plywood covering. She heard footsteps briefly but saw nothing— only heard the chain against the gate and, shortly after, the car starting.

"Goddamn goddamn goddamn!" Claire shouted, pounding the desk.

8

NEAR morning, after the evening he saw Claire, Paul dreamt that he did not stop caressing her, did not remove his mouth from her soft skin or stop her own exquisite motions. They shed their clothes and clung tightly to each other on Claire's Persian rug, Paul's face lost in her hair.

The alarm clock sounded. Paul jumped from both the dream and sleep in the still dark morning, rose up from the pillow he had been clutching fiercely, and hit the off button. The sound died abruptly, and in the hushed stillness Paul tried to reenter the dream. But he had not fallen back to sleep after waking in the morning for three years and could not do so now. Instead, he lay in bed, holding the images of Claire in his mind for as long as he could before they scattered.

Paul remembered that he had agreed to meet Claire to run with her, and that pulled him from bed. He hunted for clean sweat clothes, found them buried in a drawer, dressed, brushed his teeth, shaved, and combed his hair before going outside. As Paul loosened up on the sidewalk, Mr. Mitchell came carefully from his house across the street. Paul waved to him, and the old man slowly lifted his crooked hand, the knuckles as large as walnuts, and motioned as though shooing flies. He came down the several steps to the sidewalk, gripping the handrail, and stood facing the end of the street, back bent, head out, as though studying the terrain. During slow afternoons, when the weather allowed Mr. Mitchell to sit out front in a beach chair, Paul sat on the old man's steps listening contentedly to stories of his life.

"You're out early, Mr. Mitchell," Paul said, crossing over to him. The old man took a walk around the block twice a day, morning and evening.

"I couldn't sleep. You gonna run?"

Paul nodded.

"Mind if I walk with you to the corner?"

"Not at all."

Paul moved beside Mr. Mitchell and, without asking, the old man gripped Paul's shoulder for support before starting away from the step. Mr. Mitchell supported himself on the other side with his new cane; he had been mugged recently for the old one. With Paul taking as small steps as Mr. Mitchell, they made their way slowly in the half light of the early morning to the end of the street. They did not speak, but Paul thought of the cruelty of old age, the decay of the body, and how lucky his grandfather had been to die peacefully in his sleep while still in good health. Paul hoped that he went the same way, or in some manner just as quickly and did not have to cling to life ailing and in pain or, worse, suffering dementia.

"Well, we're here," Paul said when he reached the corner with Mr. Mitchell.

"Thank you," the old man said, letting go of Paul's shoulder. "You go and have a good run."

"And you have a good walk." Paul thought of the muggers, so desperate for drug money, so without conscience that they robbed old men of their canes, and added, "Be careful," before trotting off.

A few minutes later, Paul reached Twenty-third Street at South, where he was to meet Claire in front of the burned-out food market. She was not there, and Paul ran in place for a while. When Claire did not show after fifteen minutes, Paul gave one last look around and then jogged toward the river, disappointed, thinking she had changed her mind.

Soon Paul ran over the South Street bridge, with the green-brown Schuylkill river below it and the Expressway along its side, the traffic there not yet thick and slow. He ran through the Penn campus, through Drexel University, and soon after, on his return to Center City, past the main post office. Instead of turning to run on JFK Boulevard, he stayed on Market Street.

Paul ran south at Twenty-third Street to Walnut and then slowed to a walk. He continued straight to Pine, where he paused at the corner looking at the front of Claire's house; it appeared as though the light in the second floor room was on, and Paul wondered if Claire was inside. He looked back up Twenty-third Street to see if maybe she had started her run late and might be finishing behind him. Paul saw no one. He lowered his head and walked the rest of the way home.

Paul parked his truck outside the wood shop and watched Tut shuffling along the wall toward him, dragging his broom on the ground, eyes down and giving no indication that he had seen Paul turn onto Second Street or that he believed anyone but himself to be on it. Paul called his name when the boy came close enough. Tut looked up, startled, and clutched the broom to his chest.

"You didn't have to run last night," Paul said, walking over to the boy. "No one was going to hurt you."

Tut blinked, his eyes directed at the ground.

"But it doesn't matter," Paul said, sensing that he made the boy uncomfortable. "If you want to run, then run." Paul reached into his pocket and pulled out a five-dollar bill.

"Look, get a couple of coffees at the diner for Andre and me and anything you want for yourself." He put the bill in Tut's dirty hand. "When you come back, you can sweep up the shop again. All right, go."

Tut turned and walked toward the diner at Brown Street, the broom dragging behind him.

"So it happened," Andre said, when Paul entered the shop minutes later.

"What did?"

"I watched from the window. He grew on you."

"You don't know the half of it." Paul told Andre about taking Tut to the diner with Claire the night before.

"With who?"

"He ate like a horse."

"Wait, you said with Claire. Who's Claire?"

"That woman who showed up yesterday."

"You mean you had a date?"

"It wasn't really a date. We met in town so she could sign her check. Very innocent."

"Innocent, huh?"

"What?"

"There's something in your eyes."

"Don't give me that."

"I saw it yesterday, too," Andre said. "Chemistry."

"Chemistry? If there's chemistry, then why didn't she meet me this morning?"

"You were supposed to meet her this morning?"

"We were going to run together."

"That's romantic."

"I was thinking maybe we would have breakfast after. But she didn't show."

"There could be any number of reasons why she didn't."

Paul thought of his awkwardness on the sofa. "I think I blew it."

"Call her. I bet you just misconnected."

Tut came into the shop then with the cups of coffee in a white bag and nothing else.

"You didn't get anything for yourself again, did you?" Paul asked, taking the bag.

Tut held out the change for an answer.

"Keep it," Paul said. Then to Andre: "Let him sweep up, and if you can use him for anything else, use him." He handed Andre a cup of coffee and went into the office, where he telephoned Claire's house, but hung up after two rings, suddenly blank as to what to say.

Paul studied his "to do" list, checked off a few items, added others, and then called Claire's house again. Paul hung on until, after four rings, the answering machine was activated; he listened to Claire's voice asking the caller to leave a message, but after the beep Paul became flustered and dropped the receiver into the cradle.

Several minutes later, the telephone rang; Paul's uncle Rick was at the other end calling from the clothing store he managed. He wanted to know if Paul could meet him for lunch.

"Damn, I forgot," Paul said. "Sure. Today? I have to go into town to do a measure-up, so that's fine. Twelve-thirty?"

"Good. I'll be waiting."

Instead of putting the receiver down after Rick hung up, Paul depressed the cutoff button, waited for the dial tone, and then dialed Claire's, this time haltingly leaving a message: "Uh, Claire, this is Paul, Paul Fante. I was at the market this morning, but it looks like we didn't connect. I'm sorry. Uh, I hope we can meet tomorrow, if you're running, I mean. Uh, so long." Paul hung up, his face hot and heart wild with nervousness.

Paul found a parking spot at Nineteenth and Arch after someone pulled out and walked with his tape measure and clipboard to Liberty Place a few blocks away. Recently, a pair of skydivers had jumped from the building, the tallest in the city now, but one man's parachute had not opened and he had been killed when he hit the ground. The newspapers had shown his covered body on the front pages.

Paul signed in at the lobby desk and rode up the glitzy elevator, feeling conspicuous and out of place in his dungarees and work boots next to the men in three-piece suits and the smartly dressed women.

He met the plant manager on the Thirty-third floor and was shown an attorney's office that needed a wall-to-wall counter two feet wide, shelves all around, a cabinet with locking doors, and a desk, all in red oak. Paul spent a half hour measuring and writing notations; then he took the elevator down to the lobby, signed out, and walked the short distance to the IVB Building, where his uncle managed the clothing store in the basement.

Again, Paul felt briefly self-conscious among the racks of suits and the well-dressed salesmen and customers, but not as much as in the office building. Being the manager's nephew helped, and Paul had been at the store enough times to know most of the salesmen. He shook hands with a few on his way across the showroom floor to his uncle's office, where he found Rick talking on the telephone. Seeing Paul, Rick raised his index finger and pointed to the seat on the other side of the desk. Paul sat and tried not to listen.

Rick was more generous-spirited, open, congenial, and gracious—especially to women—than anyone Paul knew. He'd buy flowers or send kind notes to women after only a brief meeting. He was still charming and good-looking in his mid-fifties, and most people warmed to him quickly. He could be urbane and excessively mannerly and could talk with ease with the attorneys and business executives who bought their suits from him, but he was equally at ease with gamblers and criminals. Rick currently corresponded with a friend of his who was serving a prison sentence for tax evasion. Paul's uncle seemed to find something to like in everyone, although with his wife things had gone steadily downhill for over twenty years until she left him. Rick did not blame her and contested nothing during their divorce.

He put down the phone and shook hands with Paul.

"That was Catherine," Rick said.

"How is she?" Paul had met his uncle's bride-to-be only twice; an attractive woman closer to Paul's age than Rick's, she too was going on her second marriage.

"Happy. She can't wait to get married."

"And you?"

"Sooner or later, it doesn't matter to me when we hitch."

"And the happy part?"

"I'm never happy."

"But you're never that unhappy either, right?"

"I feel like sticking a gun in my mouth now and then as much as the next guy, but you're right, I'm not unhappy much. Because I don't dwell on my problems. What's the point?"

Paul had nothing to say to that, having spent a good deal of time dwelling on *his* problems.

"Anyway," Rick went on, "there's music, movies, women, and booze to give you pleasure enough to get through the day."

"You're a voluptuary, Rick."

"A what?"

"A person who lives for pleasure."

"Like suffering's better? Fuck that. Let's go."

Rick and Paul left the office and then the store, walking up the stairs and out of the building. Market Street roared with traffic and construction. New buildings were going up all along the street, and trucks of all kinds stood at the fences and rumbled to and from the sites, where giant cranes, their engines loud and jarring, swung heavy objects through space. Rick and Paul walked a block away to the Holiday Inn and were shown a table by the window.

A woman in heels and a tight skirt and leather jacket with a Pekinese on a lease walked by on the sidewalk. Rick gazed after her, eyes on her backside.

"That reminds me of Harry Moo," he said.

"The woman?"

"The dog."

"Who's Harry Moo?"

"It was Harry Moo's car that we drove to California."

"That time you left after living with us when I was a kid?"

"You remember."

"All those guys in the Buick trying so hard to look like James Dean. How could I forget?"

"Yeah. But it wasn't a Buick; it was a 1955 Plymouth."

"One minor detail. How's the dog remind you of that?"

"Well, we left for California a few days after I babysat a dog just like that for Harry Moo. It was really his wife's dog, and they asked me if I wanted to live in their house for a week while they went to Wildwood on vacation. I said sure, "Why not?" But what happens? The dog dies. I swear to God, it fucking dies on me. I get up in the morning and there's this dog on the kitchen floor with his tongue stuck to the linoleum, obviously dead, his eyes half open. Dead, very dead. I don't have a number to call Harry. And nobody who knows him—his brother or mother, who I did contact—wants anything to do with the dog. Turned out later, the dog used to bite everybody, so nobody liked it. 'The dog died? Good.' One of those deals. After all the calls, I figure it wouldn't be a good idea to put the dog in the refrigerator. I mean, I wouldn't want a dead dog in mine, so I decide to take it to the SPCA, only I don't have a car. The only person I know who does have a car has it in the shop getting a new clutch. I can't take a cab because I don't have the money for one, because I don't have a job and any gambling I've been doing hasn't been going well. All I can do is take the subway, since the SPCA is up in Kensington or somewhere, not too complicated to get to. So here I am putting this dog corpse in a suitcase that I got from my mother, who I didn't tell what I was using it for—the suitcase—and then I take it out on the street and walk the four blocks to the subway. Of course, I run into every friend and acquaintance I know in town and they ask me where I'm going. I tell them I got Harry Moo's dead dog in the suitcase. They say, 'Oh, yeah?' and have a big laugh, and then they say, 'Really, where you going, Rick?' I repeat the line about the dog, they have their laugh and ask me again, and instead of going on like that because I want to get the dog out of my hands before the end of the day, I start making up destinations: Atlantic City, New York, Saskatchewan. Finally, I make it to the subway, get on a train, take a seat near the center doors, and put the suitcase with the dog in it on the floor. I ride up past City Hall to, I think, the Spring Garden stop when—guess what? You won't believe it. Just when the doors are about to close at the stop, this guy rushes up, grabs the suitcase, and runs off the train. Robs me of the suitcase and runs off the train! The doors close right behind him and the train pulls out of the station a second later. I caught the guy's legs dashing up the stairs. Can you beat that?"

"He stole the dead dog?"

"He didn't know what he stole until he opened up the suitcase, which I would've loved to see."

Paul laughed. "What did you tell Harry and his wife?"

"The truth, though it took me a while to convince Harry's wife that it *was* the truth. She took it pretty bad, but Harry didn't like the dog anyway. It had chewed up the new furniture he got after he hit the number, and he never forgave it. His wife thought it was a plan between Harry and me to get rid of the dog, and they had some bad arguments, he told me. I even got a phone call from her wanting to hear the 'real' truth. 'I want the real truth, Rick,' she said to me. Yeah, because who would believe that story? Right after one argument where she threw a pot at Harry, he called me up and said he was going to California, he couldn't take her anymore, did I want to come? I wasn't doing anything at the time but hanging around, living with you, had no money for cigarettes let alone room and board, so, sure, I said I would go. Your father lent me some money for my share of the gas expense."

The waitress arrived and Rick and Paul gave their orders.

"We left on Friday night," Rick continued after the waitress left, "and it was like we were going to war; all the neighbors were out doing a bon voyage number, some people even waving handkerchiefs. Because who ever drove across country to California from South Philly? You may as well said you were taking a trip to Mars. Nobody did that from around there; you had to be crazy to want to go to California. People from downtown thought going to Jersey was a big deal. But we went, the five of us, with Harry Moo driving first. This is like over thirty years ago, so my memory's a little shot about it, but I remember we went through New Orleans, Texas, New Mexico, and Arizona, where we crossed the Yuma Desert at night in our underwear because it was so fucking hot. That's a sight—a carful of guys in their boxer shorts and T-shirts. We stopped at Tijuana and went to a cat house. I had a gorgeous girl, a redhead. After that, we hung around in San Diego a few days, then San Francisco, and a few other places. I think we were out there for a little over a week before we started back, stopping at Reno, Nevada, to gamble. I won and decided I didn't want to return to Philly, so I took a bus back to California and stayed about a year.

Two women in skirts walked by, drawing Rick's attention, and he gazed after them down the aisle.

"Anyway," he continued, looking back to Paul, "the rest is a blur. One thing, it's a miracle that the car made it and that we didn't kill ourselves, and I don't mean by getting in a wreck. It's easy to get on each other's nerves in a situation like that, all that time in a car, and we had guys on that trip that got in the paper years later for doing stuff, or being accused of it—some rough guys. There was Gene Monzo, who did time for stabbing a guy who got in front of him in a movie line and wanted to argue about it; and then there was Joey Dogs, who was a big numbers writer until they found him dead in the trunk of a car. That's something I never wanted to happen to me—it's so ugly, being on display like that—so I straightened myself out."

"Straightened yourself out from what?"

"You're asking for my closet skeletons."

"I won't think any less of you."

"I'm not so sure about that."

"It happened so long ago."

"So no need to bring it up."

Paul relented. "Who was the other guy on the trip?"

"Just a friend, another guy I hung with."

"See any of those guys now?"

"Well, Joey Dogs is dead, but I see the others around, at Shunk's Tavern or sometimes at the restaurants downtown; we're all still in the neighborhood."

"Are the ones that were rough guys still hoods?"

"A few." Rick sipped his drink. "Let's change the subject before we regret it."

"All right," Paul said, agreeing.

"So what's new with you?"

"I met a woman." Paul told his uncle about Claire and their meeting in the park that led to the diner. But he did not mention Tut.

"I'm glad to hear that. Bring her around, we'll have a drink."

"I kind of lost contact with her. She was supposed to meet me to run, and every time I call her there's no answer."

"It's either fate or a screwup, so don't worry."

"I'm not worrying." But Paul was.

That night, Paul worked up the courage to call Claire a second time but again connected with her answering machine. "Uh, it's Paul again," he said to the machine. "It's about eight-thirty and I just wanted . . . . I think I have to make some more measurements for your wall units. Thanks. I'll try you again later. Or you can call me, either here or at the shop. Here's my home number." He said the number. "Thanks." Then he hung up but stood leaning against the doorjamb, hearing himself and thinking he had sounded moronic.

The following morning, though Paul again waited for fifteen minutes in front of the burned-out supermarket, Claire did not show, and Paul did not see her during any of his run. Maybe she's avoiding me, Paul thought.

On the cool-down walk back to his house from Walnut Street, Paul stopped at the corner of Twenty-third and Pine and lingered there a few minutes, hoping Claire would come out of her house. The house looked exactly as it had yesterday, with light showing in the upper windows and the drapes still drawn. Claire did not come out, and Paul thought about going up to the door and ringing the bell but became nervous about it, imagining Claire stepping out just as he walked up the steps. What would he say? So he went home, telling himself that he would stop by after work if he hadn't heard from Claire during the day.

The day passed without emergencies or problems not easily remedied. Tut did not show all day, and none of the machines broke down. No salesmen dropped by. No one called to inform Paul that a piece of furniture he had built did not withstand a cigarette slowly burning on its surface or the frenetic dancing performed on it by a couple of hyperactive kids and to ask Paul to repair it.

Instead of going straight home after work, Paul drove to the Y at Broad and Pine streets, parked nearby, and soon stood in the locker room, among mostly old naked men tonight, their sagging bodies scarred from medical operations, accidents, and war wounds, their skin stippled with moles and liver spots. Paul changed into his sweat clothes and climbed the metal steps to the gym area. He began his workout by jumping rope, timing the periods by the length of the songs on the radio. A few men ran around the track, along with only one woman in bright tights, her body taut, her hair tied up, a look of seriousness on her face.

After jumping rope, Paul walked around the track while applying the wraps to his hands in preparation for hitting the heavy bag. Finishing the wrapping, he pulled on his gloves. He began to slug the bag with combinations of lefts and rights, jabbing and hooking, as he bounced on his toes, rattling the chain from which the bag hung. After three songs on the radio, Paul quit the bag and jogged around the track until the rower was free. He rowed for ten minutes, did a few minutes on the speed bag, lifted some weights, and cooled down by shooting baskets by himself. Finally, he headed for the showers.

Later, after a dinner Paul could not remember minutes after eating, after the evening news and its reports of mayhem and grief, after calling Claire's and getting her answering machine once again, Paul lay down on his battered sofa listening to the ticking clock, the creaking of the old house, the muffled voices of his neighbors in the row houses on either side of him, the rumblings of the cars that went down the street left unsurfaced for over a year because the city had run out of money—all the random city noises he now felt desperate to escape.

Paul tried reaching Claire once more. After setting off the answering machine again, he pulled on his coat and hurried out, walking toward Claire's house.

It was a chill, damp night, with halos of mist around the street lamps and something defeated about the several street people who asked Paul for money, as though they believed he wouldn't give them any but asked anyway, out of habit, so that when he did give a man his coins and a shabby woman a dollar they seemed more surprised than grateful. He saw few other people, and few cars moving along the streets; there was a feeling of bleakness in the streets, like fog, that made the effulgent house windows of yellow light seem like beacons, places where people were warm, snug, secure, and not alone.

Drawing closer to Claire's house, Paul slowed, nervous now about meeting her. What if she simply came to the door, said hello with a tight smile, thanked him emptily for his concern, then sent him on his way? What if, past her shoulder, he saw another man?

But Paul only slowed and did not turn away or stop, continuing instead to the house. He noticed the light still in the upper windows as he turned up the steps to ring the bell. He heard the bell from within, but it brought no one to the door. Paul looked through the door glass into the vestibule, noticed one of the double doors ajar, but could see only the steps leading upstairs. Holding onto the brick and leaning to the window, Paul looked through the gap where the drapes did not meet. He saw a section of the floor, the end of the sofa, and the wall beyond, where Claire's stereo system sat on a rudimentary shelf. In the shadowy light, Paul noticed that the small section of floor looked peculiar; the Persian rug was bunched up as though someone had kicked or slid into it. Claire could have bunched the rug to clean or do exercises, but Paul had more of a sense that she had left the house in a hurry. But so what? Maybe she had been late for work and dashed from the house, or maybe she had to attend to some other urgency and felt no reason to mention it to Paul. After all, they barely knew each other.

Paul stepped down to the sidewalk and started home, telling himself that if he did not hear from Claire by the following morning he would get in touch with her father and ask if he knew whether she was in the city. It would be awkward and uncomfortable, but Paul had to know.

He turned the corner at Twenty-third Street and immediately collided with the ground. Only later did Paul remember the blur and the impact at his throat.

9

ERNEST Maglio and Freddie Whale sat at a table in the club; Gus sat alone at a table nearby. At the table near the door, Cosmo sat, hardly moving, with a look reminding Maglio of a lizard. That was okay, not to have much emotions, especially in Cosmo's line of work. You asked him to go pull out somebody's front teeth and bring them to you or break their collarbones or shoot them behind the ear, you didn't want somebody who would hesitate because of feelings. You wanted a guy who would hammer like swatting flies. *Ba-bing,* then let's go eat.

Maglio wasn't feeling too well, but he never did anymore. He felt older than fifty-five, even though, with his thick, mostly still black hair, he looked younger. 'Course, what did it matter how you looked if you always had some kind of ailment like he did? If it wasn't gout, it was piles; if it wasn't that, it was his sinuses; if not that, something else. Always something. He was getting broken down little by little, from his rebuilt teeth to his toes with the ingrown nails. So much for all the vitamins he took. He ate a bran muffin every morning, stayed away from bacon and eggs, got some yogurt down his throat a coupla times a week, and still he felt like he was falling apart. What else could he do? He could retire and move to Florida, reduce his stress level like his doctor told him. Yeah, right.

At least he wasn't like Freddie Whale—fat. Too bad, but the way Freddie was going, he would probably have a heart attack any day now because his arteries had to be all clogged from the cholesterol. But anything you ate now was bad for you, plus the air and the water were all screwed up with chemicals. And how about what they called the ozone layer? Maglio didn't quite understand that, but he knew it wasn't a good thing that the ozone was being eaten up by air pollution. Something about making the sunshine dangerous. Getting a tan now was suicide. Maglio had just read that the fillings in your teeth wore away and went to your brain, the mercury screwing things up in there. With all the stuff that could kill you, you needed a lot of luck to reach seventy. The bad thing was, a lot of people went past seventy and wound up hooked up to machines getting fed with tubes in their stomachs. Which Maglio never wanted. Pull the plug, shoot him, but don't let him become a vegetable.

Gus was probably going the same way as Whale; he wasn't fat, just big, but still his heart had to pump blood through all that flesh. That's why Maglio was glad he was small, not even a hundred fifty pounds. He ate one egg a week maybe, a lot of chicken and fish, and he exercised three, sometimes four times a week. Mostly he rode a stationary bike or a rowing machine, and sometimes he jogged. Just last week he jogged on the Longport beach with his pal from childhood, Victor, who a few weeks before had asked Maglio if he wanted to go to the Bahamas with him and his wife. No, he didn't want to go to the Bahamas because he didn't want to fly—you crash and you're dead—and what was he going to do there anyway, sit on the beach all day and let the sun give him skin cancer because the ozone layer was shot? Have fun, Maglio told his friend, and call me when you get back.

He wasn't just a good friend, Victor. Maglio was the godfather of Victor's girl from his first marriage, and Victor took care of almost all Maglio's Atlantic City business, even while running a legitimate construction company. He also had some labor union influence and a few good connections with the local politicians. Bids were no problem. Vic was a talented guy, and smart, though maybe not smart about women. He had just remarried about a year ago. His new wife, Nancy, got married for the second time too. Maglio and his own wife had just had dinner at Vic's house. Nancy was a nice enough lady, still pretty, but she was a little ditzy in the head, besides being a bad cook.

It was nighttime, and the club was dim and quiet. Guys didn't talk much when Maglio was around. They were afraid to get him annoyed, afraid of him in general. Which is how it should be. Who was afraid of Carmine Tucci? Nobody. He was a nice guy, a gentleman to everybody, but that's why his thing fell apart and why he got whacked down there at the airport. It was like he was asking for it, so when it happened not too many people were surprised, especially the big people who mattered when it came to Maglio taking over; they saw the logic in it. They also saw how messy things got while Tucci was in control of the city and South Jersey, with guys running their separate little operations on the side and Tucci not doing anything about it, not even demanding regular percentages. It was free enterprise. What they did was give Tucci a payment every Christmas like a bunch of Santa Clauses. You couldn't have that and stay strong, keep those other groups from grabbing your territory—that Junior Black Mafia or those Chinese gangs or anybody else who knew Tucci's way and thought they could do what they wanted. It was a nice thing to allow, all that money-making, Maglio thought, but it caused a big problem for Maglio when he took over after Tucci. Guys were used to running their side businesses without kicking anything back, or only a little, and wanted to keep on doing it. Well, Maglio couldn't have that, not just because it weakened the organization or even because of the money he wouldn't be getting, but because these guys doing their own thing would only get bigger and bigger, and before long they would start thinking about running the whole show and getting rid of Maglio to do it. So Maglio had to straighten things out, give everybody the right message that the Tucci way was gone. So he had to bag some guys—get rid of the bad apples and those that looked like they might go bad. He didn't have a choice. Do that or don't survive. Maglio didn't want somebody telling his wife that he had gotten his face blown off, asking her if he had any scars or birthmarks so they were sure it was him.

Fear. You had to have people fear you in the kind of position Maglio was in. After he cleaned house, people feared Maglio a lot. That's the way it had to be. It was a necessary part of doing business; it made it easier to get things done. And he liked people to fear him.

Lenny's fake leg thumped on the floor as he brought the plates of linguine to the table; then he thumped away to putter behind the counter, looking miserable. He used to tell people that he lost the leg in some World War Two battle, but everybody knew it was a car accident that took it. Maglio wasn't so sure that Lenny feared him, but he was a special case; he had known Maglio when he was a kid, so Lenny didn't have to treat him any differently now than he did back then. One of those things. Whale feared him, but it didn't show like with Gus, who just about shook when Maglio talked to him. He could see it. Gus couldn't look Maglio in the eye for a whole second when they were together, and he stuttered when he spoke. Looking at Gus when he was like that, it was hard to believe the things he had done. He was Whale's man when somebody had to get smashed, and he smashed good. Cosmo was better, though—very clean, unless Maglio requested otherwise. Sometimes you had to be a little showy, get people thinking.

"As pleasant as always," Whale said after Lenny walked away.

"If you had one leg, you wouldn't be too happy, either," Maglio said, starting to eat while the linguine was still hot.

"Could be worse," Whale said, picking up his fork.

"You're right, there's always a worse." Maglio liked Whale; he was a pretty good talker, with interesting things to say. And of all the people, Maglio was pretty sure Whale didn't have any ideas about getting to the top over his body. Pretty sure, because everybody had to be watched at least some. Except maybe Cosmo, who was like a dog in his devotion to Maglio, and talked about as much.

"The eyes," Whale said. "You don't have eyes, you're screwed. A brain tumor would ruin your day, too."

"All you hear about these days is tumors. Tumors and cancer, but a lot now in people in, like, their early forties."

"If they told me I had a brain tumor, I would kill myself."

"I've been getting some bad headaches for weeks. I got it checked out but they didn't find anything."

"I had a lump on my back not too long ago," Whale said, "but it was only a lipoma, a fat deposit."

"You get it cut out?" Maglio asked.

"No, I still got it."

"I would get it cut out. You don't know what it's doing in there. Suppose it goes after your spinal cord? You got any moles, get those cut off. I got all mine cut off; it's not a big deal, takes about two seconds a mole. You afraid?"

"No. I don't like the idea of being cut."

"Wait till they go after your prostate."

"I had my tonsils out and that was enough."

"Remember the hemorrhoids I had? I was in agony. I couldn't sit; I was in the bathtub all day. I had what they call an anal fissure. It's like a cut, but it don't heal. Every time you sit on the toilet it cracks open, and it's like somebody's putting a knife up there. A week of that and you don't care how much they cut you; in fact, you're dying for them to cut you. The operation only takes about an hour. They give you a big dose of Valium, then Demerol or something, then they cut. You're half in and half out of it, and you don't feel anything but pressure now and then. Everybody's making jokes or talking about Oprah Winfrey. Afterward, you take painkillers for two weeks until the cuts heal." Maglio took a bite of bread.

"Stitches?" Whale asked, grimacing.

"Yeah, sure. What else are they going to use? Staples?"

"Oh, man." Whale laughed a little.

"That's life."

The telephone rang behind the sandwich counter, and Lenny limped over to answer it.

"Guess what," Maglio went on, "my gallbladder operation was worse. I showed you that scar. Now I hear they have this procedure where they make only three small holes and suck it out. Can you believe that?"

Lenny motioned to Maglio that the call was for him. Maglio shoved away from the table and went to the counter where Lenny had put the telephone.

It was Victor Notte, who called to say he had returned from the Bahamas that afternoon, so if Maglio needed anything, he was back. He also said he came into the house to find that it had been burglarized. Not just that, but whoever did it wrecked the place and ruined his desk by drilling holes in it.

"Holes?"

"You know, with a power drill."

"What, to open the drawers?"

"That, and just for fun. There's holes in the top, too. You have to see it; you wouldn't believe what they did."

"What did they steal?"

"It makes me sick to tell you."

"Not the coins."

"They got the coins, Nancy's jewelry, some cash."

"All the coins? The doubloon, too?"

"The doubloon, the K-rands, the whole works. They were all in one box in the desk."

"Didn't I tell you they shoulda been in the bank or a safe?"
As a wedding gift, Maglio had given Victor a Spanish dou-

bloon like one he had seen in an article on sunken treasure in an issue of *National Geographic* at his doctor's office. He had gotten the coin from a professor at Penn, though he and Cosmo had to encourage the guy a little to give it up.

"You know how Nancy was about those coins."

Yeah, Maglio thought, she was crazy in the head about them, just had to keep them in the house in case the world economy went bust. Right, that was likely. "Didn't the alarm go off?"

"Get this. Whoever did it knew the code. There's no cut wires; the thing was just turned off."

"Who could know the code?"

"I can only think of the people who have to know it to get in every day."

"Or *had* to know it."

"I didn't think of that," Victor said. "What, like Nancy's ex, her daughter? They wouldn't do something like this."

"You never know."

"But they could've used their keys because the locks are still the same from when they owned the house. Somebody *broke* in here."

"Maybe they wanted to make it look like a real burglary."

"They went through a lot of trouble if they did. The patio door off the track, the smashed cabinets, the desk, Nancy's panties all over the floor. She's pretty upset about it."

"Who can blame her?"

"And the thirty thou in coins gone."

"Does she think her ex had anything to do with it?"

"No. But she's not in a hurry to get the police in here."

"No, you don't want the cops sniffing around, getting your name in the papers."

"I wasn't going to let her call them."

"Good. Calling me was the right thing."

"What should I do in the meantime?"

"In the meantime, have Nancy call her ex and the daughter and feel them out. You call your kid."

"I already did call her; she said she hasn't left campus since the summer. And Nancy already called Philly, but nobody answered at both places."

"Well, look, the guy lives in town, right?"

"Center City."

"Good. Why don't you take a drive here tomorrow and we'll just show up at his place and watch his face when he sees you."

"All right. And Claire?"

"Who's Claire?"

"Nancy's daughter."

"Oh, right."

"I can't see her doing it."

"Well, like I said, who knows? She coulda had a friend do it. You never know about people. But if she or the ex didn't, then you might have to say good-bye to the coins."

"If I get my hands on the son of a bitch who did this to my house, I'll kill him."

"I'll help you."

They said so long shortly later and hung up. Maglio went back to his table, where Whale sat, his half-eaten plate of linguine in front of him.

"That was Victor. Somebody robbed his house." Maglio told Whale about the damage and the stolen coins.

Whale held a forkful of linguine in front of his mouth as he listened; then he put the fork in his mouth, frowning as he chewed. "Terrible," he said, looking bad about it.

"What's worse, it might be Nancy's ex-husband who did it."

"You're kidding me."

"No. So me and Vic are going to pay him a visit tomorrow."

"That's a good idea." Whale choked a little and had to drink some wine.

"Yeah, we just want to see his face when he sees Vic. You can tell a lot from a man's face when he's off guard, you know?"

Whale nodded, drinking more wine.

"The linguine's cold," Maglio said. "Lenny!"

The old man limped over and Maglio had him take the plate of pasta, telling him to heat it up.

"It won't taste good."

"I don't care how it tastes."

"If you don't care how it tastes, why don't you just eat spaghetti from a can? Why should I make sauce for you?"

"Listen to him."

"Listen to you." Lenny thumped off, mad.

Turning back to Whale, Maglio said, "He's worse than my father."

"Speaking about fathers, I'm supposed to see mine in about a half hour."

"You leaving?"

"If you're finished with me," Whale said.

Maglio thought a few moments, deciding whether there was anything more he had to talk to Whale about. He didn't think so. "Yeah, I guess I don't have anything else."

"All right." Whale wiped his mouth, left some money on the table for Lenny, and after saying so long to Maglio, started out the door with big Gus following close behind.

Maglio got up from the table and went into the back room to lie down on the sofa, one of his headaches coming on.

10

PAUL lay choking on the damp sidewalk, a man with the bright, intense eyes of a lunatic holding a gun in his face.

"You her boyfriend?" the man said.

Paul gagged. "What?"

"Her boyfriend? That you?"

"Claire's?" Paul got out, his windpipe aching.

"Claire's."

"Where is she?"

"I'm asking the questions."

Paul faltered, feeling danger emanating from this man like heat. He thought for a moment that he had seen him before—the severe face, the eyes the color of a knife blade, the madman grin. But where? "I'm a friend of hers, yes. Why do you want to know?"

"Did you jazz her?"

"What?"

"You jazz her Halloween night?"

113

"Hey!" The question struck Paul like a slap and he began to shove against the ground to get up and throw punches.

The man jammed the gun against Paul's chest. "Don't."

"What do you want? Where's Claire?"

"I can't tell you that." He straightened up and for a few moments stood over Paul, grinning, the light from the street lamp behind him. "But ask her father." Then he ran down the street to a car parked at Twenty-third and Lombard and sped away.

Bewildered, faintly sick in the stomach, Paul stood up dizzily and watched the taillights of the car until they turned at the next block. Then he started toward home, dazed but not hurt beyond the pain in his throat, trying to make sense of what had occurred.

Reaching his house, Paul immediately went to the telephone, dialed Information for Henry Lawrence's number, and called him. An answering machine clicked on after two rings. The moment Lawrence's taped voice ended, Paul began to leave his message.

"Mr. Lawrence, this is Paul Fante, Claire's friend. Something strange just happened to me. I've been unable to contact Claire for the past few days, and a few minutes ago, near Claire's house, a man assaulted me, and he mentioned you. I wanted to know—" A click at the other end stopped him.

"This is Henry Lawrence." He spoke quickly, as though afraid Paul might hang up before he lifted the receiver. "Was he a short man, around thirty, close-cropped hair?"

"Yes. Yes, he was." Paul's memory teased him again, but he could not come up with a name to go with the face or where and under what circumstances he had seen him, if at all.

"What else did he say?"

"He said you would know where Claire was. Mr. Lawrence—"

"I don't know where she is."

"Mr. Lawrence, what's this about?"

"Who did you say you were?"

"Paul Fante, a friend of Claire's. I—"

"How good a friend?"

"Good enough to be concerned about her."

"Why did he assault you?"

"What? I don't know." There was the face again, playing at the edge of Paul's memory. "Is Claire all right?"

Lawrence paused. "I don't know."

"When was the last time you saw her?"

"A few days ago."

"But you don't know where she is now?"

"No."

"Aren't you concerned?"

"She's my daughter; I'm very concerned." But Lawrence did not sound concerned, only distracted, and Paul remembered Claire saying the other day that her father had been acting strange, that he had not been himself lately.

"Tell me what's going on, Mr. Lawrence."

"It's not your affair."

"Whether it's my affair or not, Claire disappeared, and I want to know what happened to her. Does she know that man?"

Lawrence paused again but did not speak.

"Mr. Lawrence?"

"He kidnapped her."

"He what? Did you call the police?"

"No. He said he would kill her if I did."

"But why does he have her? For ransom?"

"Listen, why don't you come over here and we'll talk. I'll tell you what I know."

"Tell me now."

"No. It's too involved for the telephone." Lawrence told Paul that he lived at the Dorchester, saying he would leave word at the front desk to let him pass.

"I'm leaving now." Paul hung up the telephone and went out into the cold and damp November night. *Kidnapped?* Paul could not comprehend the notion. *Kidnapped?* He hurried down to Nineteenth Street, past two men huddled together and holding bottles of wine as if they were a heat source, and then turned north toward the skyscrapers. At South, he passed a ragged man pushing a shopping cart filled with aluminum cans, who cheerfully said hello, his voice a rich baritone. The mist haloed the bluish streetlights of the Graduate Hospital parking lot; the emergency ward sign was as garish as an advertisement. The lot was still, with only a stray dog sniffing among the cars. Just the other night, Paul and Claire had stood at the corner here beside his parked truck looking for Tut.

Kidnapped?

It was absurd, incredible. Why would anyone want to kidnap Claire? Then Paul saw the sneering face again above the gun, tried to place it, but again could not.

Paul reached Rittenhouse Square less than ten minutes later. Not having to pass through the desolate square to reach the Dorchester, Paul hurried along its south side toward the building, its lobby as bright as a stage. At the front desk, Paul told the clerk that he was there to see Henry Lawrence, and the clerk allowed Paul to pass to the elevators. He waited a half minute for a car beside an elderly woman smelling strongly of perfume, her back bent by age, and took a ride to the sixteenth floor; exiting, he read the numbers from the doors and walked down a carpeted hall to Lawrence's apartment, the air in the hallway thick with the odor of fried fish and detergent.

"Who is it?" Lawrence asked at Paul's knock.

Paul said his name, and Lawrence unlocked the door but held it open only a few inches to take a look at Paul before opening it enough to allow him to enter. Lawrence closed the door quickly behind Paul and locked it, then walked past him and into the living room, its far wall nearly entirely a bank of windows that looked out above Rittenhouse Square toward Broad Street and the Delaware River beyond. Lawrence sat down atop a bookcase that ran the length of the windows below the sill, the glittering buildings and the starless night behind him. A single lamp burned on top of the bookcase to Lawrence's right, casting his face in chiaroscuro. Standing ill at ease on the other side of a woven rug, Paul looked at Lawrence but would not have recognized him from the picture on Claire's living room end table. The difference seemed not the result alone of the intervening years, but something that, because of the poor light, Paul did not determine for some moments, and not until after he realized that Lawrence's front teeth were missing. Lawrence's puffy and dark-eyed face had been altered by recent injury, Paul realized, and the face, cheerful in the photograph, was here utterly empty of anything but despair. Paul was certain Lawrence had been beaten.

"You said you've been seeing my daughter?"

"Several times recently," Paul said, wanting to ask about the bruises and the missing teeth.

"You must like her a good deal to want to get involved in this."

"This? This what, Mr. Lawrence?"

"There's not much to tell, really," Lawrence said to the floor, his voice weary. "I had some financial setbacks that put me in a deep hole, and decided I had only one way to get out." And then he patiently told Paul about his divorce and the settlement—"My wife got the house in Longport, a lump of stocks, even a coin collection"—some particulars of his business failures, the brief try at gambling, the hounding by the IRS, who threatened to charge him with tax evasion unless he paid thousands of dollars, and finally the idea of stealing the coin collection.

"Steal?" Paul said, not expecting to hear that.

"As I said, I was desperate. Anyway, the collection was mine, after all. I researched the coins, brought them together, took care of them." Lawrence turned to the window and spoke with his head down, gazing at the square below. "My ex-wife didn't trust banks. But she didn't trust them in a paranoid sort of way, especially after all those Savings and Loans began to fail. So she kept a lot of money in the house. But not just cash, because she didn't trust the whole United States economy, believing the whole thing was going to collapse one day and paper money wouldn't have any value. The only thing that would have value, she thought, was precious metal. I don't know what survivalist tract she'd read to give her these ideas, but there you are. She liked to have the coin collection in the house. I suppose it should have been kept in a safe deposit box, but Nancy said that would mean the bank would have a key to it, too, and if the bank collapsed the door would be locked and we couldn't get to it. As I said, she's odd, extreme in many ways, and that contributed to our breakup. She wasn't always so. But we all have our peculiarities, our weaknesses, phobias, what have you. We change over time. One of Nancy's oddities was an obsession with the coins; that's why she demanded it as part of the divorce settlement and why she kept it in the house. I didn't have just rare coins, though, but also some South African Krugerrands. The price of gold is up now, and I was going to cash those first. But when I went to my ex-house to burglarize it, I found someone already there."

"The person who knocked me down?"

Lawrence nodded. "He had gotten there before me and had come in by way of the patio doors. He had apparently gotten around the burglar alarm somehow; either he cut the wires—whatever they do—or he knew the code, though I can't see how. I could have turned around and forgotten the entire idea, but I was in the house already, not really thinking anymore, just moving ahead, curious in a way. And still desperate, of course. I heard noises from the den, thumps, and went into the living room looking for a weapon, though I'm not at all a violent person. I saw the fire poker by the fireplace and took that. Then I heard a power drill and thought Nancy had hired someone to refurbish the den while she was on vacation. I went to the door of the den and peeked in. It wasn't a workman; this fellow was drilling holes in the top of the Hepplewhite desk, a pretty odd sight. I backed up and stood waiting in the kitchen. When he came into it carrying the box of coins, I hit him with the poker. I didn't want to hurt him; I didn't really want to hit him, but when he appeared, I swung, automatically, because I saw the coin box. He dropped the coins and fell down. But I didn't hit him hard enough and we wound up wrestling a bit on the floor. But because I had the poker, I got the best of him. I grabbed the coins and ran out, leaving him in the house. I hurried back to my car and then returned directly to the city. I felt strangely elated. I had agonized for days about the burglary, but, you see, I did not have to do it; the house had *already* been burglarized, and the clues left originated with someone other than me. And I wound up taking what was originally mine from a common thief. The elation was understandable. But it was short-lived."

"He found you."

"Yes. Apparently I dropped my wallet of business cards during our struggle." Lawrence told Paul about leaving the apartment the other day and, after walking several blocks toward work, being attacked by the short man with the short hair and thick build. "That's what happened to my face and teeth. I knew then what a blunder I had committed, knew how naive I had been. I had been too caught up in my need for money and had not realized that the sensibilities of a hood were ones I would never have—that I would only be trying them on like a mask, a costume. Or, at any rate, when it came to meeting one of these types in the street, one who wanted something you had taken from him, I was far out of my league. In that instance, you have to be able to give much more than you take. As you can see from the gap in my mouth and my battered face, I *took* considerably more. In fact, I gave out nothing. He ambushed me, and I was no match for him. He banged me around like you would a child; he threatened me, told me to return the coins or I'd be sorry. I believed him, and through my daze, bleeding, my teeth on the sidewalk, I nodded that I would. I fully meant to. I stumbled back here intending to meet him at a playground he mentioned. I was desperate, still am, but so is he in his own way; it's the kind of desperation you'd see in a trapped animal that will chew off its own foot to escape." He paused. "A few hours later, I left

119

my apartment building with the coins in a satchel and started for the playground. But I hadn't walked two blocks before a thin, pleasant-looking man stopped me to ask the time. I lifted my wrist to look at my watch and he yanked the satchel of coins from my hand. I shouted once as he ran, but then it occurred to me that he was working for the burglar, that he had decided not to wait for me to get to the playground. I thought the playground was a ruse in case I had alerted the police, who would be waiting there for him. Smart, I thought. After that, I came home. You could figure out the rest."

"The burglar never got the coins."

"That's what he said. He called me, wanting to know why I hadn't met him. I told him what had happened, that I thought one of his associates had taken the coins. He didn't believe me and became very angry. The following day he informed me that he had kidnapped Claire and that if I didn't want her to be harmed I should give him the coins or thirty thousand dollars. I have neither."

"How did he connect you to Claire?"

"I don't know."

"We have to call the police."

"No, we can't do that. Under different circumstances, I would have, don't you think? But it's not just that he said he would harm Claire if I contacted them or that I would have to explain to the police that I meant to burglarize the house myself and, in effect, *did*, to the extent that I took the coins from the original burglar. With the police involved, my ex-wife would likely learn what I had intended to do and from her so would her husband. It's not the shame or the reputation I would lose; I can bear that. But hers is no ordinary husband." Lawrence paused. "Does the name Victor Notte mean anything to you?"

"No. Should it?"

"He runs a large construction company in Atlantic City and, so say the newspapers, he has ties to organized crime."

"Organized crime?"

"That's who my wife married, a man whose name gets

mentioned in the papers now and then in connection with criminal investigations." Lawrence laughed slightly, shaking his head. "Can you believe that? She met him at one of the casinos. Whether she knew who he was, or cared, I don't know. But I suppose there are stranger things. He's not a fire-eater for the circus or a pornographer, for instance. The problem for me is that someone like Notte wouldn't take too kindly to the ex-husband of his wife, or anyone for that matter, breaking into his house and taking thirty thousand dollars in coins."

"But it wasn't you."

"I intended to steal them, and I doubt if Notte would bother with the distinction. Also, I wound up with the coins, however briefly."

"But on the other hand, Claire's his step-daughter, and this other person, this maniac, this—"

Paul went rigid, nearly choked.

"What is it?" Lawrence asked.

Paul did not answer, his eyes intense and fixed on the light-speckled blackness beyond the window.

"Something wrong?"

"Whale," Paul said. And then he rushed from the apartment.

Paul ran to the elevators and punched the buttons, but almost immediately ran to the stairwell, through the heavy steel door, and then down and around, down and around, down and around the concrete steps, past the large floor numbers painted on the raw walls, his footfalls echoing, blood pounding in his ears. He reached the first floor, burst through the door into the warm bright lobby, and rushed across the granite tiles, past the reception desk, and finally through the doors into the night, fleeing. But not toward home, because what he fled would trap him there, and not toward the Delaware River because that would be just as bad, and not toward South Philadelphia because that would be the worst place, and not north because it was unsafe—leaving west, the direction of his morning runs.

He ran over the Walnut Street Bridge, past the post office, through the University of Pennsylvania campus and beyond. He turned right at Thirty-eighth Street toward the church with the immense red doors, ran out of breath finally, and slowed to a walk, heart thudding with both exertion and anguish. Reaching the church, he stopped and sat heavily on the stone steps.

He saw himself three years ago, living in South Philadelphia, not quite a year out of white collar work, his new woodworking business underway but his income much less than he had been earning a year earlier. Then the restaurant job came along. Paul decided he had to land the contract if his floundering business was to get off the ground. He won the contract with a low bid, though he did not remain happy about that for long. Paul had little capital for the materials he would need and, because his was a new business, the banks would not give him a loan; he had little equity in his house and could not borrow against it. Paul was about to call the contractor and cancel the contract when his uncle Rick, after Paul mentioned his difficulties, half-seriously suggested that Paul borrow the money from a loan shark he knew. Paul dismissed the idea immediately, but that night, as his wife slept beside him, the figures ran over and over through his head. It was an eighty-thousand-dollar job, consisting of front and back bar, tables, serving stations, paneling, and booths; materials would cost about twenty thousand, the bare minimum Paul would need. If he worked with another man for six weeks, he would be able to complete the job and make a killing. He would just have to convince a worker not to take pay for that amount of time and would have to see if the loan shark would take only interest for two months. But a loan shark? Paul thought, more than uncomfortable with the idea. He had never even thought to borrow from a loan shark, did not know any, did not know anyone other than his uncle Rick who did. He would not be considering it now if the profit figure wasn't so large: at least thirty-five thousand dollars, nearly fifty percent, and just what he needed to get his business on a solid footing.

Through the sleepless night and the following day, Paul kept looking for reasons to bail out of the contract. If he couldn't hire a man to agree to defer his salary for two months, he wouldn't do it, Paul told himself. But Andre showed up and only shrugged, saying, "I trust you," after Paul explained the arrangement. If Paul couldn't get the materials he needed, if they were not in stock, he wouldn't do it, he said to himself. But the suppliers told him that stock was plentiful. If he could not finish the job on schedule, he wouldn't do it. But he went over the labor numbers and concluded again that he could finish the job inside of two months. Aside from borrowing money at usury rates, Paul could not find a single reason not to go ahead with the contract. He called his uncle Rick and asked how to get in contact with the loan shark.

"The what?" Rick said.

"What we talked about."

"You're serious?"

"I need to do it."

"You'll have no trouble paying the money back?"

"No. I worked it all out."

"Because if—"

"I know the risks."

"I'll feel responsible if anything happens to you."

"No need to. It's my decision entirely. You're just supplying a name."

"It's Freddie Whale."

Paul met Whale at the Tree Street Grill on Twelfth in South Philadelphia. A large man with a raspy voice, Whale smoked a cigar as Paul nervously explained his dilemma at a table in the rear. Whale interrupted when Paul became too detailed.

"I don't care how you use the money," Whale said. "I only want to know if you could pay back the twenty thousand on time."

"I can."

"You got collateral?"

"I have a truck, a car, and my machines."

"Machines I can't use. House?"

"Yes."

Whale puffed on his cigar, seeming disinterested. He looked around the restaurant, nodding to people, grinning occasionally but as though with effort. "I wouldn't be talking to you if I didn't know your uncle some," Whale said. "I don't know you at all and you're asking for a lot of money. You could be a bad risk. I have to feel confident that you can pay back the money no problem, and you have to understand that if you don't bad things can happen, uncle or not, which he understands. I'm not handing out charity, you know what I mean? I'm a businessman. I have cash flow problems like everybody else. Now you say you have a contract that the banks won't finance. That makes me smile, because if the banks weren't so tight-ass I wouldn't have a business. But I have to be concerned that you'll also screw me, maybe not on purpose but just the same. And if you screw me, I have to screw you. That's how it works. Now," and he puffed on his cigar, "you still want to deal?"

Trembling and trying not to show it, Paul thought again about the profit. He subtracted the interest he would have to pay Whale, went through the work schedule—bar, two weeks; back bar, a week; paneling, another week; booths and tables, two weeks; installation, a week—and again concluded that he could finish the job in two months, his considerable profit intact. He nodded.

"I'll want twenty-two hundred a week for twelve weeks."

"I can't manage that," Paul said. "Would you take only the interest per week and the entire principal at the end?"

"I don't work that way. It leaves too much money on the street for too long, which keeps me from loaning it out to somebody else."

Watching his large profit begin to vanish, Paul asked, "Would you reconsider if I offered you an extra thousand dollars at the end of the twelve weeks?"

"An extra two might help."

"Okay, two."

Whale puffed on his cigar. "All right, I'll take a chance on you. You give me five hundred a week for twelve weeks, then the balance to twenty-nine thousand at the end. Okay?"

Paul did the quick arithmetic in his head and still saw the large profit. "All right."

"A man named Gus will see you tomorrow with the money."

Paul left the restaurant. He stopped several times on the walk home thinking about what he had done and actually once turned around and started back to the restaurant to tell Whale that he had changed his mind. But the thousands in profit appeared again—what that would do for his business, the things he could buy for the shop and his family. Their car was falling apart, they needed new furniture, and wasn't it about time Paul put away a few thousand dollars for his daughter's college education? He needed money, that was certain; if he didn't get it, the business could fail and he'd have to return to a nine-to-five grind somewhere. He had done that long enough, his brain becoming duller and duller while sitting at a desk beneath shadowless fluorescent lights. He could not go back to that. So he had to borrow money from a person who ran an illegal loan business. All right. Other people did it, including his uncle. It was not as though Paul had engaged in a drug deal, stolen, or harmed someone. Anyway, he had a signed contract now. He had found a good man to help him in the shop. He had carefully gone over all the details of the job. He was ready to work.

The job went reasonably well from the beginning, with only several minor hang-ups that set the schedule back a week: the back bar mirrors had come in oversized and had to be returned, and the paneling measurements were off, necessitating an adjustment in height. But other than that, there were no more than the usual difficulties. Paul paid Whale the five hundred dollars every Monday night by withdrawing money from his small savings account and by taking cash advances on his credit cards. He met Whale or Gus at the South Philadelphia restaurant and left the envelope of cash on the seat between them.

The nightmare began with the installation. Paul had all of his product ready to be installed at the restaurant, but the other trades were behind schedule, and their work—plumbing and electric, the tile floor—had to be completed before Paul could install anything. Every time Paul called the general contractor to see if he could install, something still had not been done, preventing Paul from even making a delivery of the goods he had made. Paul argued that he had completed his work ahead of schedule and that he should be paid for it, minus the installation price. The contractor said he was sympathetic but he could not pay Paul until after he was paid by the restaurant owners.

After four frantic weeks, and on the day Paul was to give Freddie Whale the remainder of his twenty-nine thousand dollars, he was told that the restaurant was ready for his installation. Paul dropped everything, rented a moving truck, grabbed a couple of idle men off the street, loaded the bar and the rest onto the truck, and delivered it at four o'clock to the new restaurant in Society Hill. After unloading, Paul paid the men with money borrowed from Andre, and then he and Andre worked to midnight putting in the paneling. They met at the site at six the next morning and worked straight to six that evening, had a quick dinner of pizza, and then worked until ten. They finished up in mid-afternoon the following day. Paul left Andre at the site to touch up nicks and nail holes while he returned to the shop and called the contractor about payment.

"You'll get the check in thirty days," Paul was told.

"Thirty days? I can't wait thirty days." Paul had already pushed Whale off for several.

"Didn't you read the contract? It's net thirty."

"But I finished in thirty days."

"We didn't get paid yet, and if we don't get paid, how can I pay you?"

"I'm in a tight fix here."

"Look, I'll see what I can do." The contractor hung up.

Paul went to the restaurant in South Philadelphia that night with eight hundred dollars, the most money he could scrape together from the last cash advance allowable on his credit cards. He put the money on the seat between himself and Whale.

"This don't feel like enough, even if it's all hundreds," Whale said, taking the envelope.

"I got in a jam," Paul said, nervously.

"The kinda jam where now you're gonna say you can't pay me?"

"I finished the job, but they're telling me I have to wait for the payment."

"So you're telling me that I have wait too?"

"I begged the general contractor, but his hands are tied."

Whale spit a shred of tobacco from his tongue. "I don't want to hear that. All I want to hear you say is 'Here's your money.' All the rest is bullshit."

"The money's definitely coming. It's just a matter of time before it's in my pocket."

"But it's not in your pocket, and because it's not in your pocket it's not in my pocket when you said it would be."

"I'm sorry, things are complicated."

"You don't have it, get outta here. You're wasting my time."

Paul hesitated, then left the restaurant, his legs unsteady.

He called the general contractor early the next morning and was told that the best he could do was send Paul "some money" in three weeks. Paul yelled that three weeks was way too late. The contractor said that paying Paul earlier than that would be paying out money the company had not received yet from the restaurant owners. Then he said he had another call waiting and hung up. Paul slammed down the receiver.

Paul began making calls to all the clients he knew, asking if they needed work done. No one needed anything, except a woman who had six chairs that needed to be reglued. Paul called his uncle Rick and explained things, and Rick said that he might be able to lend Paul a thousand dollars.

Paul went to the restaurant with the thousand the following Monday and left the envelope on the seat.

After Whale asked, "How much?" and Paul told him, he said, "You're fucking me up. All this bullshit about the general contractor, the net thirty days, that's not my worry, that doesn't have anything to do with me. You shoulda told me about that earlier, mentioned it as a possible screwup so I coulda anticipated it, worked it into my own plans. Instead, what do I got? I got a few thousand with like twenty thousand owed to me way past the time I was supposed to get it. That's money I should be making money on. You're taking money away from me now. So get me that money by next week, all of it. Cash in your life insurance policies; sell your house; get it. No excuses."

Paul could not sleep once again that night. Janet asked him what the trouble was but he still did not tell her the truth; he could not bring himself to admit that he had borrowed loan-shark money.

Paul called the general contractor every day that week, but when he reached him was told again that nothing could be done. Obviously annoyed, the contractor told Paul that it would do no good to continue calling. Paul called anyway on Friday.

"I have some bad news for you," the contractor said. "The owner of the restaurant lost his financing."

"What!"

"It happens. The bank gets nervous and doesn't want to lend any more money, so you have to go to another bank. Now what that means is if he gets new financing, then we still get paid. If he doesn't, we have a situation where we have to sue for our money. We have signed contracts, so that helps. At any rate, nobody will get paid until the new money comes in."

"That can't be."

"I'll let you know what happens."

After they hung up, Paul stood at the telephone, stunned, sick, seeing black. He spent most of that weekend lying on the sofa watching television as though terminally ill, unable to interest himself in anything. He did not go to the restaurant to meet Whale Monday night. On Tuesday, Paul received a phone call from him.

"Is what I'm thinking the reason you didn't show last night the reason you didn't show?" Whale asked.

Paul told him about the lost financing.

"Which you're saying is the reason you don't have the money?"

"It's going to take longer. I'll get it, I swear."

Whale hung up on him.

Paul went through the day anxious and gloomy, not knowing what to expect from Whale. He had lived in South Philadelphia long enough to know what could happen. Paul saw the logic behind it, too, the vicious threats, the smashed cars, the beatings. The violence was done not only to encourage repayment but to save face, to show everyone smart enough to pay attention that Whale and his sort were not to be trifled with. It was their particular form of foreclosure.

The following week, Paul received no news from the general contractor, who would not return his calls, and no word from Freddie Whale. Waking on Sunday, Paul found the house quiet and a note from Janet on the kitchen table: "It's such a beautiful day, I thought I'd take the kid for a ride to Penn's Landing to see the ships. Meet us if you want." Paul looked into the street where the car had been parked the day before and saw that it was gone. The day was bright and not very muggy for a July in Philadelphia, and Paul thought that it was a good idea to go to the waterfront to be with his family. He left the house fifteen minutes later, taking the pickup truck, and at the first stop sign felt a sponginess in the brakes. The brakes faded more and more at the stop signs and the traffic lights, so that by the time he reached Seventh and Washington Avenue the brake pedal went nearly to the floor before the truck stopped. He drove three blocks farther, trying to reach a service station before the brakes failed completely. Then Paul maneuvered the truck to the curb along the sidewalk under the I-95 overpass, just barely managing to stop it with the help of the emergency brake, and decided to walk the rest of the way to Penn's Landing. He'd take care of the truck later.

Looking north at Delaware Avenue, Paul saw flashing lights from a knot of police cars at the river's edge. Something had happened, and Paul quickened his pace. A wailing ambulance rushed past him toward the scene. Paul noticed a figure that appeared to be wrapped in a blanket standing near a police car and facing the water. Something of the figure's posture looked familiar, and Paul broke into a trot. As he ran along the river now, with a clear view of Camden's waterfront on the other side, the figure clarified. Janet? He ran harder, faster. Janet?

"Janet!"

Not until Paul drew close enough to see Janet's wet hair did she hear her name. She turned from the water, then rushed toward Paul, her face breaking into grief.

"Where is she?"

Janet turned toward the water and pointed at the policemen lined at the river's edge, looking down at the water, several shouting. Paul hurried to the river and saw his inverted car completely submerged except for the tires and with several men in the water gulping air and diving. He rushed past the shouting policemen and dove into the river, opening his eyes in the greenish brown water hoping to see his child, flailing his arms about himself, feeling the mucky bottom hoping to touch her. He ran out of air but stayed beneath the water until his chest ached and then some before kicking to the surface, his breath exploding. He sucked air, then jackknifed downward again to peer into the murky water and to feel about. His hands struck a leg, and he grabbed it fiercely until realizing it belonged to one of the other men. He pushed away from it to flail again. Running out of air, Paul kicked to the surface, gulped air, jackknifed, and felt again in

130

the murky water. He continued diving again and again, exhausting himself, until another man grabbed him by the collar to keep him from drowning. Too weak now to resist, Paul was tugged to the riverbank and pulled out; he lay some moments on the smooth stones before trying to lurch up to dive into the river again. But a policewoman leaned against his shoulder and kept him there. Janet joined him, and shortly later two men in diving gear arrived with underwater flashlights and jumped into the water to search. After a half hour, they found her.

Paul would piece it all together later—Janet not noticing the fading brakes because the car was old and had weak brakes to begin with; the brakes becoming progressively weaker; the other car pulling out from the driveway leading to the Chart House restaurant; Janet, unable to stop, sharply pulling the wheel to the right, jumping the curb, and plunging into the river. Both doors opened as the car tumbled and the girl, knocked unconscious, Paul learned later, was flung out. Janet managed to escape the sinking car. She could not swim but struggled to the riverbank and flagged down passing cars for help. Drivers stopped, Janet frantically told them what had happened, and several men leapt into the water to look for the child. Paul arrived twenty minutes later.

He did not learn until after the funeral that the brake lines of his truck had been cut; an auto mechanic told him, and he then realized that the brake lines of his car must also have been severed, causing the accident for which Janet blamed herself. He immediately assumed Whale was responsible, but he did not tell Janet about his dealings with the loan shark, saying only that he should have gotten the brakes fixed on the car long ago, that the accident, then, was Paul's fault, not hers. He felt so, but he could not tell Janet the truth, and he could not go to the police because from them the truth would emerge. Fot the same reason, he could not, either, act on his momentary impulse to acquire a gun, go to the Tree Street Grill, and shoot Whale in the head and heart: Paul could be caught, and all the facts of his involvement with Whale and what it led to would become known. Not only Janet but his mother, in-laws, friends, and neighbors would learn what he had done. Paul imagined the story in the newspaper and on television. It would be the stolen chalices all over again and the humiliation in church that had resulted, only to a far greater degree. The shame and the grief he already felt would intensify beyond what he could bear. Paul could not face that. Better to live with the raw wound in its current size and shape.

He kept the truth from Rick, too, at least for a time, wanting to spare his uncle his own sense of responsibility.

After the funeral, Paul did not return to work; instead, he and Janet took long drives in a rented car to places they had always wanted to visit but had never had the time to see. They stayed several days in Montauk, spent a night at Lake George, and drove to Williamsburg, Virginia. They visited Janet's parents in Baltimore and Paul's mother in northwest Pennsylvania.

At night, Janet cried in the dark.

Two weeks passed before Paul returned to the shop. Beneath the mail slot he found a note from Andre asking Paul to call him and a check from the general contractor for eighty thousand dollars. Paul felt nothing.

He telephoned Andre. "I'm here."

When Andre arrived shortly later, Paul wrote him a check for all the hours he worked, giving him time and a half for every hour Paul owed him, plus a two-thousand-dollar bonus, which came close to ten thousand dollars.

"It's too much," Andre said, not wanting to take the check.

"You deserve it, so take it."

Andre stood awkwardly by. "I heard about what happened. I'm very sorry."

Paul nodded. "Thanks," he said, biting back a flash of grief and guilt.

"If you need anything—"

"I'm fine. Let's get this place cleaned up."

Returning home that evening, Paul met Gus at the corner of his block. Gus took Paul by the arm and steered him to an idling car nearby. Someone opened the door from inside, and Gus told Paul to get in, giving him a shove from behind when he didn't move fast enough. Whale sat inside, the interior cool and smoky. Another man Paul had not seen before sat in the front; he would not see him again until the night Paul turned the corner and was knocked down by him. Gus slid in after Paul so that he was sandwiched between the two large men.

"So," Whale said, "how are you?"

Paul did not answer.

"I haven't seen you for so long, I was wondering what happened to you. How's business? Did you get that check?"

"I don't have to pay you," Paul said.

The short man in the front giggled. It was that grinning, lunatic face that finally came out of the past in Lawrence's apartment and caused Paul to connect it to Whale.

"Shut up, Benny," Whale said to the laughing man; then to Paul, "Why not? Why don't you have to pay me?"

"You know why not."

"You owe me big money."

"My girl's dead because of you."

"Because of me? Whatever happened to anybody wasn't because of me, but because of you."

Paul slugged him then, knocking the cigar out of his mouth, and went to punch him again, but Gus grabbed Paul by the hair, yanked him back and slung his forearm under his chin.

"Hold him! Hold the son of a bitch!" Whale yelled as he came forward and awkwardly punched at Paul's face. "You owe me money! You owe me money! You owe me money!" he yelled with each punch, then he fell back into the seat, heaving for air. "Let him go."

Gus released Paul, and he slumped to the floor between the seats, bleeding from the nose and lips.

"Now, listen," Whale said. "We had a deal. You came to me, I didn't come to you. And I gave you a deal nobody in this business would give you, nobody in their right fucking mind.

133

Twenty thousand! I bent over backward for you. Letting you pay back what little you did a week, letting you be late for so long. But there's only so far I can go. Now maybe somebody got too creative on their own and something happened that wasn't supposed to happen. A scare turned into something worse. But that doesn't change the fact that you took my money and you never paid all of it back. Then you come in here and slug me. You're lucky I don't have Gus break your collarbones."

Paul looked up at Whale from the car floor, but without feeling now, his flash of rage gone and the throbbing from his cuts and bruises like a distant heartbeat, not his. He had no inclination even to shimmy up from the floor and leave the car.

"Now, let me show you my generosity," Whale said, lighting a fresh cigar. "Just pay me the balance of the original twenty and we'll call it even. Okay?"

Paul said nothing, only gazed at Whale.

"Okay?"

"I could talk to the police."

"Oh, you could? And what if somebody throws you off a fucking bridge? What if somebody breaks every bone in your wife's body and throws her off a bridge?"

Paul said no more.

"See, I got your number. If you wanted to go to the cops you woulda done it already. Because you didn't, I figure there's a reason you didn't. I figure you been letting people think it was an accident, not saying anything about brakes or me. I can take that as a sign of you being smart and playing by the rules or you not wanting to get your name in the papers, to have everybody finding out about you." Whale puffed long on his cigar. "I don't really give a shit which one it is. I just want my money. I'll give you two weeks. Gus, help him outta here."

Gus took Paul under the arm and pulled him from the floor; he opened the door, and, stepping out, tugged Paul after him into the evening heat. Paul started away.

"Two weeks!" Whale yelled from inside the car.

Paul continued to walk down the hot street, ignoring the voice, the sound of the door closing, the car pulling away. A group of neighborhood girls playing on the sidewalk stopped in their hopscotch, fell mute at Paul's knotty and bloody face, and watched him walk by. A short while ago, his girl had played with them.

He told Janet that he had been mugged while locking up the shop.

A week later, Paul walked into the restaurant in the Tree Street Grill and found Whale eating at his usual table. When he looked up from his food and saw Paul reach into his jacket pocket as he crossed the room, he stopped chewing and his face blanched, as if he thought Paul was about to draw a gun. Paul almost wished he had one. Reaching the table, he dropped a thick envelope into Whale's plate of ravioli, then silently walked out.

Back in the present in West Philadelphia three years later, all the sharp heartache fresh again, Paul stood abruptly, climbed the church steps, and pounded his head against the giant red doors.

11

THE vertical slits of light at the windows where the plywood did not completely cover the glass had grown dim; with her eye to a gap, Claire could see the sky and banks of mauve clouds over what she knew to be the Delaware River. Sound had shrunk, what little of it penetrated the cinder-block shed, and Claire heard only an occasional siren or brief Latino rhythms coming from a moving car. She had heard shrieking children earlier and had yelled, hoping they would somehow hear her. No one came to the door. She kicked the desk in anger and frustration and momentarily cursed her father for whatever he had done and herself for not noticing that the kidnapper had broken into her house. How stupid could she have been? There had to have been signs, something disturbed. But she had been preoccupied with Paul, first on the sofa, then after he had gone, his smell and warmth clinging to her.

She should have fought harder, she told herself, should

have let the kidnapper kill her before allowing him to bring her to the shed to languish, eating fast food and using a metal bucket as a toilet. She smelled the bucket and kicked the desk again, yelling at the top of her voice, her head thrown back, eyes shut tight, almost howling.

It did not surprise Claire that no one heard her. She could see, above the heaps of rusted metal, the upper floors of abandoned factories, every pane of glass in the windows missing or broken. Claire had to be in the old Industrial Corridor, where there were few houses and, therefore, people.

She leaned back against the cool wall. By now, someone at the office would have begun to wonder why she had not called in for two days, Claire thought, why she did not answer her home telephone. Wasn't it likely that one of her lunch friends would stop at her house, sense something wrong, and call the police? The police would investigate. Perhaps one of the neighbors saw Claire and the kidnapper leave the house; even though they had been dressed in Halloween costumes, perhaps something odd would have been noticed. The kidnapping would become clear. The search would begin. But how long before all that developed? And how would they find her? Would she be alive?

On the verge of shivering, a spasm of hysteria twitching within her, Claire hugged herself as though trying to keep all the worst thoughts contained. Her throat felt tight; the air in the shed seemed to have become completely depleted. She turned suddenly, gripped the board over the nearest window, and pulled, groaning with gritted teeth. But the plywood would not budge. Claire let go, put her back against the wall, and slid to the dirt floor.

Paul.

They were to have met to run together the morning after Halloween night. Had Paul thought it odd that she did not show? Would Paul wonder about her? If so, enough to call, stop by the house, suspect trouble? He had said he liked Claire. She knew he meant it, but did he like her enough to become concerned?

Paul wasn't particularly handsome, he seemed guarded, and Claire had known men more interesting; but he had a kindness and a sensitivity beneath his show of aloofness and disinterest when they first met; she had seen that sensitivity, felt it through his lips on her breasts and his delicate touch.

Smelling an odor distinct from that of the bucket, Claire remembered the rat and jerked her head toward where it lay beneath the cardboard, its head smashed. How had it gotten into the shed? Claire glanced at the door and saw no gap between its bottom and the steel frame, so the rat could not have squeezed in there. It either had come through a hole in the wall or had tunneled beneath it, down three or four courses of cinder block and then up through the dirt floor. Claire stood and began to search the walls where they met the ground, pulling away the tires, pieces of plywood, boxes, and a gaggle of car parts. Finally, after not seeing a hole anywhere, she pulled away the metal desk and saw an opening in the dirt floor not much wider than the rat. Claire fell to her knees and clawed at the hole, but the densely packed dirt would not yield to her fingers and she only managed to scratch the surface with her nails. She stood and looked about the room, searching for something to dig with, frantic now, as though she had only a short time to dig out. She scattered the greasy engine parts, the boxes, everything, and found a tin can of nuts and bolts. Dumping the contents out in the far corner, Claire hurried back to the hole and began to dig. The can did little better than Claire's fingers. She tossed it aside and went to the desk, where she rooted in the drawers and found a blue-handled screwdriver in the very back of the bottom one.

Back at the wall, Claire began to stab furiously at the hole's edges, chipping out chunks of hard dirt and widening it. But not a minute after she started, she heard a car door close and, soon, the rattle of the chain in the fence.

Claire dropped the screwdriver, stood quickly, and muscled the desk back to the wall, covering the hole and the chips of hard dirt. She threw the filthy shipping blanket on top of the desk, gathered what she could of the scattered items, reordered them against the wall, and with her foot smoothed the skid marks the desk had made in moving it. She forced her heavy breath to normal and sat on the desk as the man put the keys in the locks.

He opened the door a crack and peered in at Claire. "Stay where you are."

Claire thought about rushing him until she noticed the gun.

He opened the door only as much as necessary to squeeze in, then closed it behind him by kicking back with his foot. He carried the usual white bags with the hamburgers, french fries, and Coke in one hand and his gun in the other. He set the food at arm's length on the desk, then went to sit on the milk crate by the door, his back against the wall.

"Go 'head, eat."

Claire smelled the food, but had no appetite, not for another hamburger and greasy french fries.

"I'm sick of that food," Claire said without moving, wanting to divert any notice he might take of the changes in the shed.

"What do you want, veal?"

"I want some fruit and juice."

"Pray for it."

"I'll get sick if I keep eating this."

"Millions of people eat that food every day."

"But not while locked in a stinking shed day after day."

"Blame your thief father for that."

"Thief? What are you saying?"

"I'm saying your father's a crook. He stole something from me. Hard to believe, huh, a gentleman like that."

Not hard to believe, Claire thought, but impossible to believe. She obviously knew her father much less than she thought, since Claire would not ever have suspected him capable of what this man said. Claire had been less surprised to learn that the man her mother remarried was "alleged" to have dealings with mobsters. Her mother claimed not to know more than that her husband was the owner of a construction company. Maybe she didn't want to know, Claire often thought. Claire had met her mother's husband several times, and he always struck her as much more refined and sensible than she imagined he would be, although his daughter had seemed crude and vulgar, a gum-cracking, mousse-haired, cursing bimbo, as though all the qualities Claire expected the father to possess were gathered in her.

"And he hasn't given it back?" Claire asked.

"You're still here, ain't you?" He stood up from the milk crate and looked around the shed with jerky motions of his head. "Hey, things ain't right in here. Whataya been doin'?"

"Nothing," Claire said quickly.

He crossed the room and slapped Claire in the face. "You got ideas? You planning something stupid?" He slapped her a second time.

Claire jumped off the desk and swung at him with her fist, connecting with his temple, and stunned him enough to dash to the door and grab the knob. But he recovered, dashed after her, and pulled Claire back from the door before she could open it. The gun fell to her feet, but before she could stoop to retrieve it, the man spun Claire around, tripped her, and followed her down to the hard dirt, knocking the breath from her. He sat on the small of Claire's back, one hand tight on the back of her neck, the other holding her hair.

"What the fuck's wrong with you?"

"Don't hit me again, you—"

"Don't hit you? Don't hit you!" He lifted Claire's head by the hair and slammed it into the ground. "I never knew a woman like you, fighting like this, never even heard of one. What are you, a dyke?"

"Get off."

"I'll get off when I want to. Now what were you doing? Why's everything messed up in here? You got a scheme cooking?"

"Yes!" Claire screamed. "I was looking for something to bash in your goddamn skull."

He began to laugh. "Did you find it?"

140

"Get off!" Claire struggled, rocking from side to side, trying to dislodge him.

"I'll get off," he said, "but hit me or try to run again and you won't have a face when I'm done."

He stood abruptly and moved quickly away from Claire and back to the gun, sitting down again on the milk crate, with the gun between his knees.

Claire lifted herself first to her elbows, wiped grit from her face, and then stood. Her nose bled slightly. Claire shuffled back to the desk and leaned against it, looking at him. She no longer felt angry, but she hated this man now so completely that she clearly saw herself bringing the alternator she had killed the rat with down upon his head, crushing it into an unrecognizable pulp. She would either escape or kill him, or die trying; it was only a matter of time. The rest did not matter. She wrote off her father, her fears for him, the hope that he would straighten out his difficulties with this man and she would be freed unharmed. She wrote off the police, if they had even begun to look for her, because she had little faith now that in this large city, confined to a shed in a junkyard, she would be found any time soon. Finally, she wrote off Paul, because even if he had figured out she had been kidnapped, had spoken to her father, and had put the pieces together, it was far too much to expect that he would decide to look for her, or that he would find her if he did. She could count only on herself.

Minutes later, the man opened the door with his back to it, the gun pointed at Claire, and slipped out into the dark. He slammed the door, fumbled with the locks, and soon drove away, the utter silence closing in after the engine faded.

Then Claire began to dig.

12

BENNY drove away from the junkyard not believing how bad things were going. First he gets bopped and the coins get taken, then this Henry Lawrence tries to screw him, then the daughter that he grabs, thinking he might have to keep her maybe overnight at the most, turns out to be a maniac wanting to fight every time he looks at her. If things got any worse, Benny was going to freak; he could feel it, like something jittery right under his skin, dying to bust out. If this thing didn't turn around, Benny thought, people were going to get hurt.

Mainly it would be Lawrence's head that got broken, if Benny ever caught up to him again. The son of a bitch was pretty worked up when Benny told him he had his daughter, saying he would try to scrape together the money somehow but he needed time, not to hurt her or do anything "rash." I'll give him a fucking rash. It was pretty much what Benny expected to hear, but he didn't want to hear it. He was getting tired of going into different hamburger joints every day so people wouldn't get familiar with his face, buying food, and then babysitting that Claire bitch. It wasn't Benny's idea of a good time, especially with the shed so small, and because every time he saw Lawrence's daughter he had to worry that she'd start swinging or kicking, like today, and he might shoot her and then have to deal with the body. It was even worse than when he locked his pal Skinny Fuji in there for five days so he could kick the smack habit, and Fuji got so crazy for a fix it was like getting in a cage with a wild animal. Lucky Fuji was skinny and weak enough for Benny to handle.

Benny'd give Lawrence time but it wouldn't be forever. Benny told him that. The thing was, Lawrence had stopped answering his phone yesterday afternoon. Every time Benny called since then he got the answering machine. What was the guy doing? Benny wouldn't be surprised if Lawrence had taken off, split the city, and left his daughter to work things out herself. That's why Benny was glad, going back to the chick's house again to get the TV, the VCR, and whatever, that he saw the boyfriend checking things out. It felt good to knock the guy down like that and ask him if he banged Lawrence's daughter. Benny wanted to see by his reaction if he was romantic about her. The way the guy reacted, pissed, and trying to get up from the ground with a gun on him, told Benny that there was definitely something between the guy and her which Benny could count on if Lawrence totally busted. Benny could squeeze the guy.

He turned onto Delaware Avenue and headed toward Center City; rush hour had ended and there wasn't much traffic. Another minute and Benny passed the marina. That boat job was one that Benny couldn't believe how easy it went, except that Whale hadn't paid him yet. Benny had gone to the river during the day and looked around, seen where the boat was docked among the others. Then at three o'clock in the morning he went down there with a couple of half-gallon plastic jugs of gasoline with rags stuck in the mouths; he had already decided to toss them and run—in and out, real quick. The bottles would either split when they hit and blow out the lighted rag, or the rag would just burn down and melt the plastic; whatever way, the gas would spill and come in contact with the flame, and then—fire city.

If there was a guard protecting all those nice boats, he wasn't around, and the fence was not even four feet high, so Benny had no trouble getting over it. The Typhoon boat was the second one from the front of the dock, medium-sized, painted white and blue with the name in gold glitter on the sides. Benny made sure nobody was around, lit the rags, and lobbed the jugs at the boat. He scored two direct hits and then sprinted the short distance back to the fence, then to his car and sped away. He saw the video on the news the next night and smiled when they said there were no suspects. Whale would be happy, and if Benny liked him more he would be happy that Whale was happy.

Benny turned onto Dock Street and swung around the Society Hill Towers and onto Walnut Street. He drove straight up Walnut to Rittenhouse Square and circled it a couple of times, not having anything else to do, looking out for Lawrence, who might be out on a stroll, even though seeing him would be a long shot. Not seeing anybody who even looked like Lawrence, Benny parked in the lot at Twentieth Street and stopped first at the nearest MAC machine, where he fed it Claire's card, tapped the access numbers, and withdrew the two hundred dollars maximum. Then Benny stopped at the first pay phone he saw and called Lawrence. But again Lawrence didn't answer.

"Hey, moron," Benny began his message. "You there? If you're there listening to me and not picking up, you're a friggin' jit bag; and even if you're not there, you're one anyway. Where do you get off to fuck around with me like you are? I got your daughter locked up in a place where nobody can hear her and which she can never get out of by herself. Think about what I could do to her. You thinking? Now if you don't want me to do any of those things, start playing ball. I want my coins or the money. You better be home soon." Benny hung up.

He walked around the corner to the Dorchester just to see what kind of luck he'd have getting into the building and up to Lawrence's apartment; he knew there was only one way to the elevators and that was past the desk, which had two chooches at it checking everybody, so he didn't hope for much. Well, he could at least see what he could get out of the doorman.

It was this old guy in a maroon jacket and a cap, standing under the canopy and watching the cars slide by out front. He had a face, Benny thought, that was ready for death.

"Say, Pop."

The guy turned slow, like maybe he wasn't sure the sound was outside his head and not in it. But when he saw Benny looking at him, he smiled, pleasant, like nobody could say anything to him that would make him forget there was a spot reserved for him in heaven. "Yes?"

"I got a pal who lives here, and I can't seem to get a hold of him. I was wondering if I could go in and knock on his door."

"Impossible. He has to call down for you."

"Any chance that I could bribe a few people?"

The doorman laughed. Benny chuckled a little bit but he had mentioned the bribe to see if the guy would take it, not to be funny.

"I don't know his apartment number anyway," Benny said. "Maybe you know him. Henry Lawrence?"

"Oh, Henry," the doorman said, "that's 1420. But I haven't seen him in a few days."

"A few days, huh?" Benny looked at his watch, one of five Seikos he boosted, and acted like he was pressed for time, hoping the old guy would offer something, some way to get to Lawrence's place, hint at taking a bribe after all. But he only kept smiling and dipping his head at people walking by.

"Can I say who asked for Henry when I see him next?"

Benny paused a few moments. "Tell Henry that Benny Typhoon was here for him."

After a couple hits of coke in his car, Benny couldn't take the idea of spending the night in South Philly, so he didn't go that way after talking to the doorman. He couldn't take the idea of staying in any part of Philly, so not only did he not go toward South Philly, he went up Walnut Street to the Schuylkill Expressway entrance, turned onto it, and five minutes later hooked up with the highway that went toward the Walt Whitman Bridge and New Jersey. Yeah, he'd go to Atlantic City, play around in the casinos some, and then see if Audrey was around. It would be more fun than what he did the other two nights, hanging around his apartment waiting for Lawrence to come to his senses and call. What was wrong with that guy? Was he slick or a moron?

Benny hit the last toll, twenty-five cents, a little over an hour later; it was another six miles to Atlantic City, but he could see the casinos from there, the names up in the darkness, getting bigger and bigger the closer he got. Right before he entered the city he drove over the bay, which at night was about as black as you could get without closing your eyes, black but kind of shiny at the same time. Then he hit the part of the town beside the bus station where the poor people lived in the projects only a few blocks away from the casinos, which was nuts. You had ghetto right next to glitter, Benny thought, liking the sound of it.

After the casinos, the rest of the town was shit. Look at it—those projects and then the stores on Atlantic Avenue with nobody ever in them, just the Dunkin Donuts staying busy, and hardly nobody on the street but those people Benny knew right off were on welfare. He saw two bums going up the street checking the pay phones for change and twisting the knobs on the parking meters like they were slot machines, hoping coins would come out. Drunks and dopeheads slagged around. Hookers hung on the street corners, looking like nothing else but whores, one of them in high heels, a body stocking, and a fur boa, that's all. But no Audrey, because she didn't have to work the streets.

Benny made his way to Bally's Park Place and let a valet park his car. First he had a roast beef sandwich in one of the eating places inside; then he checked around for Audrey in the casino lounges and at the tables. She would do some small drinking or gambling and let herself get picked up. He didn't see her, so he sat down to play some blackjack. But less than a half hour later, after dropping like seven hundred bucks, he got up from the table and headed for Audrey's room, thinking, I better get that money from Lawrence. I better.

In the meantime, Benny was going to have to press Freddie Whale for the money owed him or grab a car or two. Claire Lawrence had a little over a thou left in her MAC account, but that wouldn't last long.

Not wanting to interrupt Audrey during her work, Benny knocked first at her door; when she didn't answer, he let himself in with the key he had gotten from Audrey after she told the front desk that she lost hers. The room didn't look like anybody had been in it for a while—the bed wasn't even wrinkled—but in the bathroom there were a couple of used towels, a bottle of mouthwash, a douche, and a neat stack of rubbers.

Benny lay down on the bed and watched an hour of television before Audrey came in. She wore a nice skirt, not too tight, a silky blouse, and shoes not too high. You couldn't look like a street hooker and work the casinos because too many old ladies complained to the management, who might throw you out.

Audrey looked tired. After the little surprise of seeing Benny, she said that he was a sight for sore eyes, happy that he had come.

"I'm glad to see you, too."

Audrey leaned over and kissed him. He smelled mouthwash on her breath.

"Busy?" Benny asked.

"There's another convention, and they all seem to have

147

southern accents." Audrey kicked off her shoes. "I'm going to take a bath before going out again. You staying?"

"I might stay the night."

"Good." Audrey walked toward the bathroom, pulling off her blouse as she went and unsnapping her bra from the front; the catch left its imprint on her skin. "See you in a tiny bit." She closed the door after herself but didn't lock it.

Benny listened to the faucets come on. He turned back to the television and watched a show for a few minutes until a commercial interrupted it. Audrey had dropped her purse on the bed when she came in and Benny reached for it to see what she had. He emptied the purse on the bed—a hairbrush, small bottles of perfume and mouthwash, lubricant, a bunch of rubbers, makeup things, cigarettes, and other stuff he couldn't believe she carried in that bag. Was she going to a deserted island? He finally got to the money. There was a black hundred-dollar casino chip, three greens, a handful of red fives, and a few hundred in cash, mostly twenties. Benny took the black and most of the cash and then started to fill up the purse again. The small things had sunk to the bottom of all the junk on the bedspread and were the last to go back in the pocketbook—earrings, a pen, a lighter, and a bunch of change. He had dumped most of the stuff back in the purse except for some bobby pins and a few pennies when he saw the gold coin.

At first, Benny didn't believe it; he thought the coin was a freak penny or something, but picking it up he saw that it was one of those small gold coins that had been in the plastic tube with the other coins he tried to steal from the Longport house.

"What the fuck?" he said, holding it between his fingers and studying it, not believing his eyes. He jumped off the bed and hurried to the bathroom.

Audrey was lying deep in the tub, her entire back touching the bottom so that if it filled the whole way, the water would rise above her face if she didn't move. The water now hadn't quite covered her thighs and the small bush between them that she trimmed. Her arms floated at her sides, so Benny saw her breasts with the big brownish nipples and the white stretch marks from the baby she had six years ago and put up for adoption. She had a tattoo on her belly, the name Zeke, a former pimp who Benny once took to a meeting at a New York Avenue boardinghouse where there wasn't nobody to meet except a pipe Benny swung at Zeke's head because he had put out a cigar on Audrey's ribs. Benny saw the burn mark now, a circular brown smudge. He had felt sorry for her then, enough to nearly kill Zeke, who disappeared after Benny cracked his skull. He looked down at Audrey now, the water at her chin, and he saw a hooker's overworked body. Meat, he was looking at.

"I have to ask you a question," Benny said, trying to stay cool.

"Sure, honey." Audrey didn't expect anything; she didn't even look at him, just relaxed half asleep in the water.

"What do you know about coins?"

"Coins?"

"Tell me what you know." Give her the benefit of the doubt, Benny thought.

"Benny, I'm tired. I want to relax in here for a little."

"Do you know a coin dealer, one of your clients?"

"What?"

"Are you investing?"

"Jesus, Benny, what are you talking about?"

Benny showed Audrey the coin. "What's this?"

She sat up slightly to look in his palm. "It's a coin."

"I know it's a coin. Where'd you get it?"

"You went in my handbag."

"No shit. Where'd you get the coin?"

"I had it." Audrey covered her breasts with her arms and lifted a knee, swinging it over so her bush was hid.

"You had it since when?"

"I don't know. For a while."

"Who gave it to you?"

"Oh, Benny, it doesn't matter."

149

"What did you do for him for a three hundred dollar coin?" Benny said, thinking that either Lawrence fucked her or the guy who owned the Longport house did and they paid her with the coin.

"Three hundred dollars?"

"Tell me you don't know what it's worth."

"I don't."

"Just for my own satisfaction, which one was it?"

"Which one?"

"Don't play stupid."

"Benny, you're confusing me."

"I have to know. What, did he come here the day after the burglary?" Benny was thinking about Lawrence, convinced now the guy was a snake.

"I don't want you to get mad."

"I won't get mad. You're a professional, doing a job."

Audrey looked down the length of her body. "It was yesterday."

"Yesterday?" So it *was* Lawrence and he still had the coins; that getting mugged stuff on the way to the playground was bullshit. "What time?"

"Last night."

That's why the bastard didn't answer his phone. Maybe he was still here in Atlantic City on a gambling bender. What a snake bastard. "Did he stay here in town, do you know, and go down to the casino?"

"They said they were going home at the end of the night."

"What? *They?*"

"Yeah." She looked at Benny. "They."

"He was with somebody?"

"He was with your friend Gus."

That hit Benny like a punch. *"Gus?* Gus was with him?"

"For a little bit, then Gus left us alone." Audrey sat up and turned off the faucets. "And I'm not going to tell you what happened after that. So you can let me finish my bath now."

"My friend Gus? The big guy with the black hair?"

150

"Yes, your friend Gus with the big black hair. I mean—you know what I mean. Now, some privacy, please."

"Wait a second. Let me get this straight. Gus was with Lawrence?"

"Lawrence?" Audrey looked at him.

"Henry Lawrence, the guy I told you about who clocked me for the coins and gave you this one." Benny showed it to her again.

"I don't know anybody named Henry Lawrence."

"Then who gave you the coin?"

"Who are we talking about? Freddie Whale. He gave me the coin." She took the small bar of hotel soap from the dish and unwrapped it.

"Whale!" Benny's legs actually wobbled.

"I thought we would never talk about me and clients you knew. See, you just get upset."

"*Whale* gave you the coin?"

"I told you. He said he didn't have anything else. He told me it was worth five hundred, which I didn't believe, but I thought it was worth about a hundred. Now you tell me it's worth three, so I feel pretty happy about it."

"Whale gave it to you for a fuck?"

"He didn't have the cash, I told you."

That's when he slapped her. Audrey put her hands in front of her face and tried to tuck her head into her shoulders. Benny swung at her again, backhand, hitting her above the ear.

"Benny, don't!" Audrey shrieked into her chest, and then said quickly, "Benny, you know Freddie sees me about once a month. Why do you have to make me say things?"

"Why?" Benny grabbed her by the hair. "Why? I'll tell you why." But he didn't tell her and instead shoved her head down beneath the water. Audrey's arms came up; she tried first to pull at Benny's wrists and then grabbed at the sides of the tub, trying to pull herself up out of the water, her legs kicking. But he was too strong for her and held her head under the water, her eyes wide open. Benny pulled her up but still held her hair, Audrey coughing and gasping, trying to speak, plead. "Why? Because he has my coins. Because he paid you with *my* coins. That's why." He paused, ready to dunk her again. "Did he tell you where he got that coin? Did he laugh about it? Didn't he care that I might find out?"

"Benny, God, I don't know, I don't know!"

Benny knocked Audrey's head back against the tub. "What did he say to you about where he got it? Huh? I told you about the coins. When he gave you one, didn't you think about me, what I said?"

"I—I thought it was part of what you paid him, that you were working together on the job. I didn't know anything, I swear, I swear on my mother's grave."

Benny let Audrey go and stood up. "I can't believe this. I can't believe how I'm getting screwed." He paced quickly back and forth in the bathroom, then punched the mirror, making Audrey yipe from the tub and cover her head as the shattered glass hit the tile floor. He turned to her, his hand bleeding. "Did he say anything that could help me figure this out? Think! Did he say anything about Lawrence or Gus? Any little thing? What, are they all in on this? Are you? If you are, I'll kill you."

Audrey pressed herself into the corner of the tub, holding her knees tight against her chest. "No, Benny, nothing, I don't know anything."

Benny looked at his cut knuckles. He ran water over his hand and pressed the washcloth against it, trying to figure things out. "Lawrence said he was mugged. Okay, so maybe that's true. Who mugged him? Who knew that he had the coins? Okay, I told Gus. Gus is my friend, so he wouldn't'ta done it. But maybe he let it slip to Whale or to somebody else, and they told Whale and Whale did it or had somebody else do it. Maybe Gus *did* do it. No, Gus wouldn't do it. But maybe he did. The thing is, Whale stole my coins, which he knew were mine. That's the thing. Whale stole my coins. That's the thing." He walked out of the bathroom, through the room, and out the door.

"That's the thing."

13

PAUL was not aware of leaving the church steps, nor of pointing himself in any specific direction, nor even of stopping on the Market Street Bridge, where he leaned against the guard rail and stared into the river below, black except for the shimmering at its edge from the lamps illuminating that part of the Schuylkill Expressway nearby. He did not know how long he stood on the bridge and thought later that he could have stood there all night, trying to disentangle his confusions, if a policeman in a cruiser had not pulled up and spoken to him.

"Everything all right there, buddy?"

Paul mumbled something and walked on.

He walked toward the center of town, past storefronts, eateries, and office buildings, and soon crossed Fifteenth Street to the City Hall courtyard, where ragged individuals huddled in the cul-de-sacs. One voice called to Paul for money, but weakly, and from the subway entrance he heard peals of demonic laughter. Paul walked on, out of the courtyard and onto East Market Street, past Wanamaker's, the banks, the various stores and shops, the Reading Terminal, and soon the Gallery. Traffic was slight, the infrequent groaning buses nearly empty. Eventually, he passed Independence Mall and the building that housed the Liberty Bell, thinking of childhood school tours in stifling heat. Several blocks later, he reached Old City.

And then, walking toward the overpass that spanned I-95, cars and trucks speeding below, Paul knew where he was heading. He crossed the overpass to Delaware Avenue and turned right, south, walking near the Delaware River, an anchored ship silhouetted in the middle, Camden lights on the other side reflected in the water. Distant sirens wailed. Thin clouds drifted across a partial moon above. When Paul reached the spot where the accident occurred three years ago, he stopped.

Not long after Paul dropped the envelope of money into Whale's plate of ravioli, he and Janet rented a blue Victorian house in Cape May, New Jersey, for a week. They spent most of their days sleeping late and lying on the beach and their nights playing the games in the arcades or making the half-hour drive to Atlantic City to gamble in the casinos. They stayed in the sun too long and burned their skin, swam so far out to sea that the lifeguards harshly whistled them back, bet large sums at the gaming tables without excitement. They made love but with an absence of passion that left them dulled and morose. They ate foods they did not normally eat—once, lobster, even though Paul was allergic to shellfish. He woke that night at four in the morning with an itchy face and a thickness in his throat; in the bathroom, he saw his face mottled and misshapened by large hives, his lips and eyes swollen as though from a beating. He did not wake Janet and drove through the deep New Jersey night to the nearest hospital where, in the brightly lit emergency ward, he received an injection and a vial of pills. Instead of returning directly to the rented house, he parked the car and walked to the beach, shrouded by predawn darkness and completely deserted. Paul sat in the cool sand facing the sea and listened to the rhythmic waves as they broke in sudden white ridges until light bled into the horizon.

"Where were you?" Janet asked when he returned. Then she noticed his face.

Paul told her of his hospital visit but not about sitting on the beach.

"You should have woken me."

"I didn't want to disturb your sleep."

"I was dreaming of her."

"I know." And he did know, because Janet's sleeping face had been knotted as from pain.

On the beach that afternoon, Paul watched as Janet, lying on her stomach, aimlessly spelled the name of their daughter over and over in the sand—spelling it, smoothing the sand over the letters, spelling it again, smoothing—until Paul reached out and took hold of her wrist.

"I still can't believe she's gone," Janet sobbed.

Paul could not believe it either. She was still so clear to her: her thick licorice hair and delicate voice; the songs she composed and sang in the bathtub; her collection of seashells and stones; the visit to the shore, and how he walked with her clinging tightly to his neck into the deepening sea, the waves breaking against them, the girl telling him to go out, go out, she wasn't afraid, daddy, but her grasp on his neck fierce and anxious. The river she had drowned in emptied into this ocean, and Paul could not keep himself from following the river in his mind back through New Jersey to Philadelphia to the place where the car had swerved and tumbled, seeing himself there aghast and frantic at the sight of the car's obscene underbelly and the splashing men, seeing himself diving and flailing his arms to find her and being pulled out exhausted, seeing the divers arriving. Later, one of the divers rose from the black-green water with Paul's daughter in his arms and handed her to the paramedics, who lay the child on a stretcher and began their futile and foregone attempts to revive her. Paul broke free of the policewoman restraining him, ran to the stretcher and saw his girl up close, drenched, her eyes slightly open, hair tangled, her lips parted to reveal her tiny teeth, and the single bruise on her forehead where she had struck the dashboard, breaking her neck. That heartened Paul a little, the frail neck snapping, all but killing her, or at least snuffing out the consciousness that would have made drowning more horrible than Paul could imagine.

"If only I wasn't driving so fast," Janet said, still looking down at the Cape May sand. "If only I insisted she wear the seat belt."

Paul put his fingers to Janet's lips, and then he told her about borrowing the money from Freddie Whale.

Janet turned on her side and stared at his eyes, her face puzzled and disbelieving, looking at Paul as though trying to comprehend a foreign language he had suddenly begun speaking. Paul looked away, unable to meet his wife's eyes. In the vacuum between them now, the seagulls wheeled and shrieked above, the children shouted happily, the waves broke and churned.

"You're telling me the truth?" Janet asked. "This isn't some made-up story to make me feel better?"

"No."

"I don't believe you."

"It's true. You had nothing to do with the accident."

"But a *loan shark?* You?" She looked at him, her face a mask of incomprehension.

"I needed that job."

"How did you meet a loan shark? Did you know one already?"

"Rick gave me the name."

"Your own uncle?"

"I'm so sorry." Paul touched her shoulder but Janet rolled completely onto her back and threw her arm over her eyes as though struck dead. He told her again how sorry he was, that he would do anything to bring their daughter back.

Janet turned to him. "Why didn't you tell the police?"

"Whale's threats to hurt us."

"But there's no evidence now, anyway, is there? The car's been junked, the truck's been fixed. There's nothing that can be used to prove anything against him."

"No." Paul looked away. "Also, I didn't want you to know what I had done."

"It's worse now." She paused. "My God, a loan shark. How could you?"

"I did it for the family."

"But we have no family now," Janet said, rising from the blanket and starting across the beach to the house.

Paul remained on the beach awhile, staring out to sea beyond the heads of bobbing children with a sharp throbbing in his chest. If his heart stopped beating now, he thought, he would not care.

A short time later, Paul found Janet packing a suitcase with that resoluteness of hers he had come to know could not be broken. She would pack and leave with or without him; it did not matter to her, and so Paul began to hurriedly pack as well, knowing that to try to talk Janet out of leaving would be useless. She strode to the car and would have driven away had Paul not thrown his suitcase in the back seat and jumped in beside her. Silent and grim-faced, Janet drove fast and dangerously all the way back to Philadelphia, remaining in the house only several minutes before she left, without having spoken since they were on the beach.

Paul learned four days later, when Janet returned, that she had spent the time at a friend's house.

She would try to live with him, Janet said, but she added that she had little hope it would work. "Basic trust" had been broken. Paul had done business with a criminal and kept the dealings secret from her, and because of that she realized she did not know him, that he possessed another level she had never suspected. If he was capable of what he had done, Janet said, wasn't he capable of another hidden act equally as damaging?

157

Paul tried to argue his side, explain himself, make his actions sensical, but it only delayed Janet's ultimate departure.

A month after Cape May, Janet left in a heavy rain.

He did not blame her, Paul thought, standing by the river, the air becoming more and more chill. If he were in her shoes, he would have done the same. There's no worse knowledge to receive than hidden knowledge, he thought, especially when it concerned a person you lived with and loved, or thought you loved. It throws all affection and judgment in doubt.

Paul accepted the blame for Janet's leaving. He could face that. He could not easily face his wife's remembered voice saying "You?" coupled with her look of incomprehension. It was the same as when his mother discovered the stolen chalices in his closet; he was suddenly thrown into a completely new and unexpected light. A man of Paul's outward sensibilities had joined himself up, however briefly and tenuously, with the underworld, with criminals, and had done it without much thought to the consequences—as he had not given much thought, while growing up in South Philadelphia, to the bookies, numbers writers, and loan sharks or to the men variously and even stylishly murdered for some transgression or because they simply stood in the way of somebody's ascent to power. The infrequent muggings and burglaries that occurred in the neighborhood affected Paul and his neighbors more. The other violence was internecine, restricted to a certain group, surgical and discriminate, and therefore did not touch Paul or his neighbors. But Paul had willingly entered that group and embraced corruption. Didn't that make Janet correct, that he possessed a potential for crime like a latent tendency ready to manifest itself at the right stimulus? That suspicion gnawed at Paul's insides like disease.

Paul did not realize that a police car had pulled up behind him until its spotlight shone on his back and cast his shadow on the water in the exact spot where the car had plunged. He turned and saw the policeman coming toward him, the beam of a large flashlight trained on Paul's face.

"Hey, aren't you the guy I saw a little while ago on the Market Street Bridge?" the policeman asked as he came up.

Paul did not answer, squinting at the light.

"You're not thinking of doing something stupid, are you?" The policeman moved the beam of light from Paul's face. "Or do you just like to stare at rivers at night?"

"I'm just walking."

"Walking, huh?" The policeman took a pad from his back pocket and jammed the flashlight into his armpit, holding it there. "You don't want to drown yourself; it's a bad way to go. What happened, had a fight with your wife?"

"I couldn't sleep."

"Right. What's your name and address?"

Paul told him, and the policeman wrote on the pad.

"You been drinking?"

"No."

"I have to write this down in case you wind up getting pulled from the river and nobody knows who you are. But you're not going to wind up in the river, are you? You'll go home now, right? I'll be swinging around this way again a few more times tonight and I don't want to see you. If I do, I'll take you to the Roundhouse, and you don't want that. So get going, and I don't mean back to the Schuylkill River either."

Paul lingered a moment longer and then started off as the policeman returned to his car and drove slowly by. Once past, he picked up speed, as though wanting to get out of Paul's sight as soon as possible. Paul did not go home but instead walked up Delaware Avenue along the river all the way to Spring Garden Street and to his wood shop on Second. Except for a few stray cats sprinting through the shadows, Paul was alone.

He unlocked the shop door, locked it behind himself, and went to the office without switching on the lights, seeing only by the light that slanted in the window from the street lamp outside the door. Legs twitching from the long walk, Paul stood motionless in the middle of the office as though bathing in the darkness, listening to the old building creaking and the infrequent cars and trucks passing on the street out front. He had no idea of the time or of how much time passed before he turned to his desk, removed everything from its surface, and then lay down on it, covering himself with one of his shipping blankets. Paul lay curled, knees up, the padding blanket smelling of wood and varnish. He did not feel sleepy, did not expect to sleep, but was surprised when the sound of Andre unlocking the entrance door in the morning woke him.

"Uh, everything all right?" Andre asked from the office doorway when he saw Paul, propped up on an elbow on the desk, the shipping blanket across his legs.

Paul nodded, vaguely confused.

"I didn't see your truck."

Paul thought for a moment that it had been stolen, but then remembered he had not driven to the shop. "I walked."

"Walked?"

Paul said nothing, the previous night coming fully back to him—Henry Lawrence, running, the walk through the city from river to river.

"What's on your forehead?"

Paul touched it and, feeling a lump and crust, remembered the red church doors he had banged his head against. "Blood."

"Blood?" Andre stared.

Paul swung his feet over the side of the desk and stood up. "I couldn't sleep last night, so I came here. I didn't want to turn on the lights at two in the morning and attract the police, and I banged my head on one of the shelves outside the office."

Andre glanced at the shelves to his right, then looked at Paul more closely. "You sure everything's all right?"

"Everything's fine. You want some coffee?"

"Okay." Andre continued to watch Paul as he left the office

and walked toward the entrance door. "The kid's out there. He was sleeping on the doorstep when I pulled up."

Paul stopped at the window and gazed out at Tut, smudged and ragged, as he worked his broom back and forth across the sidewalk. Nothing in his face or bearing had changed since the last time Paul saw him; he was just as dirty and disheveled, his face gloomy and frightful.

"What's going to happen to him?" Paul said, his breath steaming momentarily on the glass. "What happens when he gets sick? Can he just go on living year after year on the street?"

"A lot of them do."

Paul watched Tut sweep a cigarette butt all the way to the gutter. "Let him sweep the shop and stay inside if he wants; he'll stay warm."

"Going to be out all day?

"Yes. I won't be here at all."

"You have jobs to spec out?"

Without turning from the window, Paul said, "I have to find Claire." Paul spoke to the glass, gazing at Tut as he methodically swept the sidewalk.

"What do you mean, 'find' her? Is she missing?"

Paul tapped on the window and Tut, his movements frozen, looked up from the sidewalk, his eyes wary. Paul smiled at him. The boy's eyes relaxed and Paul thought he saw the sides of his tight mouth move up in a slight momentary grin before he dropped his head down and continued sweeping. Paul turned from the window.

"Yes, she's missing."

"How do you know?"

"I know."

"If she's missing, which I doubt, let the police handle it."

"No. I have to do it myself."

"I don't like the sound of that."

Paul took the few steps to the door and took hold of the handle. "I don't know when I'll be back," he said, and then he went out into the cool morning. On the sidewalk, Paul

161

emptied his pockets of cash and gave the money to Tut, asking him to buy Andre a cup of coffee and telling him to keep the change.

Before going home, Paul stopped first at the Dorchester to tell Lawrence that he meant to find Claire, through whatever means, and that he wanted his help. But the desk clerk kept Paul from going up to the apartment, and he had to settle for phoning Lawrence, using the telephone at the front desk. Lawrence did not answer, so Paul left a message on the tape for him to call. He left the Dorchester and walked home down Twentieth Street, through the cool shadows of the row houses, into the weak sun at the street corners, then into the cool November shadows again—repeating shadow to light until he reached his street, filled with autumn sun.

Entering his house, Paul immediately phoned his uncle Rick at the clothing store and asked if he knew a man named Benny. "He's short, has light brown hair, is about thirty; he's a friend of Freddie Whale's and a guy named Gus." Paul saw them all again in the car where Whale had punched him and Benny had giggled.

Rick fell quiet at Whale's name, which neither he nor Paul had mentioned since Paul told Rick about the cause of the accident that killed his child. "That sounds like Benny Bean," he said slowly.

"Any idea where he lives?"

"None. Paul, why do you want to see *him?*"

"How about where I could find him?"

"A guy like that doesn't stray far. He's probably around, on the corner, maybe eating a steak sandwich at Pat's Steaks or maybe at Mike's Bar at Eleventh and McKean or Shunk's Tavern. And I know he goes to Atlantic City a lot. Paul, this guy's not level-headed. Tell me what's going on."

"It would only get you involved."

"Maybe I want to get involved."

"I appreciate it, but I'll deal with this myself."

"Then what can I do to help you?"

"You could tell me if Freddie Whale is still in business."

"I thought you never wanted anything to do with Whale again."

"I didn't. I don't now. But it's necessary."

"It must be. Let me help."

"No."

"If you're going to be a hardhead about it, do me a favor and don't do anything foolish."

"Don't worry about me."

"I didn't before and look what happened. Paul, do you know who these guys are?"

"How could I forget?"

"Then why are you diving into the middle of them?"

"It's important."

"Important enough to get hurt or worse?"

"Rick, I have to get going."

"All right, go." Rick sounded exasperated. "But don't let me hear your name on the news."

They hung up moments later and, shortly after, Paul began his search.

He left the house in his truck near ten o'clock, with the low autumn sun bright on the windshield, and reached Washington Avenue at Broad a few minutes later. Paul turned east and drove to Tenth Street, where he turned south, reaching the playground at Wharton shortly later. He looked across the vacant playing field at the sign of Pat's Steaks a block away. Paul turned left, drove to Ninth Street, and parked. Even then, not yet ten-thirty in the morning, meat and onions sizzled on the grills, and customers, mostly young men, stood leaning against the counters that ran around Pat's or sat at the picnic tables tearing into steak sandwiches and stuffing french fries into their mouths.

Paul crossed the street and stepped to the service window. During lunch hour, there would be a long line at the window, but now only two men, splotched with paint, waited in front of Paul. The painters ordered cheese steaks with provolone,

one with onions and mushrooms, the other with peppers and onions. The cook squirted oil on the grill and slapped the bright red chip steak onto it, the meat sizzling violently when it hit the hot metal. He scooped chopped onions from a container with his spatula, dropped them alongside the steak, and then added the mushrooms and peppers. While the meat browned, the cook took two long bread rolls from a stack behind him, opened them along their precut slits, and pressed them facedown on the grill. He flipped the meat and moved the onions around with the edge of the spatula.

"Next!" the cook yelled without looking up from his work.

"I'll have the same, but hold the peppers," Paul said.

The cook nodded, slapped fresh meat on the grill, then turned his attention to the other steaks, placing full moons of provolone on them and moving the onions, peppers, and mushrooms. When the cheese had melted, the cook deftly scooped up the meat, pressed it into the rolls, and topped it with the extras. He cut the cheese steaks in half with one quick pull of a knife, put them on paper plates, and shoved them toward the cashier, a girl with large hoop earrings and moussed hair who was singing along with a tune playing on the radio, nestled in a pyramid of rolls, until she stopped to flirt with the painters as they paid her.

"I was wondering if you could tell me something," Paul said, as the cook worked on his sandwich.

"Whazzat?" the cook said, not looking up from his work.

"Do you know somebody named Benny Bean?"

"Yeah, I know him."

"I was wondering if you knew where I could find him."

"Who?" The cook flipped the meat and placed the slices of provolone on top.

"Benny Bean."

"I don't know no Benny Bean. No peppers, right?"

The cashier looked over and giggled.

"But I thought you said you knew him."

"I heard wrong. I thought you said Jelly Bean. I know a guy by that name, a big guy, six-five, sorta looks like Frankenstein

164

without the bolts in his neck. You want this for here or to go?" He pointed with his spatula to the meat and melted cheese, which he then stuffed into the long roll and followed with the onions and mushrooms.

Paul knew he had blundered with his blunt questions about Benny Bean and was not surprised that the cook treated him, a complete stranger, after all, as he had, but Paul did not know how else to inquire. "To go."

The cook shoved the cheese steak to the side for the cashier to wrap. "Next!"

Back in his car, Paul dropped the sandwich on the seat, drove up Ninth Street, and turned onto Federal, not wanting to get caught in the traffic crawling between the produce stands that lined the street from there to Christian. At Tenth and Federal, he turned south and drove several blocks, stopping at a red light where Reed Street, Eleventh, Tenth, and Passyunk Avenue intersected. Pep Boys stood on the Tenth Street side on the site of the old Acme supermarket, where Paul had worked as a stock boy one high school summer; the new Acme stood at Eleventh, where there had once been a prison; and on the triangles formed between them were Colonial Meats, in front of Paul, and the Triangle Tavern to his side. He had eaten in the Triangle once with a woman he dated before Janet, and while they were finishing dessert a man was gunned down out front, so when they left the restaurant they saw the body beyond the legs of policemen crumpled on the sidewalk, the blood, in the night, looking like oil.

At the light change, Paul continued south on Tenth Street but stopped a block later at Dickenson for pallbearers easing a coffin into the back of a hearse parked in the street in front of the Church of the Annunciation. As Paul idled, a man in shabby, dirty clothes and a tangled beard, his eyes rheumy, nostrils encrusted, shuffled up to Paul's window and asked for a quarter to buy something to eat.

Paul took the cheese steak from the seat and put it in the

165

man's filthy hands. "Here," he said, and then turned down Dickenson Street to get away from the funeral procession.

At Eighth Paul turned north again and drove through twelve blocks of row houses to Oregon Avenue, where he turned right, back toward Broad. But he turned right again at Thirteenth, not wanting to pass Pop's Water Ice and the boccie courts at the edge of the playground across the street because he had spent too many warm moments with his family there and did not want to be reminded of them. Paul drove the block to Moyamensing Avenue, crossed it, drove past the graffitied elementary school, and then continued behind the Methodist Hospital, where he had gotten X-rayed, stitched, and bandaged for a number of injuries marking the early years he had lived in South Philadelphia. At Wolf Street, Paul turned right and then left onto Eleventh, still mostly paved in Belgium block, the tracks for the trolley still running down the center of it. Paul straddled the left track with his wheels and drove to Jackson Street, where the Church of the Epiphany stood, a stone giant squatting over the neighborhood. His stomach flared briefly with the memory of his mother pulling him to his feet during the Mass years ago after the chalices had been stolen.

Paul crossed Snyder Avenue, parked near McKean Street, and walked to Mike's Bar at the corner. Only a few minutes after eleven o'clock, Mike's was nearly vacant, with only one man at the bar and two others at a table eating sandwiches. Mike stood facing the back bar, rearranging liquor bottles. Paul had gone to Mike's on several occasions with Rick; they had a few drinks and talked to Mike, though it was Mike who did most of the talking.

Paul met Mike's good eye in the mirror, his errant eye pointed elsewhere, and Mike turned from the bottles as Paul walked toward him. Paul had not seen the bartender for over three years and wondered if Mike would remember him.

"Paul, right?" Mike said as Paul came up. "Your uncle told me you might be coming. Sit down. You want something?

Juice?" Mike's good eye looked intense, the other, perpendicular to it, appeared lifeless.

"Nothing, thanks. Did he—"

"Sure you don't want something? Coffee? Rick told me why you'd show. That person, I haven't seen in a week or so. Tea? Have something. I don't know where you could find him either. You might be better off if you don't. Milk? A sandwich?"

"If I called later—"

"Fruit. I got some fruit in the 'frigerator. Grapefruit. Oranges. Sure, if you want to do that, fine, but ask for me only, don't mention names to somebody else who might be here. Actually, he lives here on McKean Street, but I don't know where. Pineapple chunks, I got. Actually, between Twelfth and Thirteenth, but I don't know the address. I don't know what kind of car he drives because they change so much. I don't know what he does for a living. I don't want to know. A kiwi? I'm only talking to you because of Rick, who's a quality guy, an ace in my book, a saint. Well maybe not a saint. Actually, this person is a thief. Where do they go during the day? They're not punching a clock, so how can you find them? They could be anywhere. Excuse me for saying, Paul, and I know your uncle feels the same way, but he wouldn't tell you because he thinks if you want to do something, no matter what it is, you should do it, go on faith and that shit—I don't think you know what you're doing. A danish?"

"Are you married, Mike?"

"What? Yeah, I'm married."

"Do you have kids?"

"I got a son in high school."

"Suppose somebody kidnapped them, took them somewhere. What would you do?"

"Well, my wife, they can have." Mike laughed.

"And your boy, what about him? You would look for him, wouldn't you? If you had no idea where he was, where the kidnapper held him, you'd look wherever you thought he'd even remotely be, check everywhere, bug strangers in trying to get information. Wouldn't you do that? Wouldn't you do that if it was your son?"

"I guess I would. But, I mean, your uncle warned you about this individual, right? This is a dangerous character we're talking about, a guy who'll strangle you with your own intestines."

"Thanks for the warning, Mike." Paul stepped away from the bar and started for the door.

"Come back with Rick for a drink sometime," Mike said to Paul's back.

Paul half turned and nodded.

He returned to the truck and swung up McKean Street, driving slowly, hoping to see Bean, but did not. Paul turned north again at Thirteenth Street, right at Mifflin, left at Eleventh, and drove past the house he had lived in as a boy for so many years. It sat across from a square of townhouses that were on a site that had once been the Francis Reed Public School, five grim stories, in whose asphalt-topped yard Paul had played touch football, basketball, and, in the summer, halfball against the brown brick wall. The trolley ran in front of the house, rattling the windows, and sounding as though it gnawed at the street as it passed. A half a block up the street stood the Saint Maria Goretti High School for Girls. As a teenager, Paul would stand on his front steps and at dismissal time watch the rivers of blue-uniformed girls as they streamed past, high-voiced and vibrant. He dated a few and visited the common haunts with them, Pat's Steaks, the musty-smelling Colonial Theater and, several times, Wildwood, New Jersey, to lie on the hot beach, bob in the surf, and rub tanning lotion on their backs. It was in Wildwood, after an hour of gin rummy, that Paul peeled a bathing suit from a girl named Linda, trembled as he touched the areas of her untanned skin, and soon sunk deliriously if awkwardly into her. When they later sat up from the moist sheets, Paul removed a playing card that had clung to the girl's naked back, the red of the queen of diamonds as red as the streaks where she had sat.

Paul made the left at Moore Street, drove one block to

Twelfth, turned south and rode the two blocks to the Tree Street Grill. But the restaurant was closed. Paul made his way a few blocks distant to Shunk's Tavern on Passyunk Avenue, parking at a meter near Moore Street in front of a clothing boutique that had once been a dusty fruit store owned by a small old man.

Completely empty and dark, except for the lighted bottle steps and the glowing juke box, Shunk's seemed cavelike, a habitat more for animals than humans. It smelled of beer and fried food. A middle-aged woman, big in the chest, came from a room in the rear.

"I'm looking for some friends of mine," Paul said, and asked if she knew Bean or Whale.

"I see them here at night some times."

"Early or late?"

"After dinner, and late sometimes, too."

"I'll stop back later."

"We're open to midnight."

Paul thanked her and left the bar; stepping outside, he noticed that the sun had gone in. He hoped it wouldn't rain.

Paul knew that the likelihood of spotting Bean at an Atlantic City casino was nearly impossible—the same as staggering blind in a dark alley—that he was following the most tenuous of threads. But they were threads, at least, and they kept him in motion. He could do no less. He could not work or spend time at the gym or lie around the house with Claire lost; Paul had to move toward finding her, even if those movements occurred in the dark and might prove fruitless.

So Paul drove the sixty miles to Atlantic City. He parked in the lot of Bally's Grand and walked the short distance to the casino, entering through the opaque doors into the synthetic air and walking down the glitzy hallway over a blood-red carpet to the game area. A low roar suddenly enveloped him. Paul walked among the tables and the slot machines, coins splashing into the metal dishes, and looked for that lunatic smile and the cold eyes. He did not find Bean and left the casino, exiting onto the Boardwalk, where he walked along the railing close to the beach. A few seagulls wheeled above the sand, their plaints half-hearted. The sky had become more uniformly gray, appearing solid, nearly as gray as the ocean, its waves slow, the foam more yellow than white. Paul had little company, most of the scarce people on the Boardwalk walking in the stunned, zombie manner of big losers or hurrying in their mania from one casino to another.

Paul entered Trop World and searched the game floor, but saw no familiar faces. He left and walked north again on the Boardwalk, going from casino to casino, from the roar of voices and falling coins and the styrene-smelling air to the weak November light, the repeating tumble of the waves, and the winter shrieks of seagulls. It was nearly four o'clock when he left the final casino, unsuccessful in finding Bean, and started back toward his car in the waning light. He could barely make out Bally's Grand in the distance; the walk would take him a half hour. He had not eaten all day, and although he walked through clouds of food smells—pizza and steak and roasting peanuts—he had no desire to eat. Paul slid his eyes from Bally's Grand left to the shore, imaginine walking south along the coast of New Jersey all the way to Cape May.

Paul drove out of Atlantic City shortly later and reached the Walt Whitman Bridge arching into Philadelphia at six o'clock. As he passed the tolls, it began to drizzle, as if Paul had brought the rain back with him from New Jersey. He took the Broad Street exit a mile after the tolls and turned onto it, driving toward Center City. He still had not eaten, and felt only a dull emptiness in his stomach with no desire for food. Paul drove to Passyunk Avenue and turned at the green light, riding between the lighted store fronts to Shunk's Tavern, his wipers squeaking against the windshield.

Paul found the place crowded and nearly too dark to see. He went to the only empty space at the bar and asked the bartender about Freddie Whale. Without speaking, the bartender pointed to the far corner with his chin. Looking, Paul made out two large forms at a table.

"Thanks," Paul told the bartender, and he crossed the room toward the men, his heart beginning to race.

14

"YOU take care of it?" Freddie Whale asked as Gus sat down across from him.

Gus nodded.

"Good."

They were sitting in Shunk's Tavern at a table in the deepest corner, and also the darkest because Whale had blown out the candle in the red holder in the center of the table when he arrived twenty minutes before Gus, who had just showed. No one sat at the tables near them, even though it was a pretty busy night, because the other men knew who they were and that Whale and Gus expected to have space around them. Most of the guys liked to crowd the bar anyway, like they did now, close enough to rub shoulders and slap each other on the back. A couple guys were shooting darts at one end of the bar, laughing, and making crazy bets, and another guy played the pinball machine at the other end. Whale liked Shunk's. Thirty years ago, he used to train in the gym above the bar on

the third floor and sometimes would knock out troublemak-
ers for Charlie Shunk's father and then drag them outside.
He was paid five dollars for the knockouts, which wasn't bad
since it usually only took one swing.

"Any trouble?" Whale asked.

Gus shook his head. "None."

Whale tapped ash from his cigar and glanced toward the
bar as someone shouted to Charlie for a beer. "Jeez, I still
can't believe it. Of all the houses at the shore, he breaks into
the one belonging to Notte. If I'da known that, I wouldn'ta–"

He shut his mouth, not wanting to hear himself say it again
because it made him feel as sick as when Maglio told him that
Victor Notte's house had been burglarized and his coins had
been stolen. While Maglio was telling him, the coins were
sitting in Whale's dresser under his socks. Whale thought of
the coins now as a time bomb, ready to go off.

"How could we know?" Gus said.

"Didn't that dope know whose house he was breaking in?"

"I guess not. I myself only saw Notte once, so I could see
where Benny wouldn't know his house from Adam's."

"But he dated the guy's daughter, for Christ's sake, isn't
that what he told you?"

"He only dated her a few times, and he didn't know that
Victor was who Victor is. Benny's crazy but if he knew who
Victor was, friends with the boss, too, no way he woulda broke
in."

"Well, it don't matter one way or the other now. We're still
looking at the same tank of shit."

Somebody put Tony Bennett singing about San Francisco
on the juke box, one of those pink and white glowing Wurlitz-
ers that looked like it could do magic.

Whale said, "If Maglio found out I had the coins—" Whale
didn't finish that sentence either, not having to say what they
both knew. Not one to ask too many questions, Maglio would
assume the worst, that Whale had been in on the burglary,
maybe even that Whale had planned it, and he wouldn't want
to hear how, when Gus learned about the coins from that

chooch Benny, Gus told Whale and they thought it was a good idea to intercept Lawrence and take the coins. Because a guy like Benny shouldn't have thirty thousand in coins and should've told Whale about it in the first place, offering him a cut. They hadn't known who the coins originally belonged to and, if they had, they definitely would not have copped them. Maglio wouldn't want to hear, either, that Whale intended to give him a share when he cashed the coins. He would only see that Whale wound up with coins belonging to Vic Notte, also known as Vic Ways, Maglio's good friend and business partner, and he would act like he had been acting ever since he took over after Carmine Tucci. Maglio'd have Whale iced and dumped somewhere in the backwoods of Jersey, where that Lawrence now was. Whale was convinced of that.

"I think it'll be pretty hard for the boss to find out now, though," Gus said, "Lawrence being out of the picture."

"We had to get rid of the guy," Whale said, thinking about Lawrence. "Otherwise, the next thing we know we're seeing our dead relatives because we're with them."

"No choice."

Because—and Whale heard himself reasoning it out again—if Lawrence got caught by the cops and told his story, or it came out some other way, Notte would be mentioned; then Benny Bean's part in the heist would get out, and because Benny was connected to Whale, that would cause Maglio to give him that cold snake look Whale never saw on any other man. It was the stare that meant the worst, because there was nothing behind Maglio's eyes when he gave that stare, nothing. So Lawrence had to go; it was Whale or him. Gus was in danger, too, because Maglio would assume that Gus had done the dirty work, which he did except for the actual grab, using Skinny Fuji for that because they needed a guy who might have to jitterbug through the city. Fuji was still a fast runner even though he had ruined himself a few years ago with dope. Whale said he'd give Gus ten thousand to take care of Lawrence, figuring on cashing the coins in another

174

state, not Jersey, and paying Gus with part of what he got, still coming away with twenty for himself. He told Gus to make sure he dumped the body in an out-of-the-way spot and, more than anything, to take any ID from Lawrence, because if the name got on the news, the wheels in Maglio's head would start turning, which was as good as being dead.

"I'm lucky I didn't cut the boss the money *before* he told me about the burglary," Whale said. "You'd be looking at a dead man." Whale gulped the rest of his drink, but it tasted sour from start to finish and he didn't look to Charlie for another.

"That woulda been something."

Whale jerked the cigar from his mouth. "Tattoos."

"What?"

"I just thought of it. Suppose Lawrence has tattoos on his body somewhere, or a scar, and they make the ID?"

"That's a long shot."

"But it could happen."

"They have to find the thing first, and they probably won't until it's rotted."

"But if they do?"

"You want me to go back with a flashlight and a knife?"

Whale looked at him, not sure if Gus was serious. Gus *would* go back to cut off tattoos if Whale asked him, but he thought now that Gus had said what he said to undercut Whale's nerves, which Whale didn't know were so stretched or that it showed until then. But who could blame him, as well as he knew Maglio? Whale took a long serious drag on his cigar, calming himself, and then felt angry again at Benny Bean.

"All this because of that nitwit," Whale said, sending a cloud of smoke outward.

Gus sat back in his chair, shaking his head a little.

"Are you thinking what I'm thinking?" Whale asked.

"What are you thinking?"

"Who knows about the coins?"

"I wasn't thinking that."

"Well, who knows?"

"Just me, you, and Benny now, unless you told somebody."

"Who the fuck would I tell?"

"Nobody. Me either."

"But suppose Bean starts blabbing about it?"

Gus didn't answer.

"How he went through all the trouble to cop thirty thousand in coins and how he got robbed and all that. He's a blabber, we both know it. I guarantee you, in three days half the guys in here'll know who burned the boat." Whale tapped ash from the cigar. "He starts blabbing and the boss finds out—" Whale put his finger to his temple and jerked his thumb.

"Maybe he won't blab. Maybe if he's not able to get in touch with Lawrence, Benny'll just drop it, think that the guy left town with the coins and chalk it up as a bad break."

"It's because he's your friend that you're trying to see it smooth."

"He's my friend, but I had Skinny Fuji steal his coins."

"Jesus, Fuji knows."

"No, he thought he was stealing something else."

"Like what?"

"I didn't tell him. I said it was secret and not to look, that I'd know if he did. He wouldn't look, I'm sure, cause I told him I'd break his arms if he did."

"All right." Then Whale remembered giving a coin to the hooker Benny liked in Atlantic City before he learned that the coins had belonged to Vic Ways. Benny finding out who gave her the coin wasn't the problem, and Whale hadn't worried about that at the time; otherwise, he wouldn't have given it to her. It was Ways or Maglio finding out through Benny that was the problem.

The Tony Bennett song ended and somebody put on Mario Lanza singing "Be My Love." It was Sammy Rose. Rose came over to the table, excused himself, said hello, told Whale that he wanted to get into the card game in the back room, and asked for a loan of five hundred. Whale planted the cigar in his mouth and, without speaking, worked his hand into his pants pocket and pulled out a roll of bills; he peeled five

176

hundreds from the center and handed them to Rose, who knew the terms.

"How's your wife, Sammy?" Whale asked.

"My wife?" Rose said, stuffing the bills in his pants. "My wife came up to me the other day waving this paper. I said, 'Whatzat?' She said, 'Divorce papers.' I said, 'Divorce papers? Who's gettin' divorced?' 'Us,' she says. I says, 'No kiddin'?' Then I grab the papers and I rip them one, two, three, four times and I throw the pieces in the air. 'Happy New Year. Fuck you.' I says. Then I leave. That's how my wife is."

"Continued happiness," Whale said.

Sammy thanked Whale for the money, nodded to Gus, and headed toward the back room.

Whale watched Rose cross the bar and then, turning back to Gus, said, "You think Benny'll let it go, just like that?"

"If he doesn't, what?"

"The boss finds out."

"We could give Benny the coins back."

"Give 'em back? No, I don't think so."

"It would keep him quiet," Gus said, jerking his head to look around and lowering his voice a little, "and if he knew he stole the coins from Notte *he* would keep quiet for the same reason we have to."

"Now that's logical if you were thinking like me or yourself. But you have to think like that bonehead, which is something else. You have to think the worst case caused by the dumbest thinking. If Bean doesn't know, he blabs about the sweet job that got screwed up and gets the boss's attention. If he does know after we give him the coins, he still blabs to a few people to make them think what a terrific big-balls guy he is that can burglarize Vic Notte's house, and soon Maglio hears, too. You're dealing with a loony personality, a guy that's dizzy on a high wire and who *likes* it. The worst thing, though, would be we give him the coins, right, and then you know what? He has leverage on us, something to use. *We* took the coins from the ex-husband. That's all the boss has to hear and we're done."

177

Gus didn't have anything to say to that and only stared at the unlighted candle holder.

"I know Benny's your pal, but—"

"Maybe we should talk to him, feel him out."

"I'd love to talk to him, but where the fuck is he?"

"I haven't seen him."

"Well, get in touch with him, and have him see me; we'll all talk and see what's what."

"If it comes to the worst," Gus said, "I—"

"Don't worry, I won't ask you."

"There's only three of us; we should be able to work something out."

"Yeah, you're right," Whale said, not believing it. "Only three, and maybe Benny's matured, can handle serious stuff now," which Whale didn't believe either.

The door opened and Whale, facing it as always, looked that way; he saw a man enter he didn't know and looked down to tap his cigar in the ashtray; then something clicked in his head and he looked up again. The man went straight to the bar and waited for Charlie Shunk to come up. Whale thought he was a stranger—he carried himself like a stranger in a strange place—but looking at him more steadily now, Whale wasn't so sure. Then, as Charlie went up to the guy, Whale remembered.

"You won't believe who just walked in."

Gus turned toward the door. "Who? The guy coming over?"

"I have a funny feeling about this."

"Isn't that—?"

But the man had arrived at the table and stood between Whale and Gus, looking only at Whale. It was Paul Fante.

"What're you doing here?" Whale asked. "Money?"

Fante barely hesitated. "Benny Bean still work for you?"

Whale didn't hesitate either. "Who's Benny Bean?"

"Does he still work for you?"

"I don't know that name." Whale puffed on the cigar, real casual, but feeling things beginning to spin out of control.

"He kidnapped a close friend of mine."

"What?" Whale jerked in his seat, couldn't help it, and felt his heart beat through his large belly, so that it felt like somebody was punching him there. He glanced at Gus. See, he wanted to say with that look, the worst.

"He has her somewhere, holding her for ransom."

"Her? Ransom?" The spinning got faster.

"The ransom is coins he stole."

Whale just caught the cigar between his teeth before it fell from his mouth.

Four, Whale thought. Four know.

"What do you know about it?" Paul Fante asked.

"What makes you think I know anything about it?" Whale said, forcing himself to recover.

"He works for you, doesn't he?"

"Who?"

"Bean."

"I said I didn't know him."

"What was he doing in your car that time?"

"What time?"

"He was in the front seat."

"When you slugged me and then I ripped into you? I don't remember anybody but Gus being there." Whale pointed with his cigar to Gus, sitting there watching closely, waiting for a signal to throw Fante out.

"Can't we cut this bullshit?"

"Listen to this guy. You're the bullshit; you're what's sticking to my shoes that I have to scrap off on the edge of the curb." Whale blew smoke.

"Just tell me where he might be keeping her."

"You in love with her or something?"

"His house? Does he have a hideaway?"

"And what would you do if you found it? Go in and rescue her like fucking Batman? Or you think he'll just say, 'Here, take her'?"

"All he wants is his coins back. Claire's father was going to

179

return them, but on the way to the meeting place he was robbed."

So that was it, Whale thought, figuring it all out in a flash. Because Lawrence took the coins from Benny and it looked like he wasn't giving them back, Benny took his daughter. Pretty ballsy for a guy like Benny, Whale had to admit, only it was a shame that Benny couldn't keep his mouth shut about the coins in the first place and told Gus, even if Gus was his best friend, or supposed to be. Gus told Whale, and that was that; Skinny Fuji was on his way, the money too big to ignore. But look what happens. Turns out that the coins belonged to Victor Notte, who's like a brother to Maglio, and now, Whale thought, I have the coins! Jesus. Then to top it, there's this guy Fante with the hots for the babe Benny took.

"So now there's nothing to give back, right?" Whale said, trying to get the upper hand, get this thing under control.

"No."

"And you're afraid Benny'll hurt this Claire unless you come up with the thirty thousand dollars or you find her?"

Fante nodded.

"You're in a jam." He meant it, because Fante was, and the jam he was in was affecting Whale.

"I never told you the figure," Fante said.

"What?"

"Thirty thousand. I never told you the coins were worth that much."

Goddamn son of a bitch fucking bastard. "So? I guessed." Whale puffed vigorously on the cigar. Was he going to have to bop this guy?

"I don't believe that you guessed."

"I don't care what you believe. Now, why don't you get outta here? Gus, show him out." Whale had to get this Fante out of his sight so he could think straight; he had already made one slip about the value of the coins. Next, he'd slip that Lawrence was dead in Jersey.

Gus began to slide back from the table.

"You're not going to help me?" Fante asked.

"Why should I?"

"Because there's no statute of limitations on murder."

"The fuck you talking about?"

"My kid."

Whale turned to Gus. "Go sit at the bar for awhile."

Gus stood up from the table and shuffled toward the bar. Whale watched him go; then he turned back to Fante when Gus reached it.

"Whatayou doin'?" Whale said, turning back to Paul. "You fuckin' with me?"

"I just need some information."

"You're either stupid or you got some big balls, coming to me like this, trying to knuckle me under. Don't you know stupidity can get you killed, and there's always somebody with bigger balls than you?"

"Just answer a few questions," Paul said.

"Fuck you."

Fante looked at Whale a while, like maybe Whale was getting through to him. But he said, "I'll tell somebody about those fixed brakes."

Whale laughed, because it really was funny, the way this guy thought he could come in and start muscling. "That supposed to scare me? You got the goods on Whale, which you're going to give to the cops? I'm shivering. An icicle just went up my ass. Brrrr."

"I'll tell them. I don't care what happens to me."

"That's good, because you might find yourself with your kid."

"Don't talk about my kid."

"You brought her up."

"Look," and Fante took a deep breath, things maybe too nervy for him and realizing it, "why can't you just tell me where I might find Bean, and then I'll leave you alone."

"If I did know him, which I don't—"

"Then how did you know about the thirty thousand in coins?"

"I told you, I guessed." That was a definite screwup, letting that out, Whale thought.

"If you can't tell me where he might be, whether because you don't want to, you don't know, or you're part of the kidnapping, then set up a meeting with Bean and me. I have ten thousand dollars I can give him. I have another thousand I'll give you to convince him to take the money and release Claire. Maybe I can raise more."

"So maybe I do know him." A thousand just for making a phone call and sitting down for a few minutes sounded like a good deal. Plus, the ten thou, together with the money Whale owed Benny for the boat job, would settle down Benny, who never had that kind of money in his hands at one time. Maybe Whale could throw in a few thou more and Benny'd let the daughter go, and then everything would blow over.

"Set something up, then."

"If I do, no cops. Because if there are, things could get messy, and nobody likes mess."

"No cops. I just want him to release Claire."

"I'll call you."

"As soon as possible."

Whale nodded, and that's when he noticed Maglio walking toward the table. His backbone went stiff. He had been too preoccupied with Fante to notice Maglio come in with his bodyguard Cosmo, standing now at the bar, watchful. "Yeah, okay, soon as possible," Whale said. "Now go."

"Let me give you my phone number."

"I'll get it from the phone book. Go."

Fante began to move away from the table but stopped when Maglio came up and froze him; he could freeze a bear with the look he had. Maglio was looking at Fante like, Who is this guy? And Fante was looking back like maybe he knew the boss but didn't care who he was. Maybe this Fante did have some balls, or he was just out on the edge because of the babe. But now that Whale hadn't gotten Fante out of there, he was going to have to finesse, something he never wanted to do with Maglio.

"All right," Whale said to Fante, "can't you see I have business." He turned to Maglio. "Boss, how are you?"

"No, let him stay, if he wants," Maglio said, sitting down.

Terrific, Whale thought, he doesn't care if the guy stays.

"I was just leaving," Fante said.

"Don't make me chase you. I just stopped by for a drink. I have a fucking migraine coming on and the only thing that seems to help is Scotch. Ever get an ocular migraine?"

Fante shook his head no.

Christ, just what Whale needed; Maglio was in a friendly mood or a weird one, which was about the same, and there wasn't anything Whale could do about it. If he blew Fante out of there now, Maglio would smell something, maybe not at the moment but certainly later.

"It's like you got somebody hitting the side of your head with a sledgehammer, plus you feel sick in the stomach and see flashing lights. You would know if you had one."

Gus placed a glass of Scotch and ice on the table and immediately went back to the bar.

"Who are you," Maglio asked Fante. "You look familiar."

"Paul Fante."

"Fante. You have family in the city?"

"He's Rick Fante's nephew," Whale said, trying to nip things in the bud, maybe leading to Fante going out.

"Oh, sure, Rick. So that's why you look familiar, you look a little like him. He's a good man, did a big favor for me once. We go back, Christ, like thirty years. I remember when we drove to California together with a few other guys when we were in our twenties; we left from right around the corner on Eleventh Street."

"I saw that," Fante said.

"What?"

"Rick was living with my family at the time; I saw you all pull up in the car and Rick leave."

"No kidding? Small world." Maglio placed the glass of Scotch and ice against his temple. "I saw Rick last week at

Marra's eating with a nice-looking woman. We had a little talk. He's getting married in a few weeks, right?"

Fante nodded.

"I had the scungilli and linguine. I was going to go to Marra's tonight but this headache killed that. I'll go tomorrow night." Maglio removed the glass from his temple, sipped from it, put it back. "Paul, how come I never see you around?"

"I live uptown."

"What're you doing down here, letting Whale get his hooks in you, if he doesn't already?"

Fante looked like he was about to answer, and Whale had to think fast because this Fante was the kind of guy who would tell his story to anybody, and if he told it to Maglio, Christ, Benny Bean's name would be mentioned, and because Benny did work for Whale, that's all Maglio would need to start thinking Whale was behind the coin theft. Whale acted like he was going to tap his cigar ash in the ashtray and knocked over his drink, careful to knock it away from the boss so it wouldn't spill on him.

"Jeez, I'm an idiot. Sorry, boss." Whale waved to Gus at the bar, telling him to bring a towel over, and hoped that now Fante would leave. Whale apologized to Maglio again and began wiping up the spill with the towel Gus brought. When he was finished, Gus returned to the bar with the towel.

"I think I'll head out now," Fante said.

Looking disgusted, Maglio barely nodded.

"So long." Fante crossed the room and went out the door.

Whale caught a glimpse of the drizzle outside and felt like he just had stepped back off a ledge ten stories above the ground.

"So what did he want?" Maglio asked.

"Fante? Like you said, money. How's your head?"

"If I could cut off half of it, I'd be all right."

"Don't they have special medicine for migraines?"

"I got medicines up to my neck. What I need is less aggravation. Like me and Victor going uptown to see that Lawrence guy, his wife's ex, you know, and him not being there. Nobody even saw him for a couple days, the doorman, the desk clerks. So maybe he did cop the coins and take off to Hawaii or someplace."

Whale was glad to hear that the boss was thinking along those lines, taking the attention that might come Whale's way.

Maglio said, "Maybe he took the trip with his daughter, because she's not around either. Maybe they're partners."

"Yeah, that's possible."

"Victor wasn't too happy about not getting in touch with them."

"I can understand that."

"Somebody breaks in his house, smashes up the place, and his wife is crazy because her coins got lifted. Not only that, Nancy won't believe that the daughter had anything to do with it, and instead, get this, she thinks something happened to her because nobody can get in touch with her. Victor's the one that should have the migraine. So can you blame him if he wants to get the guy who robbed his house, tie him to the back of the boat, and troll with him?"

"No, you can't blame him," Whale said slowly.

"One thing we know, it wasn't a one-man job."

"How do you know?" Whale tried to sound innocent.

"For one thing, it just doesn't feel that way. Plus, Victor's wife's been playing detective and one of the neighbors said they saw two guys near the house the week he was away. Maybe one guy cased the area and helped plan it and the other did the actual stealing. That doesn't mean the daughter wasn't involved, but it means not one guy is responsible." Maglio sipped some of his Scotch. "Any ideas?"

The question caught Whale off guard. He felt a little spit go down the wrong pipe and had to use all his strength not to start coughing. Whale managed to clear his throat without too much noise. "I don't know, but if Lawrence is gone and so is the daughter, that looks pretty funny to me."

"Yeah, that's what I said. So maybe that's it, cut and dry,

they needed the money, they knew the alarm code, they did the job and left the city."

Whale nodded.

"But suppose it wasn't them? Suppose it wasn't even a burglary? Well, it was a burglary, or made to look like one, but maybe it's part of this bigger scheme, somebody trying to get to Victor, and through Victor to me. Maybe New York people. They got something in the works and I'm the final target." Maglio looked around to the door as if he expected killers to walk in any second. He stood up. "I'll talk to you." Maglio left the table and snapped his fingers to Cosmo standing alone at the bar, and they hurried out of Shunk's, Cosmo checking the street before they stepped out.

"How'd that go?" Gus asked, coming over and sitting down.

"That was like walking through a thin hallway with razor blades sticking out of the walls."

"What's the problem?"

"It's with that Fante. He could make our lives very difficult, maybe end them. He knows so much, he was able to tell *me* a few things. Now the boss knows him, and they even look like they're gonna be pals. You get the idea?"

Gus nodded seriously.

"Maglio can't find out about the coins or we're dead."

"So what do we do?"

"You know what we have to do."

Leaving Shunk's Tavern and walking past the bright store-fronts of Passyunk Avenue in the silent drizzle to his car, Paul felt weak-kneed, though from not having eaten all day or from sitting down with those men, he did not know. Who had the older man been who sat down while Paul spoke to Whale? Paul had seen him before other than in the car that took Rick across country, but Paul could not remember his name.

Paul drove down Passyunk and then up Moore Street to Broad, sleepily and without hurry. He turned north on Broad

186

and had to fight off the hypnotic effect of the windshield wipers while stopped at red lights.

He remembered that he had nothing to eat at home, and, wanting to quiet the hunger pains in his stomach more than to fill it, he stopped at the diner where he and Claire and Tut had eaten and ordered a turkey breast sandwich. He sat in the same booth as the other night and gazed at the outline of the flying red neon horse on the wall at the rear or through the eight-foot plate-glass window into the nearly deserted and wet street. In the booth diagonally across from him, a group of teenagers sat joking and eating hamburgers and french fries, their voices loud and unself-conscious. Instead of looking at them directly, Paul watched the two boys and two girls by their reflection in the window. They made him feel old, not in the body because he was in better shape now than he had ever been, but spiritually; their bright eyes and unrestrained laughter reminded Paul of how long it had been since he had laughed that way.

Past their reflection, on the other side of the street, the figure of a man moving so slowly in the shadows as to be barely noticeable caught his eye. He was tall and stooped forward, but not until Paul noticed the cane did he realize it was his neighbor Mr. Mitchell. But what was he doing this far from the neighborhood, taking those slow, frail steps of his? Mr. Mitchell stopped and stood motionless at the edge of a cone of lamplight, staring straight ahead as if gauging the distance. He seemed to be reconsidering walking on or, Paul thought, could not continue.

Paul's waitress arrived with the sandwich; as she set it down, Paul told her he'd be right back and left the diner, crossing the street to where Mr. Mitchell stood.

Paul came up from behind and said hello, trying not to startle the old man.

"Oh, Paul." Mr. Mitchell's voice quivered slightly.

"How are you, Mr. Mitchell? Is everything all right?"

"I think I ran out of steam."

"Where are you going?"

"I was determined to get to the park, but I don't think I'm gonna make it. Legs quit." Rain speckled his glasses.

"It's raining anyway."

"It wasn't when I started."

"I saw you from the diner. Want to join me?"

"The diner?" Mr. Mitchell looked across the street as though aware of his surroundings for the first time.

"I have a sandwich on the table waiting for me."

"I could use a rest. All right."

"Come on, then." Paul lightly took Mr. Mitchell's elbow, and together they walked slowly across the street, sounds of struggle coming from the old man with each step.

They walked so slowly that the green traffic light turned red before they reached the other side, and several cars had to wait for them. Paul noticed heads turn their way and furtive looks as they entered the bright diner; the kids in the booth near Paul's seemed to whisper. Still holding Mr. Mitchell by the elbow as he took small, slow steps, Paul led him to the booth. The old man leaned on the table as he eased himself into the booth and then, the seat fully under him, let himself collapse, wincing as he did, as though internal organs had split.

"Want something to eat?" Paul asked as he sat down.

"Tea would do." Mr. Mitchell slowly removed his hat.

Paul motioned to the waitress and ordered the tea when she came up. "Anything else?" Paul asked. Mr. Mitchell shook his head no, and the waitress went away.

"This is the farthest I walked in years, four and a half blocks. I thought I could make it to the park. I get tired of sitting in the house all the time, but I'm always too tired to do anything about it. That's what old age is: tired of everything but too tired to change it. So do things now while you have the energy. Be like these kids here as much as you can, not a care in the world, because when you get to be my age you'll wished you'd done it more, laughed and not worried."

Paul gazed at the old bronze face with the black dots freckling it. He said nothing.

"But you don't do that too much, do you, laugh and not worry? I see you. You walk mostly with your head down."

"It's a habit."

The waitress, a sleepy-eyed woman who smoked cigarettes at the edge of the counter while waiting to serve her tables, set Mr. Mitchell's tea on the table and walked away.

"Lift your head, Paul. The weight of the world isn't on your shoulders."

They sat silent for a while, Mr. Mitchell sipping his tea and Paul eating his sandwich. When they finished, Paul asked Mr. Mitchell if he meant to walk home.

"I expected to, but I don't think I'd make it."

"I'm parked up the street if you want a ride."

"I would welcome a ride. Thank you."

Paul paid the check, and he and Mr. Mitchell left the diner. They stepped from the bright light to the rainy shadows and walked slowly to the car, Paul holding Mr. Mitchell by the elbow to steady him. At the car, Mr. Mitchell eased himself into the front seat, holding onto Paul's arm until he had settled. Paul closed the door, and they rode the several blocks to the neighborhood. After he parked, Paul saw Mr. Mitchell to his front door.

"I thank you," the old man said. He worked himself up the several steps as Paul lingered on the sidewalk. "Good night."

"Good night." Paul crossed the street to his house.

Shortly later, just as Paul finished eating an old apple, the telephone rang, and he answered it immediately.

"I got in touch with Benny," Freddie Whale said at the other end. "He's been holed up in Jersey near Hammonton. He said he'll take the ten thousand and call everything even. We bring the money to him, he gives you the girl, and that's that."

"When?"

"Tomorrow night."

"Can't I meet him myself?"

"If you want to risk Benny blowing you away, sure. But with

189

me and Gus there, he'll just fork her over and nobody'll get hurt."

"Is she all right?"

"I didn't see her, but he says she's fine."

"Where should I meet you?"

"Meet me at the corner of Ninth and Moore at six."

"All right."

"So don't go wandering around South Philly anymore. This thing'll be over by this time tomorrow night. You got nothing to worry about. So, you sleep tight."

"Ninth and Moore?"

"Yeah, and bring the ten, cash. Okay? I'll see you." Whale hung up at his end.

Paul put down the receiver and remained standing at the telephone, his forehead against the doorjamb. So, it's nearly over, Paul thought.

15

TUT heard a car come up and stop and a door open and close, and then heard the chain rattle in the fence, and he shimmied through the tunnel to the space where he could look into the clearing area of the lot, and he saw a short man carrying a white paper bag just before he went behind the shed and it reminded Tut of the time a long while ago when a short man came to the junkyard every day with paper bags and stayed a little and then left, and that time too Tut heard yelling.

The yelling scared him last night and he couldn't sleep, so he went to the shop of the nice man Paul and slept on the front steps.

Tut heard the door close on the other side of the shed and lay there on his stomach on the cold hard greasy ground to see what would happen, but it got very quiet again and there were only the usual sounds, and not even those for long, almost as quiet as when the sun came up in the morning behind the empty factory buildings not far from here, with the yellow light coming straight through the buildings in squares where the windows were, doing the same thing on the other side of the wide street, where there were also big empty buildings for the sun going down to shine through in squares, which reminded him of when he lived in Kensington.

Because when it was about to get dark, with the sun at the end of the sky, Tut would quit his playing and go home and see his house with lights in the windows, and he would go in and the house would be bright with the light and the warm smell of frying potatoes would hit him, or beef stew, and maybe one of his mother's boyfriends would be there and they would talk a little and then eat in the warm kitchen with the pictures of Jesus and the Pope on the green walls, and Tut would eat every carrot and pea of the stew and soak up the gravy with bread as white as snow.

And sometimes there was doughnuts or crumb cake or ice cream for dessert, and they would eat that, Tut having milk with it and his mother and her boyfriend having coffee, the smell all over the house.

Then his mother and her boyfriend would smoke cigarettes in the bright kitchen with Jesus and the Pope watching while Tut watched the television, hoping the beer wouldn't come out of the refrigerator, because things changed after the beer came out, but it came out almost all the time and the drinking would start and the dishes would stay on the table all night and the pots on the stoves, the stew turning white on top, and sometimes his mother and the boyfriend would start kissing, and sometimes touching and making funny noises, and if it didn't stop the boyfriend would give Tut three dollars to go to the store for cigarettes, saying to take his time, and his mother saying why not stop off at his friend's house.

But as soon as Tut jumped off the step, he ran as fast as he could to the store and back again so maybe the door wouldn't be locked, which it always was, and he would knock, knowing they wouldn't answer yet, and he would have to stay on the step in the sometimes cold with maybe Mrs. Smith down the block looking at him, not asking him in because Tut wouldn't go, and shaking her head, because she once pounded on the door herself, calling too, and Tut's mother stuck her head out the window with her hair all messed and she and Mrs. Smith shouted at each other, Tut's mother saying to mind her old business, you old bag.

So he sat on the front steps sometimes shivering if it was cold, and after a time they would let him back in the house and Tut would go up the stairs to his room because many times they were still drinking the beer, the bottles all in front of them on the kitchen table like soldiers, and would start yelling at each other, getting so bad at times that Tut had to put his head under the pillow to stop the noise, but it never worked the whole way.

Tut's mother stabbed this boyfriend in the shoulder with a kitchen knife after she was drinking and the boyfriend left and never came back.

After him, Tut's mother brought home the boyfriend who she went with to Florida.

Tut heard the yelling the next night and at first thought it was the wind going through the piles of junk or the junk itself, the way it made noises sometimes, kind of scraping against itself, but no, it was yelling, only not loud because it came from behind some wall, like in a closet or inside a car.

Then the yelling stopped and everything was quiet again in the early night except for the usual sounds of the far-off speeding cars or the sirens or the boat horns from the river or sometimes the planes, and Tut's own breathing in his buried car.

And then he heard the yelling again, but it stopped again and he thought it wasn't real.

Tut lay there for a while thinking about food, thinking about the white bag the man had brought last night and the trash can on the outside of the shed that maybe some of the food from the bag had been thrown in.

Tut shimmied the rest of the way out of the tunnel and

walked in the shadow along the wall of junk that went nearly to the shed, and then he walked around the back of the shed, not through the small light in the front, to where the trash can was, by the door with the padlock on it, and he looked in the barrel but saw right off that there was no white bag in it or food, just the same bottles and cans, rattling a little against the sides of the barrel as he looked.

Then the door pounded behind him and Tut jumped and ran straight across the greasy ground and dove toward his tunnel and shimmied back to the buried car, listening for somebody coming after him but only hearing the pounding on the door, which he then remembered had a lock on the outside and so nobody who was in it could come after him because they couldn't get out and maybe they were pounding because they wanted to get out.

Tut squirmed through the tunnel again after the pounding stopped and lay at the edge of the junk pile rising above his head, smelling the grease and the rust, and looked at the shed with the strips of light at the sides of the windows, waiting a long time in the cool darkness before he crawled all the way out of the tunnel and went slowly again along the wall of junk to the wall of the shed, but staying on the side close to him with the windows.

He couldn't reach the window to see, so he got a wooden box nearby and stood on it and peeked through one of the cracks but saw nothing but a bucket, and then he peeked through the other crack and saw hands going back and forth to the inside wall.

Tut didn't know what the hands were doing until he realized they were digging with a screwdriver and a tin can, and he thought, Why? and noticed too that they weren't man's hands but a woman's or a boy's.

Tut watched the hands in the small opening dig with the screwdriver and the can, hearing the scraping against the dirt; then the hands stopped and went away, but just after that the body sat back against the wall next to the hole, and Tut saw the shoulder and the arm and part of the head and neck and the long hair, knowing it was a woman now, the head hanging down and staying that way for a long while, not moving, almost sleeping.

Seeing half the woman's face was enough for him to see that it was the nice woman who had taken him to the food place in the city with the man Paul.

Claire!

Tut fell off the box because it frightened him, her in there and not a stranger like Tut expected.

Why was she locked up?

Tut got back up on the box to look again because maybe he didn't see right, the light wasn't very good and maybe he saw wrong, maybe it wasn't the nice lady who had given him the good food, it couldn't be.

But when he looked he couldn't see her, couldn't see anybody, and where she had been digging there was a desk, and Tut started to think that maybe he hadn't seen anything real, like at night sometimes when he thought he saw monsters in the dark or wild dogs and would want to be back in his buried car, where he could put a cover over his head and feel safe.

So he got down off the box and started back to the tunnel, but just as he reached the front side of the shed there was a noise and a motion and at the same time, before he could see anything, a smash on his chest, which he didn't feel until after he hit the ground, and he didn't know he had even hit the ground until after the hand grabbed him at the neck and lifted him straight up and threw him sideways through the dark into the wall, Tut not knowing he had crashed until he hit the ground again—not having much time to think about it or anything because the hand came again and grabbed him and lifted him up and shook him crazy like Tut saw dogs do to rats.

Claire stabbed at the edges of the hole with the screwdriver, dislodging clods of the hard dirt, which she scooped out with either her hands or the tin can and flung in the corner, where it would be hidden when she moved the desk back. Claire had dug down a course and a half of cinder block; she knew she had at least two and a half more courses to go because she had read somewhere that footings had to be at least thirty inches deep, which would be four courses of eight-inch cinder block here, unless the shed had been built cheaply and the blocks only went down three.

The hole grew wider and deeper, and before her back and legs cramped and she had to stop, Claire reached the second mortar line. At least two more courses of cinder block, she said to herself, and then some distance down for her body to squeeze under, then the same distance upward on the other side to freedom. The two courses had taken her half the night and much of the day. Thinking now about how far she had yet to go stopped her. Claire dropped the tin can in the hole and sat back against the wall. Her knuckles were scraped from striking the rough wall and her fingernails were cracked, several bleeding.

This is impossible, she thought, staring at her beaten hands. With only a screwdriver and a tin can, how would she dig deep enough to get under the footing so that she could then dig upward on the other side? How long would it take? Would her hands hold up? Where would she put the rest of the dirt so that her tunneling would not be discovered? And what would happen if, while in the hole, she did not hear the car pull up and the chain rattle in the gate, and he caught her in the hole? Would that become her grave? She pictured herself looking up from the hole into the barrel of his gun, a flash, an impact at the front of her head, then her still body in the hole as he hastily covered her with the dirt. A convenient grave. No one would ever find her. Then she heard a noise on the other side of the steel door and the sound of a bottle against a metal trash can, and for several intense moments Claire froze, knowing she did not have enough time to move the desk back to the wall before the man came in. She heard the bottle noise again, and not the sound of the keys going into the locks, and realized that someone was outside rooting in a trash barrel. Claire rushed to the door and pounded on it, then listened for a response. Nothing. She pounded again, yelling. Again, nothing. She placed her ear to the cold steel door and listened for a time for any sound on the other side. But she only heard her own rapid breathing.

"Anyone there?" she called, pausing to listen for an answer. Nothing.

"Hello? I'm locked in here. I've been kidnapped. If you can hear me, please answer. Please."

The same awful quiet. She stood listening to it until she heard the far-off bark of a dog and then shuffled back to the hole, thinking it had been a dog or maybe a cat on the other side of the door rooting in the trash.

She dug. Not long after beginning, she heard the chain in the gate. Claire jumped up from the ground and shoved the desk back against the wall, smoothed out the skid marks, threw the shipping blanket on the desk so that it draped the front, and dusted loose dirt from her knees. She did not presently hear the keys in the door locks, as before; instead, the silence expanded, as though the man had stopped some-where between the gate and the shed. Then she heard an indistinct noise outside the window, followed immediately by a thump against the wall, then a sharp cry, then another thump. It was quiet for a brief time until Claire heard the keys go into the locks. The door opened a crack, and the man told Claire to move to where he could see her, even though she stood in plain view. He tossed in the white bag of food. Then he flung the door open so hard it crashed against the other wall. Before stepping into the shed, he shoved in something that tumbled nearly to Claire's feet. It was not some *thing*, Claire saw with a catch of breath, but Tut.

"He was snooping outside," the man said. "Like I don't have enough aggravation."

"What did you do to him, for God's sake?" Tut looked dazed, a little blood coming from his nose, and Claire stooped down and held his head in both hands.

"What's it look like?"

"He's just a kid."

197

"He was putting his nose where it don't belong."

"Are you okay?" Claire said to the boy. "Do you hurt anywhere?"

"Hey kid, see what happens when you get nosey. What were you doing here, anyway?"

Tut clung to Claire's knees, looking back over his shoulder at the man, frightened.

"He doesn't talk," Claire said.

"How do you know?"

"I know him."

"You know him? How do you know him?"

"It doesn't matter." Claire wiped the blood from Tut's nose with the sleeve of her shirt.

"The fuck it doesn't matter. I want to know."

Claire told him about running into the boy in town while with Paul.

"Hey kid, what were you doing around here?"

"I told you he doesn't talk."

"Let him tell me that."

"Can't you see he's scared?"

"I want him to be scared. Less trouble."

"Let him go."

"If I do that, he'll just go tell somebody you're here. Then what do I got? I got dick, that's what."

"My father didn't pay you?"

"Would I be here if your father paid me? Let me tell you something about your father. He's no kind of father if he let you hang this long without paying me. But guess what? He doesn't have the coins anymore *to* pay me. Not only that, he either disappeared or don't answer the phone."

"Coins?"

"That's what he stole from me, your nice father."

"He stole them from you?"

"You want the whole story, I'll tell you the whole story. I copped the coins from the house of this chick I dated maybe three times, hardly enough to even know her name. But right when I'm about to go out the door, your old man bops me

198

and scoots with the coins. Simple as that. Now tell me something, don't you think I have a right to those coins that I went through the trouble of stealing?"

"Where was the house?" Claire asked.

"What do you care?"

"At the New Jersey shore?"

"It mighta been."

"Longport?"

"What're you, a mind reader?"

"I understand it now."

"Yeah? What do you understand?"

"My father was going to steal the coins, but you got there before him."

"Brilliant, real brilliant."

"That was our old summer house. My mother still lives there."

"No shit? You mean your father was going to rob his own wife?"

"Ex-wife. She remarried the mob builder."

"The who?"

"Victor Notte."

"He does mob contracts?"

"That's what the papers say."

"I don't know any mob builders by that name, though why should I?"

"Maybe you know him as Vic Ways."

"*Who?*"

"That's his alias."

"This is bullshit."

"So, you know who he is, his reputation?"

"Shut up and fuck you! I don't care who your mother married. You're staying here until I get something, I don't care how long it takes, how bad it stinks it here. I'll put bars on the door and knock a hole in the wall so I can just toss you some garbage to eat now and then. Anyway, who's going to tell Notte that it was me who broke in his place, huh? It was your father who took the coins from the house. He's the one they'll whack when they find out. I'm getting mine, no matter what." Benny opened the door without turning, stepped out, and slammed the door shut.

Somebody put the horns on me big time, Benny thought, as he sped screeching away from the junkyard. It wasn't bad enough that Lawrence clocks him and takes the coins. It wasn't bad enough that after that Whale takes the coins from Lawrence. No, the motherfucking coins have to belong to this motherfucking Victor Ways, who just happened to be a made guy tight with Maglio, that whack-happy fucker. Benny heard the name Vic Ways now and then as the guy who was Maglio's Atlantic City man, but Benny had never met him—why should he, a small fry like he was?—until on the boat ride, and then he didn't know Notte, the chick's father, was Ways, didn't hear that last name, and didn't think twice about the name Victor.

I got cursed, Benny thought, swerving onto Delaware Avenue; somebody threw the horns at me a coupla times for sure.

So now what was he going to do? The main thing was not to let Maglio find out about who broke into his friend's house. Benny punched himself in the jaw for that one, and he did it hard, no pussy shot. The car swerved a little at the blow. Good. He did it again, and felt better, except he thought he loosened a tooth.

As long as Notte and Maglio didn't find out, Benny was safe; he could do what he wanted. The only way they could find out was from Lawrence, wherever the fuck he was.

Now about Whale. He goes and steals the coins from Lawrence, not to mention he has the balls to bang Audrey and pay her with one of the coins. What kinda guy does that? And all the favors Benny did him. Now if the fat man still had the coins, maybe it was just a matter of breaking into his place and taking them, even though he would know it was Benny, meaning that Benny would have to split the city, which might not be a bad idea anyway, the way things looked. But if Whale had cashed the coins, that was something else. Maybe Benny could still break in and see what kind of cash Whale kept around the house. It wouldn't be thirty thousand in coins, but it would be something. Benny would need at least a couple of nights to case the job, to see when Whale's wife was in, when she wasn't. Whale would probably still figure Benny had broken in, in which case he'd still have to split town or whack Whale. But what did he have to lose?

Whack Whale. Benny couldn't believe he thought that. It was scary and genius at the same time. Scary because you don't whack a guy like Whale and not get yourself whacked. Genius because he would have a perfect excuse that would make him look pretty with Maglio.

"Well, Mr. Maglio," Benny said out loud as he rode past the marina still with the burned-out boat in the water that Whale owed him for, "I did it because he stole those coins from your best friend Vic. Here, I give them to you." He laughed some.

But that was a last resort, robbing Whale's place or killing him, and something he could do only if Lawrence was out of the picture and now his daughter, too, who knew everything, and that stupid kid.

Jesus, the horns!

16

AFTER the phone call from Whale, Paul watched television for nearly an hour, and then went upstairs to shower and shave. When he was through, he left the bathroom with a towel around his waist, walked into the bedroom, and stopped dead at the sight of Benny Bean sitting on the cedar chest with a gun pointed at him.

"Ask me how I got in. Ask me how I crashed your security. Ain't you wondering?"

"What are you doing here?"

"I heard you were snooping around in South Philly looking for me. I know you sat down with Whale at Shunk's. And I heard even Maglio came in and sat down with you two. Maglio? I said when I heard that, what the fuck? Because he's the big boss, in case you didn't know."

Hearing the name, Paul instantly remembered Maglio from the newspaper and television reports about his alleged part in criminal activities. With his migraine and his reminiscence about the trip to California, Maglio had not seemed so fearsome, and so Paul did not know how to feel about Rick's being on friendly terms with someone of that man's standing, even without Benny's gun pointed at him.

"I wanted to see you about Claire."

"Guess who else I got? This retarded kid your chick says you know. He was snooping around like you, and I snatched him."

"Tut?" How could that be? Paul thought. Tut must have seen where Benny was holding Claire, but it had to be in the city, not in New Jersey as Whale had told him.

"She says he can't talk. Too bad he can see."

"The boy can't help you."

"He can hurt me, though. Sit down."

Paul hesitated, then took the few steps to the bedside chair near the hamper and sat, putting his hands on his thighs.

"When I said security before, I was joking. You got no security. No bars, no dead bolts, no alarm, no maniac dog, nothing. I kicked in that diddly cellar window in your backyard and I was in. Took me maybe fifteen seconds. I been here long before you got home. If you're wondering, I followed you home that night after I clocked you. I just circled around and kept my distance. Now here I am. What can we do for each other?"

"I thought it was settled."

"What was settled?"

"Whale said that you'll take ten thousand."

"Whale said that? He knows I have your squeeze?"

"I told him what I knew. I'm supposed to meet him tomorrow night with ten thousand dollars that you're supposed to take for releasing Claire. Whale said he talked to you, that you've been holed up in New Jersey."

"I've been holed up in Jersey, huh? Let me tell you a little secret. I haven't talked to Whale for three days."

"He said—"

"You know where you were going tomorrow? To your grave. You were going to pay Whale ten big ones to get rid of yourself. I just saved your life. You'll be able to see your chick now instead of your coffin."

"Is Claire all right?"

"She's great. She's a trooper, that one."

"Take the ten thousand dollars. Let her and the boy go."

"I don't know where Whale gets off saying I'll take ten thousand. What's ten thousand? I want my thirty."

"I don't have that much money, and Claire's father—"

"Her father? He's out of the picture. Whale has my coins. That's where the thing is now."

"Whale has the coins?"

"Yeah, that fat bastard. I don't know how he got 'em but he got 'em. Lawrence said he was mugged, so I guess that was it, somebody working for Whale."

Paul remembered Lawrence's story about getting mugged on the street, suspecting now with some certainty that it had not been a chance robbery but that Whale was behind it. Paul recalled the jowly cheeks, the tiny eyes and ears, the cigar the color of a cockroach clamped in the corner of his mouth—a devious face.

"How do you know it was him?" Paul asked, suddenly thinking that Bean could be lying in the same way Whale had, each for his own purpose.

"How?" Bean stood up, dug quickly into his pocket, and tossed Paul a coin. "That's how. This is the kind of genius or don't-care pig-fucker that he is: he gave the coin to somebody I know. Somebody I know!"

Paul held the coin in his palm, looking at one face then the other; it was a gold Krugerrand. Bean snapped his fingers and Paul tossed the coin back to him.

"She told me he gave it to her," Bean said, shoving the coin in his pocket. "What other proof do I need? Now I want the rest of the coins back, and you're going to get them, the coins or the money." Bean paused. "Hey, wait a second. I just remembered you. Didn't Whale jack you up in his car once because of some bad debt? That happened, right? You were the guy whose car went in the river and your—"

"Shut up!"

"That was you."

"Shut up, I said!" Paul wanted to smash his fist into Bean's face, break bones in it, see it torn and bloodied.

"I'm the one with the gun, so calm down. But I can see how you would be upset. How can you even look at Whale knowing what you know he did? Don't you want to rip his throat out?"

Paul gazed at the floor and said nothing.

"Well, I would," Bean said. "Anyway, it's simple: I get my due from Whale and you'll get your woman and the kid. I'll give you twenty-four hours to get the rest of the coins or the money, the full thirty. Now move away from the door so I can get outta here, and stay put until I'm outside."

Paul moved to the side and, with the gun pointed at his chest, allowed Bean to walk by and into the hall; Bean never turned his back on Paul or lowered the gun.

"You'll hear from me same time tomorrow night," Bean said at the bottom of the steps, "and you better have the coins or all the money when you do. If you don't, I snuff somebody."

Paul heard the door open and close but did not move for a long while.

After Benny left his house, Paul sat on the edge of the bed thinking, and would have sat all night, he thought later, turning things endlessly over in his mind, trying to see a way out of this mess and a way to save Claire and Tut, with neither one getting hurt in the process, if his uncle Rick had not telephoned.

"Did you find Benny Bean?" Rick asked. "Mike said you showed at his place."

"I went to Mike's, the casinos, all over, and wound up at Shunk's. I met Whale and a friend of yours there who said he was one of the guys on the California trip. Ernest Maglio."

Rick was quiet for some moments. "It's true."

"You never told me you knew him."

"It's not an association that I like to broadcast."

"He says you're a good guy, and that you did a big favor for him once, but he didn't say what."

"Should I tell you?"

"If you want."

"I swore in court that he was with me miles away from a murder he was accused of. The alibi kept him out of prison."

"That is a big favor."

"I was much younger then and had less scruples, or less brains—or just less concern for the possible consequences."

"Were there any?"

"No, other than Maglio considers me his friend, not that we go out of our way to see each other."

"Could be worse."

"There were other but smaller favors since. A few years ago, when the company wanted to renovate the store, I saw Ernie at Shunk's and mentioned the job, which was ballparked at a hundred thousand dollars. He had a friend who he wanted to see get the work, and he asked me what I could do. Since I was the manager, the bids came to me, so I told Ernie the lowest one I received. A few days later, Maglio's friend came in under it. He got the contract."

"Did you get anything?"

Rick paused, as though uncertain about answering. "I got a kickback of five thousand."

Silence gathered on the line.

"Are you surprised?" Rick asked.

"I've had so many surprises these last few days that this is pretty small in comparison. I just had another one: Benny was here about an hour ago."

"Your place? Why? Or are you still not saying?"

"I have until eight tomorrow night to get thirty thousand dollars or a coin collection worth that much as ransom for that woman I've been seeing. Benny's been holding her somewhere. And Freddie Whale has the coins." Paul told Rick about Lawrence, the kidnapping of Claire and now Tut, the coins, the phone call from Whale setting up the meeting to exchange Claire for ten thousand dollars, and all of what Benny had said in Paul's bedroom earlier that evening.

There was a long pause at the other end of the line. "You're serious?"

"I wish I wasn't."

"I can see how you got in this mess, but I'm having trouble believing it."

"Getting out of the mess is what I have to figure now."

"Benny said Whale will kill you?"

"He said that's the only reason Whale would want to take me to New Jersey, because Benny wasn't going to be there."

"Benny could be lying. So could Whale. He might not be taking you to Jersey at all but might have something else in mind. They could be cutting in front of each other."

"Or could Benny and Whale be in it together?"

"Sure, and trying to get an extra ten thousand on top of the coins. Maybe you're the mark now."

"Whatever, I have to free Claire and the kid."

"They might already be dead."

Paul's stomach contracted. "Don't say that."

"I'm sorry, Paul. But you should be prepared for it, with a nut case like Bean."

An image of Claire and the boy murdered flashed in Paul's head and he immediately shook it out. Paul took a deep breath and said, "I'm going to meet Whale tomorrow night."

"And do what?"

"I don't know exactly. But I need those coins."

"Paul, let me handle it. You're not cut out for this."

"I can't sit and do nothing. Time's running out."

"Whale will have Gus with him, and Gus will have a gun. If they are taking you to Jersey to kill you, what's going to keep them from doing it?"

"I'll have a gun, too."

"Stop. You're thinking crazy."

"What choice do I have?"

"Not getting in his car is one."

"I need the coins. I need to find out if the coins are even

still around. I need to know where Benny has Claire and Tut. And I need to know by eight o'clock tomorrow night. What can I do, Uncle Rick? What? I can't call the police because Benny said he'd kill Claire if he knew the police were involved. Meeting Whale is the only option I have now."

"I could talk to Maglio."

"But does that change anything? There's no guarantee that whatever he does, if anything, will lead to Claire and Tut being released safely."

"He could stop Whale from doing whatever he has in mind for tomorrow night."

"But that's the problem. We don't know *what* he has in mind. And who's going to stop Benny? We just don't know who's doing what."

They both fell silent for a time, until Rick said, "If I didn't know he'd kill you after, I'd say you could put a gun to Whale's head and force him to give you the coins, if he still has them."

"I thought about that."

"Well, don't think about it anymore. We don't want to screw up what little chance we have of getting the coins, and we want to stay alive afterward." Rick paused. "All right, listen. You said your meeting with Whale is at six and you have until eight before Benny's deadline? That's two hours. If you insist on doing this, let me help."

"What are you going to do?"

"Something."

"I can't let you get involved in this," Paul said.

"And I can't let you get killed."

"I'll be all right."

"You love her, this Claire?"

"Do I love her?" The question surprised Paul. "I haven't known her very long."

"And the kid?"

"I just met the kid, too."

"It's the other thing, isn't it?"

"The other thing?"

"The business with Whale a few years ago, the accident, that's why you feel you have to save Claire and the kid."

"I don't know."

"You sure you're not looking for a chance to kill Whale?"

"Maybe so." Whale certainly deserved it, if only for his responsibility for the accident that took the life of Paul's child.

"Well, I'd probably do the same thing," Rick said. "Just don't make the meeting for nothing by disappearing in New Jersey."

"I won't."

"All right. Keep Whale out of the city as long as you can, and call me when you get back. I'll call you if anything develops at this end." He paused. "And one other thing. Do you have a gun?"

"No."

"I'll drop off my twenty-two."

"I appreciate it."

"Sure I can't talk you out of this, Paul?"

"I wish there was another way, but there isn't."

"Sure? These guys—"

"Uncle Rick, I'm sure."

Rick was silent for a time; then he said, "Be careful."

They hung up moments later, and Paul continued to sit on the edge of the bed, thinking, trying to see a clear line through to the safe release of Claire and Tut but picturing only vivid scenes of his own murder after meeting Whale. Maybe they would not drive to New Jersey at all, but divert to the Lakes or, more likely, Tinicum Marsh, where Paul would not be able to keep himself from getting shot in the head, Rick's gun with him or not. Or they would in fact drive Paul to New Jersey where, on a dark road, they'd stop; he'd pull his gun but fumble it, or his nerves would give out, or Gus, much experienced with violence, would simply overpower him. Some tomato farmer or a couple of lovers would find Paul's body. He would never know what became of Claire and the boy.

The following afternoon, Paul awoke from a nap on the sofa with Rick's gun on the floor beside him. He was struck for a moment by the oddity of it; then he remembered receiving the gun from his uncle and why. That morning had been the first time Paul had touched a gun, and as he lifted it from the floor now, examining its parts, it seemed foreign and rare. Its weight surprised him; it appeared lighter. The walnut grips on either side of the handle surprised Paul as well; he expected neoprene or simply a handle of blue-black metal like the rest of the gun. Paul moved a small lever and the cylinder fell to the side; he tilted the gun and let the five bullets fall into the palm of his hand. Paul pushed the cylinder back into firing position, used the sites to aim at the on/off switch of the television, and squeezed the trigger. It took more pressure than he expected. Paul sighted on the channel selector and pulled the trigger again. Then he held his wrist with his free hand, as he had seen TV actors do, and aimed at other objects in the room, imagining the noise of the gun and the destruction of the object with each trigger pull. When his finger began to ache, Paul reloaded the gun, leaving the hole below the hammer empty and the safety off.

He did not think he would be frisked that night by Whale or Gus, but Paul sewed a pouch into the inside back of his jacket in the late afternoon and slipped the gun inside before leaving the house that evening. The gun thumped lightly against his spine as he walked and dug into his back as he drove his truck toward South Philadelphia, causing him to lean slightly forward in the seat to ease the discomfort.

Ten minutes later, Paul parked near Ninth and Morris Street, feeling sick in the stomach and weak, suddenly overcome with what he was about to do. He gripped the steering wheel and took deep breaths to settle his nerves. How had he come to this? Was there nothing else to be done? Again, he imagined things going wrong, Gus or Whale shooting him.

Paul reached for the ignition and then retracted his hand.

There was no turning back now. He had painted himself into a corner, and this was the only way out.

But maybe the police should be called. His uncle Rick was right, Paul was not cut out for this. He reached for the ignition again, but again retracted his hand as a young couple, arms about each other, walked toward him in the side mirror, their heads together, murmuring. They passed, oblivious to Paul and to anyone but themselves. The girl had the same color hair, visible in the lamplight, as Claire. Paul thought of Claire running in the early morning, their quiet walk through town, the concern in Claire's face while at the diner with Tut, her smell and dizzy feel on her sofa.

Paul left the truck and walked toward Ninth and Moore.

17

AROUND six o'clock, Whale and Gus sat in Whale's Buick at Ninth and Moore waiting for Paul Fante. They were both in the front seat, with Gus driving because it wasn't necessary to have anybody behind Fante. They weren't going to do anything to him in the city, and no way in Whale's car where blood and maybe piss and shit would have to be cleaned up, and Fante wasn't the type you had to worry about sitting behind you. He was cuckoo for the woman and just wanted her free, that was all. You didn't have to worry about a guy whose daughter drowned because one of your men screwed up and he didn't do hardly anything about it except punch you. That was a guy who had something missing. It was a shame he was going to lose his life now because the same man, Benny, fucked up again, this Fante just stepping in the wrong spot at the wrong time.

Whale lit a cigar and belched, tasting the cavatelli he had for dinner. Thank God his wife could cook. Thank God she didn't ask him questions about his work, not that he would tell her anything, but who needed to be nagged? He gave her money and she kept her mouth shut. He didn't bug her when, once every month, she took the bus to Atlantic City where she'd play the slot machines until her arm got bursitis. She never won more than fifty dollars, least she never said she did, but she loved the slots. Let her have her fun.

"Is that him?" Gus asked, pointing with his chin toward the windshield.

Whale looked up the sidewalk and saw, about a half block down the street, a man in front of St. Nick's Church. He seemed to be taking his time, looking into the parked cars as he came toward Whale's.

"Looks like him," Whale said. "He looks nervous."

"Good."

"All right, let's go over this before he gets here. Where's the place that Benny's supposed to be keeping the woman?"

"Outside Hammonton."

"And we go on what road to get there?"

"Black Horse Pike."

"And where do we stop?"

"The blueberry farm."

"Where what happens?"

"I get out, and me and him take a walk to where Benny is supposed to be hiding. Then I do it."

"Don't forget to get the money from his pocket."

"I won't."

"All right, here he is." Whale rolled down the window and called to Fante as he came up. "Right on time. Get in." Whale gestured to the back seat.

Fante opened the back door and slid into the car. Gus nodded to him and started the engine. After Fante closed the door, Gus pulled away from the curb.

"You bring the money?" Whale asked.

"I had to see the bank manager about getting that much cash, but they gave it to me eventually."

"That's good."

213

Gus drove to Morris Street and made a right turn, then another right at Eighth Street, taking them south toward the Walt Whitman Bridge.

"So, everything is set?" Fante asked. "Benny Bean will hand Claire over without a problem? You've made certain of that?"

"He wants to end this thing as much as you do. Just settle back and enjoy the ride."

"Where are we headed?"

"Hammonton," Gus said, before Whale could.

"That's where Benny's been," Whale said quickly. "You want me to put on some music?"

"That's all right."

"Okay." Whale puffed on his cigar, thinking the guy seemed wound up. But it wasn't every day you took ten thousand of your hard-earned dollars on a trip to Jersey to pay somebody who kidnapped your girlfriend. "In an hour, your girlfriend will be back there with you and we'll be on our way back to Philly, so take it easy."

"By the way, here's your thousand." Fante pulled an envelope from his pocket and handed it over the front seat to Whale.

Whale didn't touch the envelope. "Nah, you keep it. I'll do you a favor."

"Are you sure?"

"Sure I'm sure. Keep your money; it's yours." This poor guy don't have a clue, Whale thought.

"Thanks."

They continued on Eighth Street. It used to be all Italian or Jewish around there, but now the blacks, the Puerto Ricans, the Koreans, the Cambodians, even Vietnamese were already up to Ninth. Some of the neighborhoods were pretty bad; some had tough gangs who did some pretty wicked things, like raping mothers and sisters of guys they were muscling or punishing for something. The bad areas ran down to about Third or Fourth, where the Irish took over; Whale didn't think it was much better living near them. The neighborhoods got better the closer they got to Oregon Avenue, where they

214

turned left and drove toward the Front Street entrance to the bridge. Not far away, the sign told them to turn right onto the ramp to the highway, which went straight for the bridge less than a minute away. Because of the time of night and its being a weekday, there wasn't too much traffic, not like weekends in the summer when you had heavy traffic practically the whole way to Atlantic City. After Hammonton, they were only going to be a half hour from the casinos, so Whale thought he and Gus might go there, see what they could do with the ten thousand they'd get from Fante, and maybe see the hooker Audrey.

Gus paid the toll and they started over the bridge. Whale thought it was too quiet in the car with practically a stranger in the back seat, but he couldn't think of anything to talk about because he didn't know the guy. What he did know didn't interest him. Besides, the guy was going to be dead in a half hour, so it would almost be like talking to a dead man. Still, it made Whale antsy that it was so quiet. Fante didn't have anything more to say, either, it looked like. But why should he? He probably felt about Whale the way Whale felt about him—nothing in common. So no wonder the inside of the car was like a tomb. Whale'd be glad when the night was over.

They came off the bridge and settled into the ride through New Jersey, Whale remembering over twenty years ago when he had ridden this way with the boss, who wasn't the boss then, after Maglio had shot a guy. They went to Atlantic City and Maglio stayed there. He did get charged with the murder, but they couldn't make it stick because Rick Fante swore Maglio was with him in Ocean City at the time the guy got shot. No wonder Maglio was soft for Rick. Who wouldn't be, he does a favor like that?

Back then, the drive through Jersey was a lot darker; you came off the bridge and—boom—it was like crossing into the dark side of the moon. Now there were a lot more housing developments and malls and exits and signs for the exits and lights for the signs and billboards for all the casinos. The thing was, now you had to go farther from the city to dump a body, and you had to take back roads that looked like they wouldn't be back roads too much longer because the back roads went mostly through the farm areas and every time you looked there was another batch of townhouses going up where there used to be tomatoes or something. That's the way it was, and you couldn't do anything about it. Not that Whale really cared. So you couldn't pick blackberries at the side of the road anymore. Big deal.

Whale turned on the radio to get a little noise in the car, but all the stations turned to static about fifteen minutes later when they reached the entrance to the Atlantic City Expressway, so Whale turned the radio off. They stayed to the right and got on Black Horse.

"Wouldn't it be faster if we went the other way and took the expressway to Hammonton?" Fante asked, leaning forward.

"We're not going exactly to the town itself," Whale said. "You think he'd keep her in town? Nah, the place is on the outskirts, near a blueberry farm, and it's easier to get to from this road."

"I see."

"You're not worried, are you? Don't worry. Twenty minutes from now, you'll see your girlfriend."

"All right." Fante sat back.

That poor sap, Whale thought. But it was Fante's own fault for getting as involved as he did, starting back when he borrowed the money from Whale and couldn't pay it back on time. If you were only a flyweight, you shouldn't get in the ring with a heavyweight. Now the only way Fante was going to get out of this jam was by dying.

They rode the Black Horse Pike past the malls and the gas stations and the motels and the houses and restaurants and curiosity shops and car dealerships—Christ, there was everything on that road, like people somewhere sat around thinking what different thing they could put there next. It was easier to see these places during the day. Now, past the lights, it was totally dark in most spots because woods or fields were right behind the buildings. In the day, also, you could see better how run-down a lot of these places were, some of the gas stations abandoned completely, the houses kind of sagging and rotting, the motels so dull they looked like they came out of some old black-and-white photograph. Every few minutes or so, there was a thin road—some that used to be plain dirt, Whale remembered—branching off from this main one, and if there was no car coming out of it when you looked, all you saw was the entrance and just deep black beyond. The road they turned off onto, after driving for twenty-five minutes, was just like that. The headlights lit up just as far as they reached and that was that; everything else was dark. After a few minutes on this road, without passing anyone, they came to the sign for the blueberry farm, which said to make a turn after a mile to get there. Fante would die with acres of blueberry fields all around him.

"We'll be there in a few minutes," Whale said. "Because he's a paranoid fuck, Bean don't want anybody around but you and Gus, so when we stop, Gus'll take you to the spot where you're supposed to look for a flashlight blinking. Then you'll go toward it and Bean'll be there with your girlfriend. You'll hand over the money, and he'll hand over the girl. Okay?"

"All right."

Another sign came up a little later, saying to make the next left turn to the blueberry farm; Gus slowed the car and made the left onto the even thinner and darker road, the headlights sweeping across the trees that the road cut through. The blueberry farm was about two miles up, but Gus switched off the headlights and began to slow down after about a mile, checking in the rearview mirror for anybody behind them. There wasn't, and soon they coasted to a stop after fading off the road and onto the shoulder.

"How did you know where to stop?" Fante asked.

Whale didn't know what to say to that. "What?"

"It's so dark; how did you know where to stop and meet Bean if you can't see anything?"

"Counting," Gus said.

"Counting?"

"Yeah," Whale said, thinking fast. "Bean's so on guard, he had us follow his count system. He said to count to sixty by one-thousands—you know, one one-thousand, two one-thousand—do that and then stop. So here we are. You go with Gus now, and I'll see you in a few minutes. Don't slam the doors."

Fante nodded and then left the car with Gus. The open doors let the cold air in and then shut it off as they closed them. Whale watched the two men through the window as long as he could, but after only a few seconds they melted into the black, and that's all he could see. He expected to see the flash of the gun and hear it in less than a minute because Gus knew the longer the car sat on the side of the road, the more of a chance somebody would come by and see it, maybe a teenage couple looking for a spot to screw. But Whale didn't see or hear anything when he thought he would, and didn't see or hear anything for a while after that.

"Come on," he said out loud, wondering if something had gone wrong.

But just when Whale was about to roll down the window, he heard the first crack of the gun and then, a few seconds later, the second one, the clean head shot. That was done. Now Benny had to be taken care of, even if it meant in this same way, and then Whale could sleep at night, not worrying that Benny would blab about the coins and the boss would hear, connect the theft to Whale, and put him where Fante now was. Tomorrow, he would go to Wilmington and cash the coins, getting rid of them once and for all.

Gus was taking longer to get back to the car than Whale thought he should, and he looked for him through the side window where he and Fante had disappeared into the dark. What was taking him so long? Gus had to clean out the pockets for identification and maybe he was dragging the body deeper off the road, so maybe that was it. But Whale didn't like sitting there.

Then the back door opened, and Whale started to ask Gus why he had opened it instead of the front and was getting in. Then he felt what he knew was a gun barrel jab him in the face.

"Drive." It was Paul Fante.

18

HE liked her, because she was very nice, because she touched his head lump from where the bad man had thrown him against the wall, saying, "Does it hurt?" and looking at it and then telling him it was a small one compared to some she'd seen, some as big as baseballs, and they were twins now because she had a hurt too on her head.

The lump stopped hurting and Tut forgot that it was there, but not how it got there, getting scared all over again whenever he thought of the man grabbing him and shaking him and throwing him, and afraid that when the man came back he was going to do it again, which made Tut cry thinking about the man and about being trapped, not able to run away or hide.

The nice lady Claire said, "Do you want to get out of here?" and Tut shook his head very hard yes, and the lady then went to the desk and pulled it away from the wall and showed Tut the hole in the ground and the dirt next to it, telling him they could dig out, they could dig a hole big enough for Tut and he could escape and get help, go to the man Paul's shop or house.

She asked if Tut remembered the house, where to find it, telling him the streets and the color of the door, blue, and she said if Paul wasn't there to try the wood shop and tell him where she was, make him understand, bring him.

Then she said, "But Tut, if you see a policeman you have to try to tell him, make him understand, and bring him here, too, you have to, okay?"

And he nodded, even though thinking about the police made him frightened because of before when they took him to that place and he had to run away.

"But we have to dig fast," Claire said, "because he's going to come back sometime today, maybe tonight if we're lucky."

Tut nodded again because he wanted to get out, he had already checked the door and the windows and looked at the ceiling and seen that you couldn't get out that way, that the only way out was through the ground, so yes he helped her dig and move the dirt and listened for the bad man's car, doing it through the night, each of them taking turns while the other moved the dug-out dirt or rested or slept.

Tut stopped his digging and stared at Claire, curled up on the blanket on the floor, her face looking sad even with her eyes closed, and her lips dry and cracked making Tut think of water and food, but there was no water and the only food was what Claire didn't eat, the half of hamburger and the french fries, which Tut had already eaten.

Tut fell asleep watching Claire but woke up before she did, and he peed in the smelly bucket as Claire slept, and when she woke up she made in the bucket too, but he didn't watch, digging in the hole so he wouldn't, and when she finished she said to tell her if he reached the end of the cinder blocks.

He did reach the end around the time the lines at the sides of the window where you could see a little outside were getting light with the new day, and he pointed to the hole and she saw the bottom of the blocks sitting on a clump of concrete and said, "Now we have to dig under them, a big enough hole for you first," and she got into the hole and used the screwdriver to dig under the bottom cinder block, loosening up small smooth stones which she scooped out, then reaching the dirt, which was softer and came out easier, scooping that out with the tin can and throwing it in the corner.

When they saw sunlight at the windows, all the dirt under the last cinder block was out, and they now had to reach behind to get more.

Claire said, "This is our last chance. There's hardly any place to put the dirt. Look at us, we're filthy, so he'll know when he sees us what we've been doing, so Tut we have to get you out before he comes back, all right?" and she looked at him and he nodded, wanting very much to get out.

Then he got in the hole and started to dig some more, now having to put his arms under the cinder block to dig forward and up, like Claire said, but it was harder and Tut's arms scraped against the rough edge of the block and got scratched and bleedy, but he didn't stop because they had to get out because of the man coming back to kill them.

Tut had to get free, and he kept digging even when it hurt his arms, then he couldn't reach any more dirt and he stopped, and Claire knew why and she said, "Let me take over. I'll stick my head under first if there's room and see how it goes."

Tut came out of the hole, his legs hurting from being scrunched up, and Claire took the screwdriver and the tin can, turned her back on the hole, and slid down into it head first on her back because there wasn't enough room to get in the regular way and then get under the cinder block, and she went sliding down and put her arms under the bottom first and then pulled herself forward so her head went under and most of her body went in the hole but her legs stuck out, from her knee to her feet up on the ground.

He heard her digging and making struggling noises and cursing and saw her body moving and saw the dirt from the other side falling on both sides of her neck, where Tut reached down and scooped it out with his hands and threw it in the corner on the pile, and heard her cough and curse, sounding like she was wrestling with somebody in there.

After not very long she started to squirm back out, one hand came out bleeding and pressed on the cinder block and she yelled to grab her legs and pull, which Tut did, helping her squirm back and up at the same time until her head came out from under the cinder block and she could grab the sides of the hole and pull herself the rest of the way out.

As soon as she got out, she just flattened on the ground, her chest going up and down fast, one hand on her stomach and the other arm stretched out halfway into the hole.

Tut could barely see her face because it was covered with dirt, and dirt was in her hair and on her neck and on her lips, in her ears too, and all her clothes were dirty and her hands were black with dirt except where the blood from the cuts made them wet.

He felt bad for her.

"That wasn't very smart," Claire said. "I didn't need to know what dirt tasted like," and she lay quiet for a while and Tut sat watching her, then she rolled over on her stomach, said "God, I'm thirsty," and crawled over to where there was a balled-up sheet, which she opened up and bit and then ripped a couple of ways into a square, then did it again, getting two square pieces, one which she gave to Tut and one that she kept, saying, "Watch me, Tut—I'm not going to make you go in the hole if you don't want, but if you do, tie the cloth over your face like this, but loosely, so you don't come out like I did."

She took her cloth, put it over her head and took the corners and tied them, then she took off the piece of sheet and looked at him, Tut knowing she did it to find out if he would go in the hole all the way, but wondering why she even asked.

He didn't go in right away but went to the paper cup that had the ice in it from the Coke last night, which was melted and now water, and handed it to Claire, then went to the hole, bit the sheet piece in his mouth, and did what Claire had done—he turned his back on the hole and lowered himself in, holding onto the sides, until his back touched the bottom of the hole, which felt cool, and then he took the cloth and put it over his head and tied the corners, seeing the light in the ceiling but nothing else, feeling it hard to breathe, and then he reached up without seeing for the screwdriver and the tin can, which Claire put in his hands, and he put them first in the tunnel going under the cinder block, then reached in to the other side and pulled himself into the darker dark.

The sides of the tunnel nearly touched his shoulders and the top of it was right above his face, this tunnel a little smaller than his own going through the metal junk from the fence to his buried car.

He took the screwdriver from beside his neck and stabbed at the dirt and felt it falling on his face on the other side of the cloth and about his ears, making it seem even harder to breathe unless he brushed the dirt off, but still stabbing until his arm hurt or he couldn't breathe at all and his head started to spin, and then stopping to brush the dirt from his face and pinching the cloth in his fingers and lifting it from his face so a space opened below his neck and air could get in, which he sucked in deep.

Claire asked, "Are you all right? Do you want me to take over? Just come out if you get tired."

But Tut only needed to rest, and after catching his breath he started to dig again, stabbing at the roof of the tunnel left and right, the dirt falling on his face and filling up the space between his head and the sides, then switching the screwdriver from one hand to the other when his arm tired, the screwdriver scraping against the wall, the cloth sucking into his mouth and nose when he breathed, stopping and lifting the cloth when he got dizzy, seeing nothing the whole time until he suddenly broke through to the bright sun right there above his face and a cool breeze and the sound of sheets flapping on a clothesline, and somebody saying his name.

It was Claire drawing his eyes away from the sun, which wasn't the sun but the light in the shed ceiling, and the breeze was Claire flapping the piece of cloth in his face as he lay on the ground on his back.

"You passed out," she said. "You went quiet in the tunnel and I pulled you out. You worked so hard, you—" but her voice got stuck and she grabbed her forehead and bent her head to her chest and she made angry and sad noises both, then just sad ones as she shook, crying and saying words Tut couldn't understand.

After a while, Claire said, "Well," and lowered herself backward into the hole again and when she reached the bottom she tied her cloth on her head and pulled herself under the cinder block into the tunnel, where Tut could hear her digging.

He sipped water from the melted Coke ice, only a little because Claire said they had to spare it, and then he went to the window and looked through the thin opening at the piece of sky above the wall of rusted junk, and for once wished that his place to stay wasn't so hidden, that somebody would be out there to hear them if they pounded on the door or Claire yelled, so they could be rescued.

Tut hurried back to the hole and Claire was pulling herself out, reaching for his hand to help her, and she got out and untied the sheet piece from her head and breathed deep over and over, her face very red, then she took the tin can and began to scoop the loose dirt from the bottom of the hole and throw it on the pile in the corner, doing it slower and slower and almost not getting all the dirt out before she stopped and rested flat on the ground.

"I don't know if we're going to make it, Tut," she said, the words coming out slow.

He looked at her.

"From the sun, it looks like it's past noon, and I don't know if that's enough time. I don't know if I can dig anymore. I'm so tired and my hands are killing me."

He handed her the water from the melted Coke ice, but

there was hardly any left and she only sipped half of it and handed the cup back to him.

Tut put the cup down and took his cloth from the desk and went to the hole.

"You don't have to, if you don't want," Claire said.

But he knew that, and he sat on the floor at the edge of the hole and lowered himself again back down into it, tying the cloth around his head, then he reached into the tunnel and pulled himself into the dark and started with the screwdriver again to stab at the ceiling of the hole, feeling the dirt fall on his face and go down the back of his neck, sucking in the cloth with his breaths but stopping as soon as it got too hard to breathe and pinching the cloth from his nose, lifting it so air could get under it, not wanting to pass out again, then digging again with both hands, blind, going by feel only, hoping he wouldn't black out again and think he was free when he wasn't, hoping the bad man wouldn't come back.

When he could barely lift his arms any more, he pulled himself out of the tunnel and the hole and stretched out on the ground like Claire had done.

"Are you okay?" she said, and Tut shook his head.

She said to rest, and she reached into the hole with the tin can and scooped out the dirt Tut had loosened, then she lowered herself down and disappeared except for her feet sticking out.

He heard her digging on the other side of the wall.

When she quit and came out, Tut still did not have the strength to move, he was hungry and thirsty, and every part of his body seemed to hurt.

"I know," Claire said, looking at him, like reading his mind again, "we'll just rest for a while."

He tried not to but he fell asleep and dreamt, as if it was real, of going to the door and just turning the knob to open it and going out and running with long gliding steps not to his tunnel to crawl back into hiding but to the fence, which even though it was almost twice as high as him he jumped over and floated down on the other side and went running not to Paul's house or the wood shop but to what used to be his home, not burned down anymore but like it used to be, only better, the windows and the door all glass and bright lights in the house and his mother inside smiling in the good-smelling warm kitchen, touching his face in both hands and sitting him down at the table for a meal of turkey, corn, mashed potatoes and gravy and pumpkin pie for dessert with whipped cream on top, everything tasting so good, and after he ate, his mother said she had a surprise and she showed him a shiny car parked out in front of the house, saying it was theirs, that they were going to Florida right now, and even though it was almost winter, when they walked outside to the car it was sunny and warm, so sunny that Tut had to squint, and the sun was everywhere he looked, but then he felt the dream going away and he knew he was staring at the light bulb again in the ceiling of the shed and he smelled the bucket in the corner and remembered that he was trapped.

He was alone and felt scared.

But then he heard the digging and turned and saw the feet above the hole.

Claire came out soon after and said, "You're awake," then went slowly to the window and looked through the crack on one side, saying, "The sun's almost down, so it's about four o'clock, I think." Then she turned her back to the wall, leaned against it, and slid to the ground, sitting there with her knees first up and then flat down, blinking her eyes slowly, looking very tired.

Tut took the tin can, crawled to the hole, and scooped the loose dirt, then he went into the hole again, tied the cloth over his head, pulled himself into the tunnel and worked the screwdriver against the dirt, clawing with his other hand, the dirt falling on his face, breathing hard, switching arms when the first became tired and switching again when the other one tired.

He was almost worn out again when a heavy chunk of dirt hit him in the face enough to hurt.

227

He didn't stop, but when he went to stab at the ceiling of the tunnel the screwdriver hit nothing.

He brushed dirt from the cloth on his face and took it off, and the real light was there shining through a hole with jagged edges as big as a soccer ball and he wondered if he was dreaming.

He wasn't dreaming, no.

I did it.

Then he heard Claire say something, and he pulled himself back into the room and saw Claire on her knees looking down, eyes wide, saying, "Are you through?" and he nodded hard, and Claire said, "Wonderful! Terrific!" and held his face with both hands and then said, "All right, Tut, listen, you finish digging out and then you run for help. Leave the screwdriver behind so I can keep digging the hole bigger for me, and maybe I won't be here when you get back, I'll be free like you, but we'll have to meet later, say at Paul's wood shop, okay?"

Tut nodded.

"Good," and she pulled him to her chest and held him hard, and then she moved him away and Tut went down into the hole, scooped out the loose dirt, then tied on the sheet and pulled himself under the cinder block and into the tunnel, where he stabbed at what was left of the ceiling, the dirt coming down now in big clods and knocking against Tut's face, but digging faster, the screwdriver sometimes missing as the hole got bigger and bigger, feeling it with his other hand, squirming forward and upward as it got big enough for his body, then wide enough to try, dropping the screwdriver back down beside him and reaching up and out of the tunnel to put both hands on the outside ground and pulling hard, the hole barely wider than his shoulders, his legs getting a little stuck at the turn under the cinder block, but he moved upward and when his head reached his hands he pulled off the cloth from his head and saw in front of his face the outside wall of the shed in the almost night and the outside light bulb above his head.

He sucked in air deep, resting, but then heard a far-off car roaring and thought of the man and started to pull hard with his hands and shove with his heels, and he squirmed more and more out of the hole, getting his elbows out and up on the ground and pushing, moving more, his chest nearly out now, then putting his hands under his elbows and pushing hard.

The rest of Tut's body came out of the hole, and he was free.

He sat on the edge of the hole with his feet still in it, looking around to the gate, then he lifted out his feet and stood up, but he almost fell because his legs were rubbery and weak.

Tut wanted to lie down but knew the man could come back any second, and so he hurried across the lot to his tunnel through the wall of junk and squirmed in and through the junk to the hole in the fence on the other side and through the fence and out of the junkyard, and ran away from it through the glassy dirty streets with the sometimes piles of tires and the once cars without tires toward the river in the growing dark.

Claire watched Tut's feet leave the hole, and her heart jumped and pounded in her throat with excitement. She put her ear to the cold cinder block and heard him struggle through the hole on the other side of the wall and then, after a pause that had her calling to him, asking if he was all right, she heard Tut's steps running away. She closed her eyes, cheek and arms flat against the wall, relieved and happy that he was now free and away.

Now it was her turn to get free. Weak from hunger and aching from the digging she had done already, Claire moved away from the wall to the hole and slid backward down into it. She needed to see to widen the tunnel large enough for her to pass through and so did not tie the cloth over her head. Claire reached under the cinder block and pulled herself into the tunnel; immediately she saw the hole three feet above her head and the outside wall, lit by the light cast from the front of the shed. She reached under her neck for the screwdriver Tut had left and began to dig at the sides of the hole, widening it. Clods of dirt and specks fell against her face, but she tried not to let the dirt affect her. It was near five o'clock, she estimated; though he had come earlier, the man had never arrived at the shed after seven, so she figured she had at the most two hours to dig. Two hours might not be enough time, she thought, and she could not allow dirt in her face to slow her. If he returned while she was still in the hole and the hole was still not big enough for her to pass through, she would have to scramble back into the shed and fight him. There was no way to hide the hole now, and if he found her in the hole it would be convenient for him to just shoot her in it, then cover her with the loose dirt. She would not give him that opportunity.

Claire's arms tired quickly now and she found herself switching the screwdriver from one hand to the other frequently; it slipped from her weakened grip several times and fell against her head. When her arms gave out entirely, Claire shifted to the side as much as possible and worked the loosened dirt from her chest and the sides of her head down her ribs, hips, and back into the shed. Still without the strength to continue, Claire would lie in the tunnel unmoving, listening to the far-off sirens and yipes of dogs, and for the kidnapper's car. Once, she remained still for too long and found with a start that she had dozed off. Claire went rigid, listening for the car or footsteps, but heard only the distant city sounds. Then she grabbed for the screwdriver and began to dig again.

When Claire became stuck as she tried to wiggle through the hole, she was not surprised. She had widened the hole to the width of her shoulders, but because she was able to slide down into the hole and under the cinder block without much difficulty, she had failed to realize that her jackknifed legs would need room to move either straight back or, bent at the knees, to the side and then be pulled under the wall as she pulled herself up out of the hole. But there was certainly not nearly enough room to the back of the hole in the shed for her legs to fall straight back, and although the hole was just wide enough for her legs, bent at the knees, to fit as Claire twisted on her hip, it was not quite wide enough under the wall to pull the legs through in that position. Had she not been digging for most of the last twenty-four hours and if she had normal strength in her arms and legs, she might have been able to pull herself through while pushing with her feet on the back wall of the inside hole. But her hips were jammed under the bottom of the wall. She tried to twist her hips to the side but could not. All she could do was take the screwdriver again and dig at the dirt under the wall in front of her knees and widen the hole. But with her left arm tight against the wall of the hole and the dirt she needed to dig away at the end of her reach, Claire could do little with the scant energy she had.

Exhausted, hoping to gather strength by resting, Claire dropped the screwdriver in her lap, rolled her head back and went still. Gazing past the roof line of the shed at the sky, Claire saw no stars.

Tut's stomach hurt from wanting food, and then his side from the running, but he kept running through more dark streets this way and that to the big street that ran along the river, reaching it where the park was where he used to sleep sometimes before he found the junkyard, glad now because there was more light along this road and moving cars and some big loud trucks rumbling, and the black river on the other side and across that the other city with its light, too.

He felt better when he reached the breakfast and lunch diner where they let him sweep the sidewalk sometimes and gave him breakfast for doing it, but it was closed now, nobody to try to tell about Claire, and Tut only stopped in the back where the trash bins were and lifted the lid and poked around and found some parts of sandwiches and almost a whole doughnut and lots of cups of ice with still tastes of Coke or something in them, but he only drank the melted water right away and chewed the ice, his head hurting from the cold, and put all the pieces of food in one bag and then started away because if he stopped to eat the man might come back and get Claire.

The water was good, though, and as soon as he chewed and swallowed the ice he started to run again.

He passed the lumberyard but did not see the big barking dog behind the fence and passed where all the trucks were parked and the office building that used to be a warehouse, now all the windows bright when they used to be black.

"Hey, kid." It was a policeman in a car driving slow beside him.

Tut got scared, and then he remembered Claire said to try to tell a policeman, make him understand, but he was still scared.

"Why are you running?"

Tut stopped and the policeman stopped, leaning now across his front seat talking to Tut through the open window, saying, "Are you running away?"

Tut went two steps toward the car but stopped, he shook his head, and the policeman got out of the car and came around it toward Tut, saying, "Where do you live?" but Tut ran because he got scared, and the policeman yelled, "Hey, hey kid!" but Tut kept running, away from the wide street along the river and toward the small ones where there was a stable of horses and a pretty big lot of grass where they stood around, this being the place the horses who pulled the carriages in the city stayed, not the police horses.

He ran that way toward the stable because the streets were small and ran crisscrossing into each other and the old closed-down beer factory was around there too and other lots which in the summer had weeds growing as tall as Tut and where it would be easy to hide from somebody.

The policeman had not gone after him, Tut thought, and if he had he gave up looking for Tut, making him feel happy, but sad too because Claire said to try to tell a policeman if he saw one and Tut had seen one but didn't try to tell him about Claire still in the shed.

Tut was mad at himself, and said to himself if he saw another policeman on his way to the wood shop he would try to tell about Claire and take the policeman there and she would be free like him.

It was on the 2 Street that would take him straight to the wood shop if he stayed on it, that Tut saw not only one policeman but two, sitting in their cars side by side pointed in different directions, just talking, and at first Tut hurried up toward them, then slowed down, then hurried up, then stopped and started to turn away, then stopped again thinking about Claire in the shed and the bad man, and he turned back to the police cars and hurried toward them again, then slowed the closer he got, but still going up to them, and when he got closer he saw that one of the policeman was the first one who called at him, and now this policeman saw Tut and recognized him and said something to the other policeman and then got out of the car but stood without moving, and Tut stopped but then started forward again, with the policeman saying, "Is everything all right?"

He was tall and his shoes were very shiny even in the dark.

Tut tried to say about Claire, trying, but he couldn't say the words, and the policeman looked at him, then at the other policeman getting out of his car now, then back at Tut.

Tut could feel his lips shaking and could hear the policeman say "Son?" and then they stood beside each other and then the other policeman came up and said "Are you lost? How'd you get so dirty?" and Tut tried to say about Claire but couldn't and the policemen looked at each other and one said "You want to take me where you live? I'll drive you there. You ever been in a police car before?" and Tut just tried to say about Claire, tried to say but couldn't, and he kept twisting up the paper bag with the food in it and trying to say.

"Better take him down," the one policeman said, and the other said "Yeah," and then "Want to see the police station? We'll call somebody for you."

Tut tried to say again about Claire but couldn't, and when the policeman touched his shoulder and moved him to the car, Tut didn't run away because he kept trying to say about Claire and knew at the station there would be many policemen and there he could tell them about Claire, so he got in the back seat of the car and the policemen said to each other, "So long, Mike. So long, Julio," and Tut's car drove away first and went straight down the street, soon past the wood shop, Tut looking at it, trying to say something but nothing coming out, and then to the wide street, where the police car turned and went up to the 12 Street toward the tall buildings and past the very widest street to one of the Chinese streets, where Tut often saw Smash Louie but not tonight.

They turned, then turned again at the end of the block and went almost another block but stopped where the police cars and vans were parked, the policeman pulling into a lot and saying, "Okay, let's see what we can do," and getting out of the car and opening the door for Tut and walking with him to the doors with the sign above them saying something with a number, and then they went into bright white light with the telephones ringing and the other policemen and policeladies and the desks and people sitting around and barking dogs from somewhere, walking through with the people looking at Tut to a warm room where the policeman said to have a seat and talked to a woman at a desk and then said, "So long, champ," and left the room.

The woman said to Tut, "Hi, what's your name?" and Tut tried to say it but couldn't and reached into his pocket to get the piece of paper his name was written on, but his bag of food fell to the floor, the bottom breaking and a piece of tomato coming out, and Tut picked it up, putting the tomato back in the bag and holding the bag at the bottom.

He did not have the piece of paper with his name.

The woman said, "I can't call anybody if I don't know your name," and Tut tried to say it again and then tried to tell about Claire, but couldn't, and the woman shook her head and got up from her desk and went to another part of the room to talk to a man who looked at Tut and said something, and then they both came over and stood in front of Tut.

"You have a home?" the man said.

Tut shook his head no, and the man said "I thought so," then turned to the woman and said "You'll have to call DHS," then went back to his desk.

The woman went back to hers and pressed the buttons on the phone, not looking at Tut, and Tut stood up from the chair and went over to the desk, forgetting about the ripped bottom of the paper bag, and as he tried to say about Claire the pieces of sandwich fell out the bottom of the bag and onto Tut's shoes, and he looked down and then put the pieces back into the bag, holding it at the bottom again and then trying to say about Claire again, but the woman said to please sit down, that somebody would be there to talk to him soon, and she bent her head down over her papers and seemed to forget that Tut was there, except looking at him once when she got up and walked away to where he couldn't see her.

That's when Tut got up and just walked out of the room and then through the bigger room and then out the front doors with the sign with the number in it above them and then started running again back to the shop, knowing the way easily, running straight up the 13 Street across the widest street and then to the wide street that ran to the river, holding the bag of food like a football, going past the small buildings where you heard noises during the day but nothing now and some other buildings that Tut didn't know what they were for and an apartment building only for old people and the gas station and the big office building lighted up but no one around it, and turning two blocks later on the 2 Street, and walking a block and a half past the houses and the shops for laundry and pet food and the fire station where he sometimes saw the shiny fire trucks but nothing but the closed door now, and finally getting to the wood shop.

The lights were out, and he looked through the window, and saw only dark.

He started to run again, and his bag of food fell from his

hand when he reached the wide street and turned, and the pieces came out the bottom again, tomato and bread, but this time Tut left them on the ground and kept running, sometimes walking to catch his breath, straight back toward the Broad Street, where he turned toward the City Hall and the yellow clock high up in the sky, and he started to run that way but passed the subway entrance and then thought and then turned back and crossed the street and went down the stinking steps and crawled along the bars until he reached where you go through but waited there sucking air, out of the sight of the person in the booth who took the money, until he heard the train rumbling in the tunnel louder and louder and then screeching and then showing, humming and hissing, and even when it stopped Tut waited for a little bit and then dashed under the thing that let you pass when you put money or a token in, and he jumped through the open doors just before they closed and the train pulled away with a bump.

People looked at him, then looked away.

He saw himself in the black window, his messed hair and dirty face, and he looked down at his dirty clothes and shoes, and he knew why they looked away and two women shook their heads.

Tut sat in one of the seats by himself and watched the window as the train rumbled and screeched through the dark tunnel and slowed into the blasting white lights of the stops, Race–Vine, City Hall, Walnut–Locust, the signs said, and then Lombard–South, where Tut got off the train and climbed the steps to the bars and the way out and then up more stinking puddled steps out into the cool night again, turning to Paul's house, remembering the way from the other night when Tut ran away from him and Claire . . . Claire in the shed, in the hole, Claire above his face when he woke up from the dream in the hole, Claire.

Tut ran to the 15 street, then the 16, then 17, going all the way past some bright fixed-up houses and some boarded-up houses and some lots filled with trash, past few people, all the way up to the 19 street, where Tut turned and tried to run some more but couldn't because of his legs and his chest and now his head spinning more and more, and so walking as fast as he could, the air as thick as syrup, to the street where the house was, turning up the street, hurrying past a tall old bent man walking very slow with two canes halfway up the street, sort of groaning, getting to the house and pushing the button, hearing the buzzer inside, then knocking when no one came to the door, then knocking some more but no one answering, then trying to hold onto the doorknob as the sidewalk came up on one side and went down on the other, which wasn't a sidewalk at all but a pool of black tar that Tut fell in and sunk through.

19

SO they really intend to kill me, Paul thought as he crossed the Walt Whitman Bridge in Whale's car, and he thought it again as they continued straight onto the Black Horse Pike instead of splitting left to take the Atlantic City Expressway, and then again as Gus turned left onto the thin road that led through the countryside to Hammonton. Each time Gus did not turn in another direction, away from the eventual dark road, Paul felt his fear rise, but also, beyond the mounting fear, an increasing anger. All along the ride, Paul felt compelled to pull out Rick's gun and force Whale through the threat of putting a bullet in the back of his head to give him the coins. But with Gus close by, Rick's instruction to keep Whale out of the city as long as possible, the certain retribution for taking the coins, and Paul's own need for privacy and the cover of darkness to execute his risky plan, he sat still, alternately fearful and seething, as the miles accumulated behind them.

When Paul stepped from the warm car with Gus out into the chill country air, he thought for a moment, Maybe they are only going to leave me here as a form of threat, teach me a lesson for meddling in their affairs. But it was two words from Gus that made Paul realize beyond a doubt that he had been brought to this back road in New Jersey to be murdered.

"This way," Gus had said as they walked away from the car and into the deeper darkness.

Which "way"? Paul thought, while walking over brittle grass at Gus's right side. They were surrounded by thick darkness, and behind them even the frail light reflecting from the glossy surfaces and windows of Whale's Buick faded after a short distance. If there were no lights to be seen, no darker shadow where a structure stood, where was Gus taking him? His "this way" had that empty sound of something expressed only to puncture tension or unease, a comment about the weather between strangers on an elevator, no direction or destination indicated by it.

"It's certainly dark out here," Paul said, voicing his own empty comment, though it was meant to distract Gus from Paul's slow drop behind the large man's pace while at the same time reaching to his back for the .22.

"Yeah."

Paul took a quick glance over his shoulder and saw that the darkness had completely swallowed the car. He sensed that the vanishing of the car into the darkness marked the optimum distance away from it in time and space that would spin Gus into motion.

"Not even a moon," Paul said, certain that the tremor in his voice would alert Gus.

But Paul had gripped the gun by now and faded to nearly a full step behind Gus, whose head just began to swivel to glance at Paul, now no longer at his side. Heart wild, Paul released the .22 from the pouch and brought it quickly from behind his back and up to poke Gus's turning cheek. Gus's head jerked away at the feel of the snout and he halted, startled.

"It's a gun," Paul said. "Throw yours on the ground."

Gus did not move.

"I'm not dying out here. If you want to, that's fine with me." Paul moved the barrel of the gun into Gus's ear. "Get rid of the gun."

"What gun?"

"I know you have one."

"You want it, you take it."

Paul jerked the gun out of Gus's ear and, leaving the cylinder pressed against the side of his head with the barrel pointed away, pulled the trigger. The noise was much louder than Paul expected. So close to Gus's head, the sound of the gunshot staggered him as his hand went up to cover his ear. Paul had also not expected the gun to recoil as sharply as it did, and the shock of it against his hand, with his already weakened nerves, caused his finger to twitch, and the gun fired again. Gus dropped to his knees and Paul thought he had shot him in the head.

"All right, all right," Gus moaned, holding his head. Paul saw with relief that it was only the pain in Gus's ear that had dropped him and not a bullet.

"Throw the gun in front of you." Paul stood behind Gus, the gun pointed at him, ready to shoot should Gus turn with his gun.

Gus reached into his jacket and tossed the gun, which thumped on the hard ground. Paul circled around to Gus's front, felt with his feet for the gun, found it, and picked it up. It was heavier and larger than the .22. Paul stretched out his arm and hurled the gun as hard as he could.

"Take off your jacket and spread it on the ground," Paul said.

"What?"

"Whatever's in your pockets, toss on the jacket."

Remaining on his knees, Gus slowly removed his jacket and placed it inside up on the grass, then reached into his pockets one at a time and tossed their contents onto the jacket.

"Pull the pockets out; I want to see them."

Gus reached into the pockets again and withdrew the cloth. "All right, tie your shoelaces together."

"Where'd you learn this, the Boy Scouts?"

"Do it."

Gus shifted from his knees to sit on the ground and undid the knots of his shoelaces, then tied them together.

"Take your belt off and tie it around your ankles."

"That's a good one." Gus undid the buckle, pulled the belt through the loops, and began to bind his ankles with it. "You want a square knot or a hangman's noose?"

"Cross your ankles and tie it tight."

When Gus finished, Paul squatted over the jacket; he took the several coins and threw them over his shoulder, followed the coins with Gus's keys, and then heaved the wallet in the opposite direction of his gun. Paul picked up the jacket, checked the pockets, and found a knife and comb; he threw the knife into the darkness and dropped the jacket to the ground.

"You didn't have to do all that," Gus said. "It's not like I can catch a taxi out here."

Paul wanted to make sure that even if Gus hitchhiked to the nearest town, he would not have the money to buy a bus ticket. Gus would have to be very lucky to find the wallet by groping on hands and knees in the dark for it. Paul could simply have taken the wallet, but that felt too much like theft to him. At the very least, Gus would have to call somebody collect to pick him up. There was also the chance that Gus would flag someone down, assault them, and steal the car; Gus would then drive around looking for Whale. Paul would still have enough time to reach Philadelphia before them.

"One last thing," Paul said. "Where are the coins?"

"*You* want the coins now?"

"Does Whale still have them?"

"Ask him."

"Were you the one who cut my brakes?"

"What? What brakes?"

"On my car three years ago."

"If I did, you think I'd tell you?"

Paul swung the gun and struck Gus in the jaw with it, knocking him onto his back. Fante sprung to the big man before he could move and jammed the gun under his chin.

"The bullet will come up through your tongue, enter the roof of your mouth, and come out the top of your head. Who cut the brakes?"

"Benny. Benny did it."

"Thank you."

Paul left Gus flat on the ground and hurried toward the road. Shortly later, he made out the silvery light that marked the windows and chrome of Whale's car.

"Drive," Paul said from the back seat of the car, pressing the gun into Whale's face.

"Hey, watch it. Watch it!" Whale jerked his head back away from the gun, but Paul kept it pointed at him.

"Drive or you're dead." Paul's heart pounded rapidly and his throat quivered.

"Okay, okay." Whale slid over to the driver's side and started the car. He hooked the Buick sharply back onto the road and drove through the darkness.

"Turn on the headlights."

"Somebody might see us."

"It's your car they'll see. Turn them on."

Whale touched a switch and the headlights instantly carved sharp arms of light from the country darkness. Paul sat back in the middle of the seat, the gun on his knee; he was prepared to shoot Whale if necessary, even as he drove. Whale glanced nervously at Paul in the rearview mirror every few seconds, as though wanting to catch the exact moment Paul pulled the trigger.

"I heard two shots back there," Whale said after a short time. "Tell me you didn't shoot Gus."

Paul met Whale's tiny eyes in the mirror. "You brought him out here to kill me."

"No, we were just going to rob you, leave you out here."

"That's not what Benny thought."

"You've been talking to Benny?"

"I walked in my house last night and there he was; he had broken in. He told me that if I wanted Claire released, I would have to pay him the coins or what they're worth. This was after you called to set up the meeting between him and me."

"And I guess he said he didn't know about a New Jersey meeting and that I never talked to him."

"That's right, and that I'd be coming here to be killed."

"What does he know? I was only trying to make a buck out here."

"More than a buck. You were going to take my ten thousand *and* you wanted to keep the coins. I know you took them. Benny showed me a coin he said you gave to someone he knew."

"The hooker. I was feeling rich at the time."

"Where are they now?"

"My house. You want 'em, they're yours. You'd be doing me a favor."

"Why? Because of who they belonged to?"

"You know that, too?"

"Henry Lawrence told me that Benny took the coins from somebody named Victor Notte."

"Notte's practically my boss's brother. They're like this." Whale raised his hand with the first two fingers crossed. "If Maglio knew I wound up with the coins, I'd be dead."

"You mean, you were going to kill me because you were afraid Maglio would somehow find out from me that you had the coins?"

"It would work that way if I wanted to cover all my bases to protect myself. But we were only going to take your money, believe me."

"Was Henry Lawrence one of the bases?"

"What happened to him?"

"You tell me." Paul looked steadily at Whale in the mirror.

"I don't even know him."

"Did you set up this whole thing?"

243

"Did I steal from Victor Notte, Maglio's best friend? Do I look like an idiot?"

"You and Benny weren't working together?"

"I wouldn't partner with that dope for a million dollars."

They drove without speaking through the darkness.

"All right, stop the car," Paul said at a spot in the road as dark as where Gus had stopped earlier, without any electric light anywhere visible.

Whale looked at Paul in the rearview mirror. "Here? What're you going to do?"

"Turn off the lights and pull over."

"Don't make me do that."

"Stop the car."

"Come on, we can work something out, we—"

Paul fired a shot into the back of the passenger seat, causing Whale to jump and swerve the car. The shock nearly threw the gun from Paul's hand, and the loud noise hurt his ears. "Pull over."

"All right! Don't get crazy." Whale jammed a finger in his ear and slowed the car. "You made me deaf. And look, you put a hole in the glove compartment. You mighta even shot the engine."

Paul smelled the cordite, and he barely heard Whale above the ringing in his head. "Get out," Paul said as the car stopped.

"You don't have to shoot me."

"You're disgusting. Why I didn't kill you three years ago, I don't know."

"You're not a killer, that's why."

Paul leaned slightly forward in the dark car and pushed the barrel of the gun into the back of Whale's neck. "Tell that to Gus."

Paul allowed Whale to believe that he killed Gus because to say otherwise, Paul thought, would have made Whale think he was safe from harm; that would cause Paul to lose an edge he needed to manage Whale.

After walking Whale from the car a distance into a grassless

244

field, Paul had him empty his pockets as he had done with Gus, throwing his keys and wallet far away, and checked him for a gun. Whale did not complain or comment, except to ask that Paul not take the cigars and the matches from Whale's jacket pocket. Paul left the cigars where they sat and had Whale sit on the ground.

"You didn't kill Gus, did you?"

Paul said nothing.

"I know because you're not killing me. You wouldn't have left me the cigars if you were."

Paul said, "How do you live with yourself?"

"Huh?"

"Doing what you do, hurting people, blood on your hands."

"It ain't hard."

"Is it true that Benny cut the brake line of my car that time?"

"He tell you that?"

"Gus told me."

"You work Gus over some back there?"

"I want to know the truth."

"Benny's a wrench in the gears," Whale said. "Yeah, he did it, trying to be cute. He wasn't supposed to go that far and cut your brakes." Whale clamped a cigar in his mouth. "You gonna take care of him now?"

Paul hesitated a moment. "Yes." And he meant it.

"Well, good luck."

Without speaking further, Paul hurried back to the car. He drove quickly away on the dark road, meandered back to the road they had turned onto from the Black Horse Pike, and followed the signs to Hammonton. Before reaching the town, he turned toward the Atlantic City Expressway and soon rushed at sixty-five miles per hour toward Philadelphia.

He did not notice the ascending needle of the temperature gauge until a few miles before the Walt Whitman Bridge, and then, a minute later, could not miss it as a red light within the gauge blinked on. Steam began to seep from beneath the hood as Paul crossed the bridge, and by the time he reached the tolls, with the needle of the temperature gauge as high as it could go, steam billowed from the engine.

"You gonna make it?" the toll operator asked. "Or you want me to flag you to the side?"

"I'm taking the Seventh Street exit."

"Okay. Hope you make it."

The Seventh Street exit branched from the highway about a hundred yards from the tolls and Paul sped toward it, trailing a thick tail of steam, and with the engine beginning to sputter. The bullet he had fired in the car to scare Whale must have nicked a part of the engine, as Whale had feared—the heater, some hose, or the radiator itself—and the coolant had slowly leaked out. Paul was thankful that the leak had been slow enough to allow the car to reach Philadelphia, but now, ten minutes before eight o'clock, Bean's deadline, the engine seized and Paul coasted down the exit ramp. The car had enough momentum for Paul to ease it onto Seventh Street and out of the way of traffic. He jumped from the car and ran toward Broad Street, hoping to flag down a taxi or, if necessary, take the subway at Oregon Avenue. But even if the train came as soon as Paul reached the platform, he would still have to run the five blocks to his house. He would not reach it by eight.

Paul reached Broad at five minutes of. Looking north and south, he saw no taxis. A bus chugged toward him, but he did not consider taking it; he could run the several blocks to Oregon Avenue faster, and did so, reaching the wide street as the bus lumbered up just behind him. Paul gave one final look up and down Broad Street for a taxi, as well as east and west on Oregon; he spotted none, hurried to the subway entrance, and rushed down the stairs.

On the platform in the uniform fluorescent light, Paul was alone, and the only sounds, instead of the distant rumble from the tunnel that he had hoped to meet, were the traffic noises from the street above and the slow gurgle of water from somewhere. He paced up and down the platform, the creo-

246

sote smell of the track ties sharp in his nostrils, and peered into the tunnel for signs of the train—a splatter of blue sparks, the cyclopic headlight—but saw nothing.

It was six minutes after eight. As he paced, his hands tightening and untightening, he felt the gun thump against his spine, and for a moment considered quitting the subway and rushing back up the stairs and out to the street, where he'd jump into some stranger's car at a red light and force him with the gun to drive Paul home. But he immediately pictured the terror on the person's face and shoved the idea from his mind.

At eleven after eight, Paul heard the low rumble from within the tunnel, but the sound came from the wrong direction, north. He went to that side and watched the front of the train enlarge, sparks bursting from the darkness beneath its wheels. Screeching and shuddering, the air brakes hissing, the train strained against the motion of its tremendous weight and came to a stop in front of Paul. Five or six passengers emerged, pallid and lethargic, as though made ill by the damp, cryptlike air of the tunnel, a place where Paul imagined cholera and anthrax would flourish. The people dragged themselves up the stairs as something in the bowels of the train thumped; the train lurched and rolled away, the air collapsing in behind it as the last car receded, squeezing sparks from the rails. Before turning away, Paul noticed the face of a child in the window of the back door; she waved as the train shrank.

At seventeen after eight, Paul's train appeared in the tunnel, shoving air before it, and a half minute later it shuddered to a halt, the doors slid open, and Paul stepped onto a car with only three passengers inside. The train lurched into motion soon after and went pounding and rocking through the tunnel, intermittent lights attached to the tunnel walls streaking past the windows, the mechanisms of power humming and vibrating beneath Paul's feet. He did not sit down, too agitated now to be at rest.

At nineteen after eight, the train pulled into the Snyder

Avenue station; at twenty-two after, it arrived at the Tasker–Morris stop. Elsworth–Federal took another minute, but the train sat at the stop longer than it usually did. Paul leaned out and looked toward the front of the train, and saw a man conferring with the engineer.

"Hey, what's the holdup?" Paul shouted.

The men glanced down the length of the train at him with that mild annoyance shown to disruptive crazy people, then went back to talking.

"Hey! How long are you going to sit here?"

The men shook their heads and chuckled a bit.

"Come on, Goddamn it, I'm in a hurry!"

The men did not even look at Paul this time, but they seemed to be saying their parting words, and the man on the platform stepped back from the train and the engineer ducked into his compartment. The doors slid shut, and soon the train battered through the tunnel darkness for another short time and finally pulled into Lombard–South at eight-twenty-six, with Paul close to the sliding doors. He sprang from the train as the doors opened and ran up the steps to the mid-level, through the revolving bars and then up the reeking steps to the street. Paul ran up South Street, past the shops, the apartments, the food places, the laundromat, the vacant buildings, the defunct Royal Theater, the parking building for the Graduate Hospital, the hospital itself, turning at the new diagnostic center and running south on Nineteenth the several blocks to his street, turning there and then up, reaching the house at eight-thirty-one. As Paul fumbled for his keys on his doorstep, his breathing short and fast from the run, he heard his name, recognizing Mr. Mitchell's voice.

Half-turning, the key eluding his fingers, Paul said, "I'm in a big hurry, Mr. Mitchell. I'll talk to you later."

"Wait—"

Paul turned from the door, the key now in the lock, and saw Mr. Mitchell on his front step, waving him over. "It's very important, Mr. Mitchell, I can't now." Paul turned the key in

248

the lock and, turning the doorknob, shoved open the door and hurried to the telephone.

The red light on the answering machine blinked and Paul pressed the button to hear the messages.

"It's eight o'clock on the button," Benny Bean had said. "Okay, I'll assume maybe you're in the bathroom, you can't get to the phone." The beep sounded to end the message and another came on: "My watch says ten after. All right, maybe your car broke down somewhere, you're not even home yet. You should allow for these inconveniences. I'll be nice and try again." That message ended with a beep and a third began. "Now I'm thinking," Benny's voice said, "Is this guy screwing me or what? Did he cut a deal with that fat fuck Whale? Hey! Where the fuck are you? Look, I'll call once more and you better be there." He said he made the last call at eight-thirty; it was now eight-thirty-four. "All right, motherfucker, she dies. The bitch dies." No other messages followed the loud click.

Paul's face burned as his jugulars throbbed. He quickly telephoned Rick but no one answered.

The doorbell rang. Thinking Bean had come to the house, Paul hurried to the door, with no idea what he would say about not having the coins or the money, except to tell him that Rick was due at the house any moment with the coins. If Bean would not accept that, Paul was prepared to point his gun at Bean's heart and attempt to force Bean to take him to Claire.

It was Mr. Mitchell, standing on the sidewalk in front of Paul's door.

"Mr. Mitchell, I'm sorry, I—"

"There's somebody come for you."

Paul went rigid for a moment. Bean?

"He's in my living room. Go on over."

Paul crossed the street and, pulling open the storm door, walked into the house, smelling of chicken soup, and dark except for the light from the kitchen and a lamp at the end of the sofa, where Mrs. Mitchell stood. Arms folded across her midriff, she watched Paul come in, then looked to the sofa.

Paul's eyes followed. "Tut."

20

"WHO do these people think they are, fucking with me?" Benny said out loud as he slammed down the phone and then kicked the table it sat on. The leg broke, making the phone and the lamp topple to the floor, where Benny kicked both.

First Lawrence, then Whale, now this bastard Fante, they think they can just walk all over you. Benny slugged a closet door, then pounded the refrigerator as he entered the kitchen.

"But not no more!" Benny went into the bedroom and took his Beretta from the dresser. He strapped it on and then went to his closet, removed the panel on the inside wall, and cleaned out the hiding place, taking all his cash and drugs. He didn't figure to come back for a while, because he was going to blow people away. Benny swallowed two tabs of Dexedrine, then sucked a few fingers of coke up his nose before putting the drugs in a duffle bag and throwing some shirts and pants and other clothes on top of them.

"Not no more!"

First he gave the street a look before leaving the house, just in case, because you never knew when somebody got it into their head to hammer you. Nothing looked funny. He jumped off the step and walked fast to the car, tossing the duffle bag into the back seat, where it looked more innocent to a cop than if he saw it in the trunk. Besides, he was going to have to put the chick in there for the drive to Jersey and didn't want her bleeding on the bag. Too bad he couldn't just leave her, but then the body would be Selligrini's problem. Benny couldn't screw Selli like these pricks had screwed him.

The car started right up, and Benny worked his way out of the parking spot and drove the six or whatever blocks to Whale's house. The fat guy still owed him for the boat job. First, Benny would talk to Whale, be professional, say, Now the coins are mine and you took them and I want them back so there won't be any bad blood between us. But if Whale gave him a rough time, well, then Benny would just have to take out his gun and do what he had to do. Maybe just shoot him in the knee to get him talking, tell where he had the coins. And if he didn't have the coins, take whatever money he had, fuck the consequences. And if Gus was there, well, Benny wouldn't know what to do about that, unless he knew for sure that Gus had taken the coins from Lawrence. Which, if he did, he had to die, too, because those coins were Benny's biggest score, his ticket for a nice ride for a while, and they had been stolen from him by fuckers.

Benny parked around the corner from Whale's house and zipped up his jacket to hide his gun before leaving the car. But what if Whale wasn't in, or nobody was home? That might be better, now that he thought about it, unless he couldn't find the coins in the house. Benny went into his trunk and took out his pry bar, large screwdriver, and glass cutter, because the one time he was there he remembered Whale had a front door that, if you got through the glass, you could just reach in and turn the door locks from the inside. A cinch.

But after Benny knocked, a woman came to the door, who

he figured was Whale's wife, a woman about fifty and a lot smaller than Whale.

"Freddie in? I'm a friend of his. Sal," a name Bean liked.

"He's not here."

"Where is he?"

"I don't know."

"When's he coming home?"

"I don't know. But if you see him, tell him to come home right away. Tell him I left bingo early because I wasn't feeling good, and I came home to trouble."

Benny noticed something was bothering this woman, something was on her mind. "What kind of trouble? He'll want to know."

"You're one of the guys?"

"Yeah. I'm Gus's cousin," Benny lied.

"Gus? I like Gus."

"He'll want to know, too. About the trouble."

This woman was daffy, Benny thought, a loony. Another second of this and Benny was just going to slam into her and shove her back into the house.

"We were robbed," she said.

"Robbed?"

"They came in the back. Want to see? Go ahead, look."

She couldn't step aside fast enough and when Benny walked in he bumped her and nearly knocked her off her feet. Benny rushed through the living room, dining room, straight to the kitchen where he saw, on the table, nice and neat, a section of cracked windowpane with two-inch masking tape holding it together. Benny knew it came from the back door before he looked and saw the neat cutout in the glass panel. Jeez, it was a thirty-second bust-in, tops; a high school kid could've done it. Look at that security; it was just a doorknob with a standard twist lock and above it a deadbolt lock with a knob and not a key to drop the bolt. Not too bright. But the tape to keep the glass from making noise was a professional touch; it wasn't a kid just banging into houses, seeing what he could get.

"He's going to be mad at me, Sal," Whale's wife said from behind him.

Benny spun around. "What did they take!"

"I don't know."

"The coins?"

"What?"

"Did they take the coins?"

"What coins?"

"You don't know about the coins?"

"No. I—"

"They just broke in for the fun of it?"

"I don't—" She paused. "Are you sure you're a friend of Freddie's?"

"Fuck Freddie." Benny pulled out his Beretta and pointed at Whale's wife. "Stop chirping bullshit. What did they take?"

"I said I didn't know." She squeezed the fingers of her hand with the other, nervous and scared.

"You don't know what's missing from your own house?"

"Nothing of mine is gone. Please—"

"Nothing of yours, huh? What about Whale's? The coins?"

"I said I—"

"Where are they!"

"There was something in Freddie's drawer that isn't there now."

"Whataya mean 'something'?"

"I don't touch his things, so I don't know. I only saw it when I put away the laundry, and now it's not there. A box."

That's when he slugged her, one shot to the stomach, which was enough to drop her. Then Benny took the stairs by twos and went into the front bedroom, where the closet doors and the dresser drawers had been left open, as if Whale's wife wanted her husband to see exactly what had been done by the burglar. Benny rifled all the drawers and the closets, and flipped up the mattress and then the boxspring to look under the bed. Nothing but dust. He went to the other rooms, ransacked those, but found nothing. One last try, he tore apart the linen closet in the bathroom, shoving towels and washcloths and a hundred drugstore things like shampoo, cough medicine, stomach tablets and hemorrhoid creams onto the floor—but not finding the coins.

"Son of a bitch bastard!"

When Benny returned downstairs, Mrs. Whale was crawling up from the floor and reaching for the dining room telephone. She had just grabbed the phone and sat down in a chair when Benny lifted his arm and shot her. The receiver flew into the air as she slammed back against the wall, and the second shot, catching her on the rebound, knocked her sideways out of the chair and onto the floor.

Then Benny left the house to go kill the bitch and the kid in the shed.

21

"WE found him on your front step," Mrs. Mitchell said to Paul. "Passed out."

"He was a mess," her husband said behind Paul. "All dirty like he was doing I don't know what. We asked him why he was knocking on your door but he didn't answer. He didn't answer anything. Do you know him?"

Paul nodded, looking down on Tut, lying on the sofa with a blanket up to his chest, face and hands recently scrubbed, and wearing a white T-shirt twice his size that must have belonged to Mr. Mitchell. Tut gazed up at Paul but as though seeing little more than his own reflection.

"He was fevered when we brought him in," Mrs. Mitchell said. "His teeth were chattering. I made him some chicken soup, which I think did some good."

Paul knelt down beside the boy and touched his flushed cheek. "Tut?" His eyes blinked and focused. "Tut, is Claire safe, too? Just nod or shake your head. It's very important."

Paul did not know how Tut had gotten away from Bean, and did not care at the moment. He thought only that if Tut had gotten free so had Claire, and hoped that Tut would somehow be able to communicate that one way or the other. If she had not escaped, Paul had no idea what he would do, except to finally call the police. They had to be better than Paul at finding missing persons, and the police would have known how to handle someone like Bean and threats to kill Claire. Surely they had experience with that. But if he had called the police, the questions they would ask would lead back to Paul's involvement with Whale and all the misery surrounding it. Paul's errors would then come to light. So be it, they would come to light. He had been a fool and a coward to concern himself with keeping them hidden.

"Is Claire safe, Tut?"

Tut's head turned sharply toward Paul, and his hand gripped Paul's wrist. His mouth opened and closed and opened, as though gasping, and from deep in his throat he made a sound, and then another.

"Ca-laire," he said.

Paul's chest fluttered at the sound of the boy's voice.

"Ca-laire . . . I . . ."

"Yes, Tut, is she safe?"

Tut shook his head no.

"Then show me where she is, Tut. Take me there."

The boy's eyes widened; he looked frightened.

"What's going on, Paul?" Mrs. Mitchell said behind him.

"I'll explain later. Tut?"

Tut looked from Paul to Mrs. Mitchell, glanced at Mr. Mitchell, then back to Paul, as though trying to decide whether to stay with the old couple or go with Paul. He held Paul's eyes, seeming to search for a meaning for himself, something that would make whatever he did right.

With fear remaining in his face, Tut released Paul's wrist and sat up, dropping his feet from the sofa and removing the blanket from himself. He wore clean white socks, also plainly Mr. Mitchell's. His wife went across the room and returned with Tut's dilapidated shoes, handing them to him. He hesitated for some moments at the sight of the clean socks, bright white against the grimy, torn shoes, before pulling them on. Tut stood without tying the laces, but immediately swayed. Paul gripped Tut's bony shoulder for several moments to steady him. The boy then took Paul's hand and led him a little unsteadily toward the door.

"Thanks for what you've done," Paul said as he and Tut started out.

"You take care," the Mitchells said.

Paul and the boy hurried across the street to the pickup truck and jumped in. The Mitchells watched from their front step as Paul gunned the engine. But as Paul began to pull from the parking space, he saw his uncle Rick in the rearview mirror half-running down the sidewalk, waving one hand and carrying something in the other. Paul rolled down the window.

"Get in," he said as his uncle came up.

Tut slid sideways toward Paul as Rick hurried around the front of the truck, opened the door, and joined them, placing a small box on his knees. The instant Rick closed the door, Paul screeched out of the parking spot and sped down the street.

"I have the coins," Rick said between breaths and patting the box in his lap. "I hope it's not too late."

The coins meant nothing to Paul, nor was he curious about how Rick had gotten them; other matters were more pressing at the moment. "Bean left a message on my machine saying he was going to kill Claire."

"Is that where we're going?"

"Yes. Okay, Tut, straight, left, or right, that's all you have to tell me. Just point, okay?"

Tut pointed straight ahead across Nineteenth Street as they slowed for it.

"He knows where Claire is?" Rick asked.

"Yes. He escaped the place."

Paul crossed Nineteenth Street and sped to Eighteenth,

meeting a block of townhouses that prevented him from continuing straight. He swung left. At Bainbridge, Paul asked, "Straight or right?"

Tut pointed right.

Paul turned and raced toward Seventeenth Street. "Tut, do I keep going until I reach the river?" That would be Spruce Street and Delaware Avenue. "Or do I turn again somewhere?"

"River," Tut said.

Paul turned to the boy briefly and put his hand on Tut's head, happy for both of them that he had spoken. "Then what, left?"

Tut nodded.

Paul sped toward Broad Street, barely stopping at the stop signs. It was as though he could sense the direction, could feel Claire and would only have to pay attention to a particular vibration in his head to find her.

"I waited for your call until about twenty after eight," Rick said, "then I figured something happened. I called you a few times but the line was busy."

"Bean left four messages on the machine."

"That explains the busy signal."

They halted for the light at Broad Street, though Paul would have crossed it had traffic allowed. He pounded the steering wheel, but it made Tut jump, and he stopped. Paul crept up beyond the parked cars so that he could see the oncoming traffic running north and south, but it was uniformly too thick to cross the street before the light changed. "Damn, damn, damn," he muttered.

"I made some calls between calling you, but Whale and Gus weren't around anywhere," Rick said.

"They're still in New Jersey."

"So they did take you there? What happened?"

"Let me tell you later."

The light changed to green, Paul popped the clutch, and his tires screeched as he rushed across the wide street. Bean's last call came at eight-thirty, Paul thought, and if he phoned from South Philadelphia that would give both of them roughly the same amount of time to reach Spruce Street and Delaware Avenue. Paul lived closer, but he had been called into the Mitchell house for Tut; to get an edge in time, Paul hoped that Bean had been slowed as well. If not, Bean would arrive at the place he kept Claire before Paul. Paul could not think beyond that.

"When I didn't get your call and couldn't get a hold of you, I figured I'd come to your house," Rick said.

"I'm glad you did."

"But now what?"

"I don't know."

Paul rushed from stop sign to stop sign on Bainbridge Street until Eleventh, where he turned left against the red light and sped to South, then to Lombard, then to Pine Street, where he hooked the screeching truck right because the lights were sequenced on Pine and, catching the greens, Paul could make better time to Delaware Avenue. Paul picked up the green-light sequence immediately at Tenth, and was even luckier to find himself behind a taxicab, which seemed part of the emergency and eager to run interference. Paul chased the taxicab past the antique shops and the townhouses all the way to the stop sign at Second Street and Headhouse Square without slowing for a single red light. The taxi turned onto Second and Paul rushed to Front, then left toward Spruce, turning sharply onto the Belgium block that paved the street there, throwing Tut against his shoulder. The truck rumbled over the lumpy street the short distance to Delaware Avenue and the river beyond it.

"Left, Tut?" Paul asked to make sure.

"Left."

Turning left, north, toward Northern Liberties, Fishtown, and the old Industrial Corridor, made sense. There were countless deserted pockets in those parts of the city, abandoned factories, toxic waste dumps, overgrown lots. Hiding someone there would be much easier, far less conspicuous, than in any other part of the city.

The traffic light at Delaware Avenue stopped Paul. He looked right and left at the oncoming traffic and cursed; it was not as thick as on Broad Street earlier, but it kept him from crossing.

"I know you're thinking about ignoring the light," Rick said, "but if we get stopped by the cops, we'll be held up a while."

"Do you see any?" Paul asked, looking in the rearview mirror as well as on the road and the parking areas of Penn's Landing.

"No, but—"

"Neither do I." Paul moved as far out into the roadway as possible without getting hit by oncoming vehicles. As soon as a break opened in the traffic, he floored the gas pedal and shot across to the other side of Delaware Avenue, pausing only for a horn-blowing car speeding by in the direction Paul meant to take. Then he rammed the truck into gear. In a few seconds, he was driving at fifty miles an hour over a road cut here and there by railroad tracks, ruts, and potholes. The truck bounced severely, and all three of them were jostled wildly in the cab.

"Straight, Tut?" Paul asked as he neared the incinerator at Spring Garden Street.

"Straight."

"Good boy."

Tut looked at him a moment, then turned to the windshield again, hands squeezing his knees.

"You have the gun?" Rick asked.

Having forgotten it until now, Paul felt the gun against his spine in the pouch of his jacket. He nodded as they bounced and joggled over the gully in front of the incinerator gates and then bounced again as they drove over railroad tracks a short distance farther before the street arced right and ran between odd structures whose function, even in daylight, Paul could not determine.

"Because we should plan on what we're going to do when we get there," Rick said.

"Just give him the coins."

"It might not be that simple."

"That's all he wants."

"That's all he *did* want. We don't know what he's thinking now."

"I don't see how we can do anything but play it by ear."

"You're right, but it's his turf. We have to expect that—"

"Don't say it."

"I wasn't going to say it."

"Don't think it."

Rick turned to the window in the direction of the river, showing intermittently through the breaks in the odd buildings.

"I appreciate what you've done," Paul said.

"Don't mention it."

"If she's dead, I—"

"She won't be."

Tut pointed suddenly. "Turn!"

They had come to Columbia Avenue. Paul braked hard, downshifting at the same time, and turned the truck at a speed so high he felt the tires on the left side leave the road. For several moments, he thought the truck would continue rising on the driver's side and they'd flip over, but the wheels came down with a screech and they sped away from the river. From there, Tut leaned forward, hands gripping the dashboard, his face near the windshield, telling Paul to turn right, left, or to go straight. He led them first to American Street, bordered on either side by the dark hulks of defunct factories or junkyards dimly lit, and then onto branching streets sided by dilapidated housing or squat buildings behind tall fences topped with razor wire or lots strewn with debris, and then onto smaller streets, taking Paul and Rick deeper into a labyrinth of decay. The extreme poor lived here, Paul thought, people with Third World lives, poverty like part of their genetic makeup, thirteen-year-old mothers, ninth-grade dropouts, ten people living in crumbling two-bedroom houses, the houses vermin-plagued, their plumbing faulty, roofs leaking, houses where children died in fires because there was no smoke alarm. This area had its own urban geology, the decay so complete and uniform it seemed a natural, physical phenomenon, the buildings, cars, sidewalks, and streets succumbing to forces of erosion—and the people, too, steadily wearing away. In the warm summer days, they would crowd their stoops or lean shouting out windows or shoot craps against a wall or soak themselves in the powerful gush of fire hydrants. Tonight, few people were on the street, and still fewer the deeper Tut brought Paul and Rick into the area, and eventually none, as though he and Rick and Tut were headed toward a core of decay too fearsome for human flesh. Paul realized that this was where Tut lived, this was his neighborhood; Tut knew it too well for it not to be. Paul's heart sank at the thought.

"Stop," Tut said.

He pointed to what appeared to be a junkyard. Mounds of metal towered above the surrounding fence, some of it glinting in the distant lamplight.

"Is Claire in there?" Paul asked, looking beyond the fence, just making out a small, squat building, a single bulb attached to it near the roof.

Tut nodded, the fear back full in his face.

Paul turned off the ignition. "Okay, let's go."

"Wait," Rick said, "we can't just—"

"There's no time," Paul said, leaving the truck and hurrying to the fence. Through a break in the mounds, he spotted a gate on the other side of the yard and ran toward it, broken glass crunching under his shoes. Turning the corner of the fencing, Paul saw that the wings of the gate were parted. He ran faster toward the opening and slipped through, his hip jangling a chain and lock looped through the poles of the gate. He smelled rust and engine oil as he crossed the open area between the piles of metal and the shed. Rick called from behind him, but Paul continued to the shed, spotting the door in the shadow opposite a wall of fenders.

"Claire?" he called, reaching the door.

There was no answer. The door stood slightly open, the lock in the hasp attached to its surface unlocked; a strip of light came from a crack where the door did not meet the frame.

"Claire?"

Paul shoved against the door and entered the shed as Rick showed in the corner of his eye. A single lightbulb hung in the ceiling, throwing thick shadows. Paul saw a metal desk nearly in the middle of the room, shelves, a tire, boxes, and, along the far wall, a heap of dirt with a hole beside it—but no Claire. Paul looked in the hole. Empty.

"So?" It was Rick, stepping into the shed.

"Nothing." Paul gestured to the hole.

Rick came around to the other side of the desk and looked at the hole and the heaps of dirt. "I noticed a hole on the other side, but I didn't know it went through to here. You think she got out?"

"I hope so. Tut did."

"You have to admire them for what this had to take."

Paul nodded.

"If she's free, it's over," Rick said.

"If she's not free?"

Rick looked at the ground. "He could've taken her."

Paul put his hand to his forehead and squeezed. Not that, he thought. Not the blind, cramped, suffocating ride in the trunk, where Bean would surely put her, each shock of the road jarring her shoulder and hip, the smell of exhaust and tire rubber thick and sickening, the complete not knowing of where he was taking her, but knowing now it was to die—not that, please.

"But Tut got out, you said, so maybe she—"

"Where is Tut?" Paul asked, looking over Rick's shoulder.

Rick turned. "I thought he was right behind me."

"Tut!" Paul called. He took one step toward the door before stopping at the sound of footsteps from outside.

Tut showed first, walking stiffly, his hands straight down at his sides, shoulders hunched, both terror and pain in his face.

He lurched into the shed, sounds of hurt and fear coming from his throat.

Paul began to speak and then he saw him, Bean, emerge from the darkness, one hand gripping Tut's hair, the other holding a gun behind the boy's ear.

"Here he is." Bean smiled cruelly.

"Let him go," Paul said.

"I went through this routine the other day with your girlfriend, and I did let him go. 'Course, I locked him in here. But it seems like he escaped, and the beautiful Miss Claire, too. Imagine how pissed I was to see that. I come in and—fuckin' Houdini!—she's nowhere. I'm freaking the fuck out, going nuts, but what happens? I hear a truck pull up and then I see the cavalry coming. Rick, how are you? So you got involved too. This is turning into a fuckin' Broadway production."

"Let the kid go, Benny."

"This is my insurance policy. I can't let him go."

"We have the coins."

"So you did that beautiful job at Whale's. I didn't know you were in the business."

"I'm not."

"You coulda fooled me, it looked so professional. Now, put the coins on the desk."

Rick placed the box on top of the desk. "All right, you got what you wanted. Let the kid go."

"I'm sorry, I still need the kid."

"You got the coins," Rick said. "All the rest is bullshit."

Paul began to slowly reach behind his back for the gun.

"Think about it," Bean said. "It's smart that I get out of town for a while, which, to do, I need some time and not no fucking cops coming after me or, worse, guys wanting to sit me on a meat hook. Yowl. So, I don't need you two heroes talking to anybody for a while. Locking you in here won't be enough because there's a tunnel now. I need the kid so you won't talk when you get out. It's that—hey, you fuck!" Bean jerked the gun from Tut's head and pointed it at Paul's face. "I shoulda thought you would bring something. You got a piece there behind your back, hero? Rick, you believe this guy? He was about to pull a piece on me. Drop it, wiseass."

Paul took the gun from behind his back and let it fall to the earth floor.

"What is that, a twenty-two?" Bean laughed. "What were you going to do with it, shoot rats? You didn't really think you could get a clean shot at me, didja?"

"There's no need to take the boy," Paul said.

"Don't worry, I won't have him long. I'll even do you a favor. I'll put him on a bus back here from the state I wind up in. How's that?"

"Don't take him."

"You think I want to? You think I need the hassle? I got no choice. We were anywhere else, I'd think seriously about offing all of you and not have to worry about talk, but this place belongs to a friend of mine and I couldn't have him coming back from his vacation and finding dead bodies in here. So feel lucky." Bean looked at Paul. "All right, you, move away from the desk." He cocked his head to the side.

Paul backed away from the desk, slowly, keeping his eyes fixed on Bean.

"All right, Rick, the coins," Bean said.

Rick took the box from the desk and walked toward Bean.

"That's close enough. Stretch out your arm."

Rick stopped several feet from Bean and lifted the box at arm's length. Bean brought Tut and himself a few steps forward and grabbed the box, his gun hand holding Tut by the back of the shirt. He stepped quickly back to the doorway, the gun pointed at Rick and Paul now, and brought the box into his armpit, where he clamped it against his ribs.

Bean said, "I don't have to tell you if you make a move I'll drop you. So don't try anything." Bean took another step backwards toward the door. One more and he would be out of the shed.

"Come on, Benny, leave the kid," Rick said.

"I told you I can't do that." Bean glanced to his side to see the doorway before stepping backwards through it. "Now, I'll be locking the door when I get outside, so I get some head start if you guys decide to come after me, by yourselfs or with the cops. I hope you're not whammy about small spaces like me." He laughed a little. "See ya."

Bean took the final step back. Half in and half out of the shed, he began to turn. But as if it were part of the same motion, he shuddered at a noise Paul could not identify and immediately lurched back in. The box fell from Bean's underarm. He began to raise the gun, though not toward Paul or Rick but toward the darkness beyond the door. Something blurred shot from the darkness and struck Bean on the wrist with the same sound as moments before. He made a noise and the gun fell from his hand. Bean let go of Tut and started after the gun, but as he stooped, the blur came again and struck Bean on the back of the head. That's when Paul rushed.

He drove his shoulder into Bean's ribs and knocked him through the doorway and onto his back, landing on top of him but knocking the wind from himself. Bean easily shoved Paul to the side and began to get up. But the blur came again and struck Bean on the chest. From the ground, Paul followed the object as it rose and fell again, catching Bean in the shoulder as he rolled away and gathered his arms and legs beneath himself as he made to stand and run. Paul scrambled and dove for Bean's leg, catching him by the ankle. But Bean kicked back and caught Paul in the cheek, stunning him enough to loosen his grip. Bean jerked his foot free and tried again to get to his feet and run before getting struck another time by the thing swung in the darkness. He managed to stand and start away, but Paul sprang up and tackled Bean before he ran four steps. They went down together, pitching into the outer rim of light from the bulb on the outside of the shed.

Bean threw back an elbow that caught Paul above the temple, separating them. He scrambled to his feet first and kicked at Paul's face as Paul came up from the ground. The boot grazed Paul's cheek; then Bean threw a long looping punch at Paul's head. Paul saw the punch the moment Bean threw it and easily ducked it. As Bean's fist sailed over his head, Paul shifted to the side and drove his own fist upward into Bean's stomach. Bean went "Oof!" and bent sharply over at the middle. As his head shot down, Paul came around with a downward arcing left hook that caught Bean on the ear, spinning him around. Bean righted himself, and threw a wild punch. Paul slipped that one easily, too, and countered with two left jabs, a right, then a left hook, all to Bean's face, all solid punches.

Paul continued to knock Bean around the small space of the junkyard, into and out of the weak half circle of light, against clattering piles of steel and iron, hammering him in the stomach, the ribs, the eyes, the already torn lips and bloodied nose, the ears, steadying Bean when his legs began to wobble, slugging again, Paul outside of himself now, beyond fury, beyond sense, painless and heartless both, his rage pure and unconscious. He would have killed Bean with his bare hands and felt neither satisfaction nor remorse over it. It was Tut who stopped him.

He had not heard the voices of Rick and Claire as they called for him to cease, but he heard the boy's, a new, unique sound akin to the primal shriek of a newborn infant anguished by the frightening sights of an alien world into which it had been thrust.

The boy wailed, and Paul froze in mid-punch. Bean collapsed.

Paul turned to his right and saw Rick and Claire, with Tut between them, standing at the edge of the shed. Paul blinked at them in the sudden stillness and quiet. Rick looked solemn. Claire, smudged from head to foot with dirt, still held the length of exhaust pipe with which she had struck Bean. In Tut's face Paul read fear, horror, confusion, and sadness.

Paul started toward them across the oily ground and, as he did, Claire dropped the pipe and stepped toward him. They came together and held each other tightly, their faces pressed into each other's neck, until Rick spoke.

"Uh, Paul," he said, and pointed to Tut running across the junkyard to a wall of metal.

"Tut!" Claire and Paul called, as they watched the boy drop to his belly and shimmy into a hole in the junk. "Tut!" Claire called again and started after him, with Paul quickly following. Without hesitating, Claire dropped to her hands and knees before the hole, then onto her stomach and elbows.

"Be careful," Paul said.

"Okay." Claire began to crawl into the tunnel. "Tut?"

When Claire's feet disappeared, Paul got onto his stomach and shimmied into the dark tunnel after her, moving along with his elbows and echoing Claire as she called Tut's name. Paul realized then that tons of steel and iron balanced above them and that any shift in one part could bring the metal crashing down. He crawled on.

"Tut?"

Paul heard a noise to his right and, at the same time, felt the tunnel expand; reaching out for what sounded now like a whimper, he felt nothing but space. But rotating his arm, Paul touched what he made out to be the frame of a car door.

"Claire?"

"Yes?" Her voice came from in front of Paul.

"I think he's this way. Come back."

Paul could sense the boy, hear him as he crawled into the car shell, his arm extended. Paul felt cloth beneath him. Yes, Tut was here. This was his home, where Tut slept nights.

"It's okay, Tut. Everything's okay."

Paul crawled toward the whimper and touched the boy, huddling under a blanket in the corner of the car, shaking. Claire drew herself up then beside Tut, and Paul felt her arm encircle the boy's thin shoulders and draw him close. Paul moved closer to them and slid his arm atop Claire's, putting his other arm around her back.

Shaking and whimpering between them, Tut did not resist their touch, and for a long while, wombed by metal in the solid dark, they held each other as Tut quieted and their own hearts became peaceful.

22

MAGLIO called up Whale the morning after the funeral for Rita and said to meet him at the club with Gus; they would go take a trip to the shore and do some gambling, help Whale get over his wife's death. The boss had been nice to Whale when he heard about Rita's murder and called him to say how sorry he was, and that it was a goddamn shame a thief would shoot a woman. Anything he could do for Whale, the boss had said, just ask. He sent two gigantic flower arrangements to the wake, and another couple big ones to the church for the funeral. And now he wanted to take Whale to Jersey to cheer him up. Maglio really wasn't a bad guy once you got to know him, Whale thought.

"Sure, okay," Whale said; then they set a time to meet.

But no trip to the shore was going to get Whale over his wife's death; the only thing that would do that, Whale thought, was if he strangled Benny Bean and put a bullet between the eyes of that bastard Fante. He wasn't sure which one broke into his house and took the coins, but he was pretty certain Bean shot Rita. It didn't matter either way because they were both going to die. Gus had been looking for them for two days, but Fante wasn't at his house or his wood shop, and Bean wasn't around, either, which wasn't a surprise. You do what they did to somebody like Whale, you better disappear.

"I don't like the way this feels," Gus said, during the ride to the club.

"What?"

"Going with him to the shore."

"If I didn't think it was all right, you think I would go?"

"How do you know we're going to come back?"

"It's been three days already since Rita got killed, which is plenty of time to whack us if he wanted to. Number two, Benny disappeared, and so did Fante, so the boss can't know any more now than he did before. But mainly, he told me at the funeral that Victor bought his wife a whole new collection of coins worth about the same amount of money as the stolen one and that he just forgot the others got boosted. Victor just took the lump." It had made Whale glad to hear that because Maglio, who had other things to think about anyway, would start to put the whole thing out of his mind, which wouldn't start turning toward Whale. "All that pretty much has us in the clear."

"I hope you're right."

They met Maglio and Cosmo at the club. One-legged Lenny served them coffee and doughnuts, and they sat around talking for a while, though Whale didn't talk much. And for once he didn't feel like he had to say anything, figuring the boss would blame his silence on his wife's death and understand, not think Whale was plotting an overthrow or something.

When they left around noon, Cosmo drove the BMW with Maglio in the front seat and Gus and Whale in the back. The sun was shining; it was a pretty nice day to be riding on a highway that ran through South Jersey, and Whale tried to

270

enjoy it. He wound up thinking about Rita. Okay, he hadn't felt much more than a lukewarm brotherly feeling for her for the last ten years, but he felt bad that she went the way she did, two shots in the chest. He figured she went quick, though, and didn't suffer much.

When Whale finally made it home from Jersey at six o'clock in the morning after the night Fante left him stranded, he found Rita dead on the dining room floor, more blood than he had ever seen soaked in the carpet around her. Any other night, any night that he hadn't already walked through who knew how many miles of backwoods Jersey, trying to get to a phone so he could make a call to Philly and get somebody to pick him up, he would have felt some shock at seeing his wife on the floor with two bullet holes in her. But when he saw Rita and saw that the house had been robbed, the way the night had already gone, it all seemed logical. Or maybe he was just too tired to feel much of anything.

He sat in one of the dining room chairs for almost an hour before calling the cops; it was starting to get light out when he did. Then he had to go through the aggravation of answering a lot of questions that Whale knew were meant to make sure he wasn't the one who shot Rita instead of some burglar. After they took the body and the cops left, Whale called Gus to tell him what happened, but he hadn't gotten back from Jersey yet. Skinny Fuji had picked up Whale at a pay phone on the Black Horse Pike, but when they went looking for Gus they couldn't find him, so they returned to Philly. Gus called Whale later in the morning, after getting a ride from a truck driver, saying he was in Philly now and what did he want to do about Fante. "Nothing yet," Whale had told him, "because I have to make plans to bury my wife." Then he filled Gus in on the story. But that night, Whale told Gus to find Bean and Fante, and to kill them.

His wife was in the ground now, and he and Gus were going over the Walt Whitman Bridge with Maglio and Cosmo, a guy who talked so little you thought maybe he didn't know how.

First, they met Victor Notte at Caesar's in Atlantic City and had lunch. Then they did some gambling, mostly craps, which Maglio liked but couldn't play well, betting those silly long shots of his, snake eyes and boxcars. Whale kept his eye open for Audrey and told Gus to watch for her too, because there was a good chance she would be around and maybe Bean was with her, hanging out in her apartment, since he wasn't anywhere in Philly. If they saw the hooker, Whale would have to get away from the boss long enough to strong-arm her and see what she had to say.

After gambling, they went to dinner at the Showboat because Maglio had never been there and wanted to see it. The boss was in a good mood and for once wasn't talking about his health; he told jokes and a couple of funny stories that made everybody laugh, and even got a smile out of Cosmo, half of his tight mouth coming up at the side. If Whale had been thinking about Rita, he would have stopped because of Maglio's distractions, but he wasn't thinking about her. He was thinking about Bean and Fante most of the day, wondering where they were. One good thing about the burglary of Whale's house if Bean did it, and because Rita was killed it looked like he did, was that Benny was gone from the city; that would make it pretty hard for Maglio to hear about Bean's theft of the coins from Victor's house. The down side of Benny's skipping town was that now Whale wouldn't have the pleasure of seeing Benny get killed. He'd have to settle for only Fante.

When they finished at the restaurant, they got into the car, but instead of heading toward Longport to Victor's house they drove to Brigantine, Maglio saying he wanted to go to Harrah's and play blackjack there. But when they reached Brigantine, the boss said he had changed his mind about the casino.

"My sinuses are starting to clog up. Victor, you feel like taking me out on your boat for ten minutes so I can clear my head?"

"Sure," Victor said.

"You guys don't mind, do you?" the boss said, like they had

a choice about it, Maglio taking a refusal as an insult or a reason to become suspicious.

"Boat?" Gus said.

"Yeah, the air'll do you good, too."

"I get seasick."

"We're not going to be out long, just a few minutes."

Sitting beside Whale in the back seat, Gus gave him a little pressure in the ribs with his elbow, meaning that he was concerned about going on the ocean in a boat with Maglio. Whale gave it back, meaning he was concerned too. But he wasn't much, knowing this was one of Maglio's home cures, like the Scotch for his migraines. Anyway, what choice did they have? Whale and Gus walked from the car with both Cosmo and Victor behind them, so they couldn't exactly run even if they wanted to. If they did run and were wrong about the boat ride, they wouldn't only look like idiots but the boss would assume they felt guilty about something and the questions would start. So when Gus caught his eyes, Whale tried as best he could without speaking to tell Gus to stay calm and play it out. There was nothing else they could do.

It was a pretty big boat, a forty-footer, Victor said, and it had a pretty nice size cabin, red and green lights on the side, and two motors in the back, which made a low, growling noise when they chugged through the bay toward the ocean in the dark. Whale sat in one of the seats along the side next to Gus, and Maglio and Cosmo sat on the other side while Victor steered in the cabin. There was light in the cabin coming up from the console where the gauges and dials were, and it lit up Victor's face from below. The boat smelled like fish from one of the recent fishing trips Victor had told them about, and the exhaust from the motors got up Whale's nose too. He was worried about getting seasick, especially on a full stomach, but so far he was all right. Gus was the one who didn't look so hot.

"Perfect night for a boat ride," Maglio said as they left the bay and started to pick up speed, heading into the ocean.

"Yeah," Whale said over the motor noise, "perfect." But it

wasn't perfect at all. If it was such a perfect night, here in the middle of November, where were all the other boats? They saw one, and that was coming in. Whale wasn't shivering like Gus, but he felt cold and wished he could go in the cabin with Victor and get warm, or at least get the wind off him. But as long as Maglio sat out in the air, Whale would have to stay with him and act like he didn't mind.

"The thing I like about being in a boat on the ocean," Maglio said, "is that you can go any way you want, you know? Not like in the city, on a road, whatever, where you have to go straight and can only turn at certain spots. Traffic lights and all that bullshit."

"Yeah. The freedom of it," which did make sense to Whale.

They were picking up more speed, and the lights from the casinos along the shore were getting farther and farther away. The darkness in front of them was very black because there was nothing out on the ocean to give off light except other boats, and there weren't any that Whale could see. There was a little light from the cabin and it wasn't easy to see anybody, but you could see enough.

" 'Course, you don't get seasick in a car," Maglio said. "Whale, you get seasick?"

"Not yet."

"That's good, because otherwise you can't enjoy yourself. Gus, how 'bout you? You all right?"

Gus looked miserable, but he nodded and tried to smile.

"It is a little chilly, though," Maglio said, getting up from his seat. "I'll tell Victor to put on the heat." He gave a little laugh and went into the cabin, where Whale watched him say something to Victor and then come out. Victor didn't even look at him, turn from the windshield or anything; he didn't even nod, and Whale thought that was a little strange. Maglio sat down again and hunched his shoulders a little, like he really was cold, and he looked back to the shore at the shrinking casino lights like he suddenly didn't want to talk anymore. He didn't.

They started to slow down about five minutes later when the

casino lights looked like they were about as far away from the boat as the last toll on the expressway was from Atlantic City. So they were about six miles out in the ocean. You fell off a boat six miles out without a life jacket, you drowned, unless you were an Olympic swimmer. Even then, sharks probably got you.

The motors quit entirely and the boat drifted forward a little bit, then seemed to settle in one spot, though it bobbed up and down slightly. With the motors off, it was very quiet, except for water slapping against the boat and Victor moving around in the cabin. That's one thing Whale didn't like about the country—too quiet—and this was worse.

Whale heard scraping noises and watched Victor come out of the cabin with a cinder block in each hand. He set the blocks down in the middle of the boat and went back into the cabin, coming out with another pair of cinder blocks.

Before anybody could ask, Maglio said, "Ballast."

"What's ballast?" Gus said, his voice a little shaky, Whale wondering if only he noticed.

"It helps stabilize the boat, keeps it from rocking so much."

"Oh." Gus stared wide-eyed at the cinder blocks. "What's making it unstable all of a sudden?"

Whale wanted to know, too.

"Ask Victor."

"Victor?"

But Victor had gone back to the cabin. When he came back with two more cinder blocks, Gus said his name again, but Victor didn't seem to hear. He set down the cinder blocks and went into the cabin again. Gus looked at Maglio but he was turned away, looking out over the black water. Gus looked at Whale, but before he could say anything with his face Victor returned with another two cinder blocks. He put those down and then stood by the cabin door.

"Victor?" Gus said.

He had to have heard that time, Whale thought, but Victor didn't even look at him. Gus looked from him to Maglio, who was still looking away, to Whale, then back to Victor. Victor was looking at Maglio. Turning to look too, Whale watched the boss elbow Cosmo, who stood up.

Whale knew instantly it was all over.

"I can explain, boss," he said, as Cosmo brought out a gun.

"What's to explain?"

"It was this big misunderstanding."

"If it was a misunderstanding, you shoulda explained it a long time ago. Now look what you got yourself and Gus into."

Gus turned and threw up over the side of the boat. Maglio waited for him to finish before he spoke again.

"The only good that came out of this was that Victor got the coins back, minus a coupla of those K-rands."

"You got them from that little bastard Benny? Good."

"Not exactly." Maglio reached up and tapped Cosmo on the arm, holding his hand open for the gun. Cosmo gave it to him and first patted down Gus for a gun, which he did not have, then started to lift the cinder blocks from the deck and line them up on the side of the boat, holes to holes.

Gus retched again.

"I'm sitting in Marra's the other night," Maglio said when Gus stopped, "and Rick Fante walks in with his nephew, who looks like shit—he's had his face banged up some—and Rick comes over and hands me a box and says he thinks it belongs to me."

"Boss, I can explain."

"You know what it is, right?" Maglio went on. "But I didn't, and I look in and I see the coins. I don't get it. What's Rick doing with the coins, and why's he giving them to me? I have him and his nephew sit down, and they tell me this story I can't believe, it's so wild. The nephew—what's his name? Paul?—Paul tells me he just got back from Jersey where you and Gus were going to pop him, and after that he fought Benny Bean, which explained his messed-up face. He told me all about Henry Lawrence, how Benny stole the coins from Victor's house, and the kidnap of Lawrence's daughter. Then there was a bit about a street kid that Benny also locked up in the shed. It was wild, like I said. I don't know if you knew

276

about the kid, but you knew about the other stuff and didn't tell me."

"I—"

"But the thing that killed me was Rick then saying he got the coins from your house, Freddie. Your house. Okay, I gave you the benefit of the doubt. I figured after your wife gets shot and the coins get taken from you, you would come to me and tell me what went on. But did I hear from you? Nothing. Not a word. All this time and nothing."

Gus turned and retched. Maglio waited, occasionally glancing at Cosmo as he balanced the cinder blocks on the side of the boat.

"I didn't know the coins were Victor's when we took them from Bean," Whale said.

"That's not the point, which I don't even know if it's true," Maglio said. "The point is, you did know a lot and you still kept your mouth shut. What am I supposed to think after that? What is Victor to think? We figured you wanted to keep the coins, what else? You may as well've stole them yourself in the first place."

"I was afraid."

"Afraid? Afraid of what? Me? But see what it looks like now? It looks like it was your job, Freddie, and even if it wasn't, you keep something like this quiet from me, I have to wonder what other stuff you're hiding now or in the future."

"Boss, I made a mistake, I know. I shoulda told you."

"That's too late now."

Cosmo finished lining up the cinder blocks and went into the cabin, where Whale heard a metallic rattle. He came out with a chain looped over his arm and dropped it on the deck. The boat leaned to that side now because of the weight of the blocks.

Maglio got up from his seat. "Stand in the middle of the deck, you two, so we don't tip over."

"Boss, please," Whale said, as he moved to the middle.

"You, too, Gus."

Gus looked like he was about to cry as he joined Whale.

Maglio and Victor moved to the opposite side of the boat, balancing it somewhat, and faced Whale and Gus while Cosmo pulled at the loops of the chain looking for the end of it. When he found the end, he stood up and started to pass the chain through the holes of the cinder blocks, one after the other.

"There's nothing I can do?" Whale asked.

"What could you do? I can't trust you. I'll never know for sure that you weren't behind the coin boost. Benny wasn't saying, not that it mattered anymore. You know where we found him, where he was keeping Lawrence's daughter? Selligrini, the chop shop guy, he's got a shed in his junkyard, and that's where Benny had her. After beating up Benny and taking the coins from him, Rick and Paul locked him in the shed for me. They had to put a barrel with heavy stuff in it on the other side so Benny couldn't crawl through a tunnel that Claire and the kid had dug and got free, believe it or not. Then Rick and Paul came to the restaurant." Maglio paused and glanced at Cosmo, then looked back to Whale and Gus. "Benny's still there, in the tunnel that Claire and the kid dug. That was so convenient, it wasn't funny. All we had to do was fill up the hole and move this desk over it on the inside. Benny's gonna be a fossil."

Gus dry-heaved.

"Gus, that's why you couldn't find Benny when I know you went to look for him. You couldn't find Fante, either, right? You don't think they would stay in town waiting for you to visit them, did you? Even Rick took off, just in case; he went on his honeymoon a little early. That was my suggestion. Paul, my friend's nephew, and Claire, the daughter of Victor's wife, you stupid fuck, you know where they went? I'll tell you since it won't matter. They spent a couple nights in a hotel with Cosmo hanging around for protection; then Cosmo took them to the train station where they and that street kid took a train to Florida. What, you think they went to Disneyland?"

The chain stopped rattling behind Whale and he knew Cosmo had finished snaking it through the cinder blocks.

Cosmo took a few steps and stood to the side of Whale, looking at Maglio, waiting. Maglio nodded his head, and Cosmo reached into his jacket and pulled out two pairs of handcuffs.

"Boss, don't," Whale said.

Maglio didn't speak.

Cosmo clicked one cuff on Whale's wrist and the other on Gus's, who stared down at it like he couldn't believe what was happening. Cosmo did the same thing with the other handcuffs, bringing Whale's other wrist to join with Gus's, so that now they faced each other, the top of Whale's head about level with Gus's chin. Cosmo then walked them, shuffling, over to the row of cinder blocks with the chain through them. He took one end of the chain and passed it over the handcuffs, running it to the other end of the chain. Then Cosmo took a large padlock from his jacket and joined the end links with it. He looked to Maglio.

"Boss?" Whale said.

Maglio nodded to Cosmo. Cosmo went to the side of the boat and kicked the end cinder block, which plunked into the water and brought the next one quickly after it and the one beside that and the next one, all of the blocks plunging into the water like dominoes falling and jerking Gus and Whale closer and closer to the ocean.

"Boss!"

Whale and Gus braced themselves against the side of the boat, straining against the weight of the cinder blocks pulling at their wrists. The handcuffs cut through Whale's skin and his knees felt as though they were about to snap.

Then Cosmo shoved them, and Whale and Gus pitched over the side of the boat and into the cold water, where the cinder blocks tugged them down through the dark sea toward the bottom. They had not reached it when Whale's mind went black.